More books by (Availabl

Get Wet: A C
S
Shower Club
Breaking Brad
Two Weeks in Provence
Once Upon a Time in the Closet
Bathhouse Brian

Coming soon:
19/46: A Hot & Steamy MM Age Gap Romp!

Please feel free to get in touch:
@EganSheridan
EganSheridan@gmail.com
http://sites.google.com/view/EganSheridan
http://www.amazon.com/author/egansheridan

If you enjoy this book, kindly consider leaving a positive review on Amazon. It would be greatly appreciated.

© Copyright Egan Sheridan 2024

CLEARWATER
A Novel by Egan Sheridan

Available in Hardcover, Paperback and eBook formats

Dedication:

To all of those who have felt the loss of love.

A special thank you:

Many thanks to Amy for your time proofreading and for your helpful editing notes. It is greatly appreciated. You're a five-star person.

Prologue

Love is a magical thing. I can still picture his face and the way his smile lit up my darkest days. But now my thoughts are laced with bitterness and regret.

Love… oh, love. What an absolute bastard you can be. You sweep in like a thief, stealing my breath and turning my world upside down. You promise ecstasy, a high that makes every moment feel vibrant and alive, but you also bring the chaos of vulnerability, where one misstep can shatter everything. I've tasted your sweetness, felt the warmth of your embrace, and yet here I am, shackled by the weight of what I've done.

Love… It slips through your fingers like sand, elusive and shimmering, promising warmth and comfort, yet it can also leave you with scars you never thought you'd bear. It has this uncanny ability to elevate you to heights you didn't think were possible, making the mundane feel extraordinary. But in its shadows lurk darker truths, where joy can quickly spiral into chaos, and the very thing you cherish most can become a source of unbearable pain.

I learned this the hard way. Love has a way of distorting our perception, warping our better judgment until we can't tell where the line between passion and pain truly lies. It can push you to protect, to fight, and even to hurt the one you hold closest to your heart. And that's where it gets dangerous.

As I sit here in this cold courtroom, the walls feel like they're closing in on me, each tick of the clock echoing my own pain. I can almost hear the whispers of what could have been, the laughter that once filled the air between us, now replaced by a silence so heavy it's suffocating. There was a moment, not long ago, when everything felt right—a single kiss that ignited something profound within me. But that moment quickly turned into a nightmare, with shadows lurking behind every corner, threatening to unravel everything we had.

Now, as I await the judge's decision, I know that I crossed a line I never intended to approach. I was desperate to protect what we had, to hide from the storm that loomed over us. But love can blind you, make you act in ways you never thought possible, and suddenly you find yourself in a place where your own choices haunt you.

The weight of my actions is heavy, and guilt washes over me like a tidal wave. I keep replaying the moments leading up to this, questioning every decision, every word spoken. Yet all I can think about is him. His laughter, his warmth, the way his eyes sparkled when he smiled. I've done irreparable damage to the one person I wanted to protect the most. My heart aches with the thought that I hurt him.

And as the judge asks me what happened, I feel the weight of my choices bearing down on me. This isn't just about bad decisions or a momentary lapse in judgment; it's about the love that has been twisted into something I can hardly recognize. It's about the haunting silence that fills the space where joy once thrived. And as I face the repercussions of my actions, I realize that love, in all its complexity, can lead us to places we never wanted to go.

Chapter One

Aston Carter stared down at his hands, his fingers interlaced in his lap, nails pressing into his skin. They were shaking, though he tried not to let anyone see. The cold weight of the handcuffs had been replaced with the unfamiliar freedom of his hands unbound, but it didn't feel like freedom. The room was too bright, too loud with the murmurs of voices around him. Yet it was the silence between those voices—the anticipation of the inevitable judgment—that made his skin prickle with cold sweat.

How had it come to this?

He couldn't stop the flood of memories rushing through his mind. Love, they always said, was supposed to heal. But they never mentioned the way it could rip everything apart, leaving you raw and exposed. They didn't tell you that love could push you past your limits, make you act in ways you never thought possible. He clenched his fists tighter, the knuckles turning white as he replayed the events that had led him to this moment.

Aston felt a nudge on his arm, jolting him back to the present.

His lawyer, a middle-aged man with salt-and-pepper hair and a weary expression, gave him a small nod. The bailiff called his name, and Aston felt the eyes of everyone in the courtroom shift to him. A sea of faces blurred together as he stood on legs that felt far too unsteady, his heart pounding so hard he could hear it in his ears.

"Mr. Carter, please approach the bench," the judge's voice boomed, steady and authoritative.

Aston's lawyer rose beside him, placing a reassuring hand on his shoulder as they made their way to the front. The judge, an older man with thinning gray hair and glasses perched low on his nose, glanced over the papers in front of him before lifting his gaze to Aston. His expression was unreadable, a practiced neutrality that made Aston's stomach twist.

"Mr. Carter," the judge began, his voice measured but firm, "you are here today facing charges for an offense that carries serious consequences. Do you understand the gravity of the situation you're in?"

Aston's throat tightened. His mouth felt dry, like sandpaper, and the words stuck as he tried to respond. He managed to nod, but his lawyer stepped in, clearing his throat. "Yes, Your Honor, my client understands the charges."

"I am sure your client can speak for himself," said the judge.

Aston's lawyer looked at him, willing him to speak.

"Yes, sir. Your honor," said Aston softly.

The judge's eyes lingered on Aston for a moment longer, as if assessing him, weighing the choices that had brought him here. "Arson is not a charge we take lightly in this court. The actions you've taken, regardless of motive or circumstance, have consequences. I need to be clear that you are facing potential jail time and a permanent mark on your record."

Aston swallowed hard, his eyes lowering to the floor. He didn't need the judge to remind him of the stakes. He'd been replaying them in his mind every night since that day, watching as everything unraveled, helpless to stop it. What had started as something simple, something pure, had become tangled, knotted in ways he couldn't undo. It had consumed him, pushed him to the edge until all that remained was the aftermath—the wreckage of what he'd done.

The judge continued, his voice cutting through the fog of Aston's thoughts.

"I understand that this may have been an emotionally charged situation, but that does not absolve you of responsibility for your actions. This court will consider all the facts, and you will have your day in trial, but I advise you to reflect on the choices that led you here."

Choices. That word echoed in Aston's mind, taunting him. As if this had been a series of logical steps, as if he'd made some conscious decision to throw everything away. But it hadn't felt like that. It had been instinct, emotion—something primal and desperate that had overtaken him. And now, standing in this courtroom, it all felt like a distant memory, something that had happened to someone else. How could he explain it when he didn't fully understand it himself?

"Do you have anything you'd like to say at this time?" the judge asked, his voice softer now, as though offering Aston a chance to speak.

Aston looked up, meeting the judge's gaze for the briefest moment before his eyes darted away again. What could he say? That he hadn't meant for any of this to happen? That it had all spiraled out of control in ways he hadn't anticipated? He could barely find the words to explain it to himself, let alone to a courtroom full of strangers waiting for him to confess.

"No, Your Honor," he whispered, his voice barely audible.

The judge gave a slow nod, as though he had expected that answer. "Very well. I will set the date for your trial, and you will remain out on bail until that time, but under house arrest, monitored by an ankle bracelet." He paused, his eyes searching Aston's face one last time. "I hope, Mr. Carter, that you take this time to reflect on your actions and what led you here. This is your opportunity to consider what comes next."

The gavel came down with a sharp crack, and the sound reverberated through Aston's chest like a final, heavy note. It was done, for now. The trial was looming, but this part of the process was over. The room, which had felt so stifling moments before, now seemed to expand around him, emptying of air and meaning. The whispers in the gallery grew louder as people began to move, but Aston remained frozen in place.

His lawyer leaned in, murmuring something about next steps, but Aston barely heard him. His mind had already drifted back to the day everything had changed, to the heat of the moment, the rush of anger and hurt that had propelled him forward.

He could still feel it in his bones, the weight of that decision—the moment when everything had shifted, and he'd crossed a line he couldn't uncross.

Aston felt his legs move, carrying him toward the exit as if on autopilot. The doors of the courtroom swung open, and the cool air from the hallway hit him like a splash of water to the face, jolting him back to reality. He sucked in a deep breath, but it did nothing to ease the tightness in his chest. Outside the courthouse, the world continued on, oblivious to the weight of what had just happened in that room.

The sky was overcast, gray clouds hanging low, as though reflecting the storm brewing inside him. His lawyer walked beside him, talking about legal strategy, about the importance of keeping his emotions in check during the trial, but none of it registered. All Aston could think about was the moment that had led him here, the moment that had altered everything.

He remembered the way the tension had built, the way the air had seemed to thicken with unspoken words and emotions too heavy to bear. He had been walking on a tightrope for weeks, maybe months, and it had finally snapped beneath him. And in that moment, everything had gone wrong.

It wasn't supposed to happen like that. It wasn't supposed to end this way. But now, with the trial looming, Aston knew there was no going back.

He was left to face the consequences of that one moment, and the slow, unraveling truth of how love had turned to something else—something darker, something that had brought him to this very point.

As they stepped out into the parking lot, Aston's lawyer stopped and looked at him with a mix of concern and professionalism. "Aston, you need to stay focused. We'll work through this, but you have to keep it together. Don't leave the house, or else the leniency that I think the judge might show you, due to the circumstances, could evaporate. Do you understand?"

Aston nodded, though the words felt hollow in his chest. Keep it together. Like it was that easy. But that was the only thing he could do now, even as everything else seemed to be falling apart.

"Yeah," Aston said, though his voice sounded far away. "I understand."

But as he looked out over the gray horizon, Aston wasn't sure he did.

He wondered how it had all gotten to this. All he knew was that it all started many months ago when he and his mother moved to Clearwater.

It was supposed to be a new start.

Chapter Two

Aston stood at the edge of the sandy beach, the salty breeze rustling his light brown hair as he gazed out at the vast, undulating sea. Waves crashed rhythmically against the shore, each swell a reminder of the change that had washed over his life in the last few weeks. Just a year ago, he had been navigating the familiar halls of his old school, surrounded by friends and the echoes of laughter. Now, he felt like a ship adrift, the shoreline of his past fading into the horizon.

"You okay, sweetheart?" A voice broke through his thoughts. Aston turned to see his mother, Laura, approaching with a soft smile that belied the worry lines etched across her forehead. She was always so positive, always trying to infuse some light into the shadows that loomed over their lives. The sun was setting behind her, casting a golden glow around her figure, a stark contrast to the heaviness in Aston's chest.

"Yeah, just… thinking," he replied, forcing a smile. He wanted to assure her he was fine, that the move had been a good idea, but the truth was tangled up with feelings he hadn't yet unraveled.

Laura placed a gentle hand on his shoulder, her warm brown eyes searching his. "This is a new beginning for us, Aston. I know it's a lot to take in, but I really believe we can start fresh here. It's a beautiful place. You'll see."

Aston nodded. They had moved to this coastal town hoping to escape the memories of his father's illness and death. Aston was only 17 when cancer took him, but the absence of a father had left a huge void in his life, one that had grown larger with each passing year. His mother had fought to fill that void with love and support, but sometimes, it felt like an insurmountable chasm, as she also battled with grief.

Laura had decided back then that as soon as Aston was done with high school, they would move. She couldn't get over all the reminders of her husband.

"I just don't know what I want," Aston admitted, his voice barely above a whisper. "I don't know anyone here. I don't fit in anywhere."

"You will," Laura assured him, squeezing his shoulder lightly. "It takes time. Just give yourself permission to explore. Try new things, meet new people. I want you to find what makes you happy. Someone who makes you feel secure." She smiled at him, her expression brightening.

"Just look at this place! The beach, the sunsets… It's perfect for a fresh start."

The waves lapped at the shore, their rhythm soothing yet maddening in its reminder that time was still moving forward, whether he was ready or not. Aston watched the horizon blend into vibrant shades of orange and pink. It was beautiful. It felt like a promise, yet it also reminded him of the uncertainty that lay ahead.

"I don't know if I'm ready for all that just yet," he said, feeling a twinge of guilt at his hesitation. He knew his mother was hopeful, her spirit buoyed by the prospect of a new life, but he felt the weight of expectations pressing down on him. What if he couldn't find happiness? What if he never fit in?

"You don't have to be ready right away," Laura replied gently. "Just take it one step at a time. Besides, till then, you've got me."

The comfort in her words warmed him, but the reality of his life still loomed large. They had left behind their old home, their old friends, and everything familiar. Aston felt like a stranger in his own skin, and the thought of starting over felt daunting.

"I just wish things were different," he admitted, his voice cracking. The memories of his father, the way he had been taken too soon, pressed heavily on his heart.

Laura's face softened at his admission. "I know, sweetheart. I wish that too. But you have so much ahead of you. Dad would want you to live fully, to embrace life. You owe it to him to find your happiness."

Aston looked at his mother, seeing the glimmer of hope in her eyes. She had always been his anchor, grounding him even when the storm raged around them. He wanted to believe her, to believe that they could forge a new path together. Yet, the fear of failure gnawed at him, whispering doubts that wrapped around his heart like vines.

"Let's take a walk," she suggested, breaking the weight of silence. "There's a little café not far from here that apparently has the best coffee. I hear they have a great view of the ocean."

Aston nodded, grateful for her distraction. They began walking along the beach, the soft sand shifting beneath their feet. As they strolled, the sound of seagulls echoed above them, and the ocean breeze carried the scent of salt and freedom. With each step, Aston felt the tension in his chest begin to ease, if only slightly.

"Maybe I'll find a job," he mused, thinking aloud. "Something to keep me busy while I figure things out."

"Absolutely!" Laura beamed, clearly pleased with his idea. "There are always opportunities in towns like this. You could work at the marina, or even help out at one of the local shops. You'll meet people that way."

"Yeah, maybe," Aston replied, but the prospect felt overwhelming. What kind of person would he meet? Would he fit in? He was still grappling with the feeling of being uprooted, the absence of his friends weighing on him like a heavy cloak.

As they approached the café, its cheerful facade stood in stark contrast to Aston's inner turmoil. The large windows offered a panoramic view of the beach, the sun beginning to dip below the horizon. They found a table outside, the warm glow of the sunset casting a golden hue over everything.

"I'll grab us some coffee," Laura offered, leaving Aston to ponder his thoughts. He watched her walk inside, her movements graceful yet tinged with the fatigue of a single mother starting over.

Sitting alone, Aston gazed out at the ocean, feeling the vastness of it all. Each wave that rolled in seemed to echo the uncertainty that churned inside him. He longed for clarity, for a sense of direction, but the future felt murky and undefined.

As the sun sank lower, painting the sky in deep shades of purple and blue, Aston felt a flicker of hope emerge amid his anxiety. Perhaps this new beginning could bring him closer to understanding himself. Maybe he could discover who he was away from the expectations of his old life, away from the shadows of loss that lingered around him.

With a deep breath, he resolved to take it one day at a time. He could not predict what the future held, but he could choose to embrace this moment, this chance for a fresh start.

Laura returned with two steaming cups of coffee, a smile on her face that lit up the dimming light around them. "Here we go!" she said, setting a cup in front of him.

"Thanks, Mom," Aston said, lifting the cup to his lips, the warmth spreading through his fingers. The rich aroma filled his senses, reminding him of cozy mornings back home, where laughter and familiarity intertwined.

They shared small talk as they watched the sun disappear, the sky darkening into a canvas of stars. Aston felt the pull of the ocean, the call of new adventures waiting just beyond the horizon.

As they finished their coffee and prepared to head back, Aston thought that perhaps this new beginning wouldn't be so bad after all. He was still navigating the unfamiliar waters of grief and identity, but with his mother by his side, he felt a little less alone.

In the stillness of the evening, with the sound of the waves crashing softly against the shore, Aston took a step forward into his new life, embracing the promise of tomorrow. It was time to explore, to discover, and maybe—just maybe—find a piece of himself in the process.

Chapter Three

Aston sat in the passenger seat of his mother's car, staring out the window as they drove toward the local supermarket. Not the most glamorous outing, but he was bored with sitting at home and took his mom up on her invitation to go with.

"Anything in particular you would like?" Laura asked, her voice light and upbeat.

"Not really. I'll maybe grab a couple packets of potato chips," Aston replied absently, though his mind was elsewhere.

As they turned onto the Clearwater boulevard, the gentle sway of the car provided a brief sense of laziness. Laura hummed along to the radio, and Aston leaned back, watching the palm trees blur by.

"I think we should get some fresh fruit too." Laura said, glancing over at him.

"I guess," Aston answered, his thoughts drifting.

Just as they approached the supermarket parking lot, Laura turned her head to check for pedestrians. In a split second, a blue sedan came barreling out of nowhere, catching Laura off guard. She slammed on the brakes, but it was too late. The sound of metal crunching against metal pierced the air as they collided with the car lightly.

"Mom!" Aston exclaimed, instinctively bracing himself against the dashboard.

Laura let out a sharp gasp, gripping the steering wheel tightly. After a brief moment of silence, she took a deep breath, her shock turning into action. "Are you okay?" she asked, checking on Aston, who nodded, still a bit dazed.

"Yeah, I'm fine. Are you?"

"I think so. Damn," she replied, her voice steadying as she put the car in park.

Stepping out into the warm breeze, Aston felt a rush of adrenaline. The blue sedan was slightly crumpled, and a man was already climbing out of the driver's seat. He appeared to be in his late thirties, with dark hair, bright blue eyes, and a friendly demeanor.

"Oh dear." the man said, offering a reassuring smile. "I wasn't paying attention, I apologize."

Laura stepped forward, concern etched across her face. "I'm really sorry! I didn't see you coming either."

"It's alright. You guys good?" he asked, his tone light.

"Yes, we are fine, thank you. And yourself?"

"Just a little embarrassed that I didn't see the stop sign," he smiled. "I'm Alex, by the way."

Laura responded with a light giggle, smiling, making Aston frown.

As they exchanged insurance information, Aston hung back, arms crossed. He couldn't shake the feeling of annoyance. There was something in the way Alex smiled at his mother —something he didn't like.

While Laura scribbled down her contact details, they engaged in small talk. Aston caught snippets of their conversation. They laughed lightly at their shared misfortune, and Aston noticed the warmth in his mother's eyes as she spoke.

"So, do you live around here?" Alex asked, genuinely interested.

"My son and I just moved to Clearwater a few months ago," Laura replied, her voice brightening. "I'm still getting used to everything."

"That's great. Hi there, I'm Alex," said Alex, extending his hand towards Aston.

"Aston," he replied, reluctantly extending his hand and shaking it.

"My pleasure, Aston."

Alex smiled and turned his attention back to Laura, "Clearwater has its charm, especially this time of year," Alex said, glancing back at Aston and offering a friendly nod. "You're lucky to be near the beach. It's perfect for unwinding."

Aston shifted uncomfortably, feeling like an intruder in their moment.

"Yeah, it's nice," Laura agreed, her smile lingering longer than usual.

Once the exchange was complete, Alex gave Laura his contact information. "Just in case we need to follow up about the insurance. But I hope we can keep it simple. No need for any headaches, right?"

"Of course," Laura replied, and Aston could see a flicker of excitement in her eyes. It made his stomach churn.

"Thanks again for being so understanding. It was nice meeting you both!" Alex said, waving goodbye as he got back into his car.

As Laura returned to the driver's seat, Aston couldn't hold back. "You know he's just going to forget about it, right? It was a fender bender, Mom."

Laura shot him a look, half annoyed, half amused. "Aston, it was just an accident. He seemed really nice. You can't just assume he's going to be a jerk because of a little bump."

"Nice? You just crashed into him!" Aston argued, feeling defensive.

"I think I am a good judge of character and he most definite seems nice to me," she replied, her tone firm. "And it's good to meet new people."

"So that's your strategy for meeting new people… Crashing into them," he said.

"Oh Aston, lighten up. It was nothing," she smiled.

Aston sighed, glancing out the window again, trying to shake off feeling overly protective of his mother.

As they walked through the aisles, picking out groceries, Aston couldn't help but glance back at the blue sedan, now parked outside of the same store, with its dented bumper glinting in the sun. He shook his head, feeling a mixture of annoyance. Why did it bother him so much? It was just an accident, after all.

But as they finished their shopping and headed back to the car, he couldn't shake the image of his mother smiling at Alex.

Chapter Four

The sun had barely risen over the coastal town when Eli Taylor arrived at the marina, the salty breeze tousling his dark brown hair as he stepped onto the familiar wooden dock. The world was still quiet, the only sounds coming from the gentle lapping of the waves against the boats and the distant calls of seagulls awakening with the dawn. For Eli, this was more than just a job; it was a sanctuary, a place where the pressures of life faded into the background, at least for a few hours.

Eli slipped into his work shirt, the fabric worn but comfortable against his skin, and surveyed the scene before him. The marina was a hive of activity, a small business his parents had built from the ground up. His father, Samuel, chartered boats for tourists, skillfully navigating the waters while his mother, Rebecca, managed the financial side of their family business and provided bookkeeping services for the local fishing community.

The sight of his father at the dock, preparing the charter boat for a day of fishing, brought a sense of pride to Eli's chest.

Samuel was in his early fifties, sturdy and weathered, with kind brown eyes that sparkled with joy when he spoke about the ocean. Eli had grown up watching him work, listening to tales of the sea that felt like legends to him.

"Eli!" Samuel called out, his voice booming across the dock. "Can you help me load the gear?"

"Coming!" Eli replied, his heart swelling with eagerness.

He crossed the dock, the wood creaking softly under his feet. The air was thick with the scent of salt and fish, a smell that felt like home. As he approached the boat, he could see the well-worn tackle boxes and fishing rods waiting to be loaded. Each piece of equipment carried its own story, a testament to countless adventures on the water.

Eli grabbed a tackle box, the weight familiar in his hands. He and his father worked in sync, moving seamlessly as they prepared for the day ahead. Samuel's weathered hands moved expertly, demonstrating the patience and skill that came with years of experience. Eli watched as his father maneuvered the gear with ease, a smile tugging at his lips.

"Just make sure you double-check the knots this time," Samuel said, a playful glint in his eye. "Remember what happened last week?"

Eli chuckled, shaking his head. "I won't forget, Dad. No more loose knots."

As they loaded the final piece of gear onto the boat, Eli caught sight of the office where his mother was busy with her spreadsheets. Rebecca was the backbone of their operation, the one who kept everything running smoothly. Her bright red hair was pulled back in a tight bun, and she often wore a crisp white blouse that contrasted with the casualness of the marina.

"You'd think she'd enjoy the ocean a bit more," Eli mused, half-joking. "Maybe take a break from the numbers."

Samuel chuckled, his eyes twinkling. "Your mother loves the sea, but the books pay the bills. Besides, someone has to keep us afloat—figuratively and literally."

Eli nodded, appreciating the blend of their roles within the family business. While his father charmed customers with his stories and fishing expertise, his mother ensured everything was in order behind the scenes. They worked tirelessly to keep the family business going, and Eli often felt the weight of their expectations resting on his shoulders.

As tourists began to arrive, Eli retreated to the background, never one for too many people.

Samuel took over, understanding his son's reluctance and ways, his voice warm as he explained the day's itinerary. He effortlessly slipped into the role of the enthusiastic host, showing them around the boat and introducing them to the equipment they would use.

The boat gently rocked beneath their feet as they set off, the engine rumbling to life, and Eli watched the boat retreat into the distance.

As they made their way out to deeper waters, the sun glistened on the waves, creating a dazzling spectacle that took Samuel's breath away. He could feel the worries of his family life drifting away, replaced by the rhythm of the ocean and the laughter of the tourists around him. But he always had a bit of tension in those moments. He knew from experience how quickly things could go wrong on the ocean. And he kept a close eye on everyone.

"Captain, look!" a young boy exclaimed, pointing at a school of fish darting beneath the surface. "Can we catch them?"

Samuel grinned, the boy's excitement infectious. "We'll try! Just keep your lines ready."

As they spent the day fishing, Samuel engaged with the group, answering questions and sharing stories about the local marine life. He enjoyed their enthusism, feeling a sense of purpose in his role. Each time a line tightened or a fish broke the surface, cheers erupted, and Samuel couldn't help but feel a part of something again.

Later that afternoon, back at the docks, Eli ate a sandwich, watching the boat coming back in, still far off in the distance. He had been working on a particularly stubborn engine of one of the boats he was fixing. Beneath the surface of his calm demeanor, a current of uncertainty flowed.

As the sun began to set, casting a warm glow over the water, Eli found himself momentarily lost in thought. The pressure of his family's expectations weighed heavily on him, particularly his father's want for him to take over the family business one day, and his mother's desire for him to find a girl... Namely Ava, the girl his parents had picked out for him, it seems.

Eli's mind drifted to thoughts of what lay ahead. He loved fishing and the family business, but part of him longed for something more—an adventure beyond the confines of the marina. Each time he watched a boat leave the dock, a pang of desire washed over him.

He often dreamed of sailing away, of exploring new horizons, free from the expectations that bound him. But the boats always came back to Clearwater, making him feel strangely trapped in a life he felt was suffocating him every now and then.

That evening, after the tourists had departed and the boat was cleaned and docked, Eli sat on the edge of the dock once more, his feet dangling over the water. The horizon blazed with colors, the sky a canvas of fiery reds and oranges. He took a deep breath, letting the salty air fill his lungs, feeling the tension in his chest slowly dissipate.

The marina was his sanctuary in many ways, but it also served as a reminder of the life he felt trapped within. As much as he enjoyed working with his father, he disliked the tourists. It wasn't their fault. It was what they represented. Freedom. Something he felt he never had. The weight of his mother's expectations always loomed large too. He wanted to pursue something more, something that felt true to who he was.

"Hey, Eli!" His father's voice broke through his thoughts, and Eli turned to see Samuel approaching. "You ready to head home?"

"Yeah," Eli replied, forcing a smile. "Just enjoying the view."

"Tomorrow you need to continue fixing up Mr. Enston's old boat. How is that coming along?" Samuel said, joining him on the edge of the dock.

"I'm running behind. These tourists are keeping me busy."

"Yeah well. It needs to be done. He says he wants to go out with it next month. And from the looks of it, there is still a bit to be done."

"I'll work harder," said Eli, as he looked down into the water.

"I know. But I put out a few ads last week to see if we can find someone to hire for the Summer. Difficult to find someone with experience in this town. But maybe you can teach them."

"I don't need help, dad. I can do it on my own."

"We can't afford to lose customers. And besides, you never go out unless forced to do so. So, having some outside company here might do you some good."

"I really don't—"

"Not up for discussion, my boy. I'm interviewing someone tomorrow morning. Hope he has what it takes."

Eli sighed, but did not go against what his dad said. They sat in companionable silence for a moment, both lost in the beauty of the sunset.

"You've been quiet lately," Samuel finally said, his gaze fixed on the horizon.

"So," Eli said, his voice steady.

Samuel turned to him, concern flickering in his eyes. "Just making an observation."

Eli hesitated, unsure of how to voice the turmoil within him. "Yeah, I guess. It's just—"

"You're upset with mom for forcing you on a date with Ava, right? Take your time," Samuel replied, placing a reassuring hand on Eli's shoulder. "You're still young. You'll figure it out."

Eli nodded, grateful for his father's support.

But as they made their way back to the office, the familiar feelings of expectation and staying in the family business lingered, intertwining with the warmth of his father's words.

As they drove home, the sun dipped below the horizon, casting a warm glow over the coastal town.

"So Eli, you excited for your date with Ava this evening?" Asked Rebecca, his mother.

"I suppose," he said.

"Oh come on. A boy of your age should be excited to know a lovely girl like her."

"I'm not going out with her, mom. She is just a friend."

"Don't close yourself off from the possibility of something more, my boy. It's about time you get a girlfriend. I want grandkids. And the way you are going, if I don't push you into something, I'll die without them," she chuckled.

"Stop, mom."

"Oh lighten up, Eli. Just have fun tonight."

Eli watched the landscape blur past, the familiar sights merging into a haze of uncertainty. The weight of expectation loomed large, but he couldn't shake the feeling that there was something waiting for him just beyond the horizon—something that would help him break free from the confines of his quiet world.

And in the depths of his quiet world, Eli knew that a change was coming, even if he couldn't yet see what it would be. He liked Ava, but he could not see a future with her. She was a good friend though. He would have to find a way to navigate the currents of his life, to seek out the freedom he craved, and to embrace the possibilities that lay ahead without hurting her or upsetting his mom.

A sigh escaped from his mouth.

Chapter Five

Aston walked along the unfamiliar streets of Clearwater, his sneakers kicking up small clouds of dust with every step. It was one of those sunny days where the sky seemed endlessly blue, and the town was alive with the faint hum of activity—families wandering along the boardwalk, couples heading to the beach, the occasional sound of laughter in the distance. But for Aston, the carefree mood of the town seemed worlds away. He felt restless, a gnawing sense of frustration building in his chest as another door closed behind him with a polite but firm, "Sorry, we're not hiring right now."

This was the third place he had tried that morning. First, there was the small café near the boardwalk, which was already fully staffed for the summer season. Then the hardware store—an old man behind the counter had apologized before Aston had even finished asking. And finally, the surf shop. The guy behind the counter had barely glanced up from his phone to tell him they weren't looking for anyone new.

Aston stuffed his hands into his pockets.

It wasn't like he expected to find the perfect job immediately, but being turned down again and again was starting to wear on him. He was bored—bored of the same routine, bored of having nothing to do, and bored of feeling stuck.

With no other options, Aston made his way back toward home, kicking at a small pebble as he walked. The neighborhood felt too quiet, like it was holding its breath, waiting for something to happen. He wondered how long it would be before he could find something to fill his time, something to keep him occupied and distracted. He hadn't realized how much he needed that until now. It was tough not having friends in Clearwater yet. Sometimes he felt he would never make any.

As he neared the house, he saw his mother, Laura, standing by the front steps, her face lighting up as she spotted him. She waved him over, her expression a mix of excitement and something else—like she had news.

"Aston!" she called as he approached, tucking a loose strand of hair behind her ear. "How did it go?"

Aston shrugged, shaking his head as he climbed the steps. "No luck. Seems like everyone's fully staffed for the season."

Laura gave him a sympathetic look, but there was a glimmer of hope in her eyes that Aston couldn't quite place. "Well, thank goodness you have the best mom in the world then, right? I might have some good news for you," she said, leaning against the porch railing. "I ran into someone earlier today. He mentioned that they were looking for help down at the marina."

Aston's eyes widened slightly. "Really? The marina?"

Laura nodded. "Yeah, it's not glamorous, but the pay's decent, and they need someone to start right away. I told him you were looking for something, and he seemed interested. I can take you down there tomorrow morning, if you want."

Aston felt a surge of excitement—finally, something that wasn't a dead end. The marina wasn't what he had been thinking of when he imagined getting a job, but it was better than nothing. And the thought of being around the water, even if it wasn't always pleasant work, was strangely appealing.

"That sounds great, Mom," Aston said, a smile tugging at the corners of his lips. "I'd definitely be up to checking it out."

Laura smiled back, relief softening her features. "I thought you might be. It's long hours, though. You'd be working a lot of mornings, afternoons, and possibly evenings… sometimes weekends. But I figured you'd be okay with that, considering how bored you've been."

Aston laughed lightly. "Long hours sound perfect right about now. I've had enough of sitting around doing nothing."

Laura patted his arm, her warmth and reassurance steady as always. "Good. I'll take you over first thing tomorrow morning. They seemed pretty eager to get someone in, so you might be starting as soon as you walk in."

Aston nodded, feeling a strange mix of anticipation and nervousness. It wasn't just about the job; it was about having something to focus on, something to pull him out of the aimlessness that had been weighing him down lately.

That evening, as he sat in his room, staring out the window at the fading sunset, Aston let himself imagine what the marina might be like—the boats, the water, the smell of salt in the air. Maybe, it was exactly what he needed right now.

Chapter Six

Aston Carter lay sprawled on the couch, his fingers idly scrolling through his phone, the glow of the screen illuminating his face in the fading light. The rich aroma of garlic and herbs wafted through the air, a comforting reminder of his mother, Laura, bustling around the kitchen.

"Aston, your dinner is done. Do you want to eat now, or warm it up later?" Laura called from the kitchen, her voice carrying a note of cheerfulness that warmed the room.

He sat up, stretching as he asked, "We can eat now. I'm starving. Smells good."

Her tone shifted slightly as she took a breath. "I'm not eating here tonight."

"Huh?" Aston asked, feeling a twinge of curiosity and anticipation as he stepped into the kitchen.

"I'm going out tonight," she said, her tone casual, though there was a hint of nervousness in her demeanor.

"Where are you going?" Aston asked, tilting his head, intrigued.

"Just… out," she replied, a sheepish smile creeping onto her lips.

"Out?" he repeated, eyebrows furrowing. "Out where?"

Laura hesitated for a moment, her cheeks flushing slightly. "Um… Well, I've been meaning to tell you. But to be completely honest, I've been a little nervous. I'm going on a date," she finally confessed, her voice light but edged with uncertainty.

Aston's heart sank. "A date?" he echoed, trying to keep his tone steady. The word felt heavy in the air, like a weight he hadn't expected to carry. "With who?"

"Alex," she said sheepishly.

Aston felt a knot twist in his stomach, an emotion he couldn't quite pinpoint mixing with jealousy. "Alex! The guy from the supermarket?" he asked, a note of disbelief creeping into his voice.

"Yes, Aston. We talked for a bit afterward, and it just… He is really nice.

And we seem to be clicking," Laura explained, her excitement tempered by his obvious discomfort. "I thought it would be fun to get to know him a little better."

"Fun?" Aston echoed, incredulous. "And what about Dad? Are you just going to forget about him?"

Laura knew this was coming. How could it not? She looked at him with understanding and compassion.

"Absolutely not," Laura said firmly, stepping closer and placing a comforting hand on his shoulder. "Your dad will always be a part of our lives. This isn't about replacing him; it's just me trying to find some happiness again. It's important for both of us."

"But what if it gets serious?" Aston pressed, the thought gnawing at him. He hated feeling this way, but the idea of his mother moving on felt like a betrayal.

"It won't if you don't want it to," Laura reassured him. "This is just a step, and I want you to know that no one could ever take your dad's place in my heart. He will always be here with us. But it's been more than a couple of years now. And this feels like it is something I need to do. For me."

She patted her heart. Aston stared at her, feeling bad for even questioning her, but unable to shake the anxiousness he felt, thinking about his mom with a new man.

"And besides, you'll always be my number one guy, you know that."

Her words settled over him, providing a flicker of comfort amidst the storm of emotions.

"Just be careful, mom." he said quietly, searching her eyes for reassurance.

"Of course," she said, her smile returning, brighter than before. "You're my son, Aston. That bond doesn't change, no matter what happens. And we will both love your father till our dying day. Nothing in this world can ever change that."

Feeling the tension in his chest loosen just a bit, he nodded. "Okay," he said softly. "I guess it's cool. Just… keep me in the loop, alright?"

"My Aston. I'm very proud of the man you are turning out to be. I'm the luckiest mother in the world," Laura replied, her voice filled with warmth.

"Now, how about you get to dinner? I made a chocolate cake for dessert. Keep me a piece, please!"

"Sure," Aston said, a small smile breaking through the remnants of his unease.

She went to go get ready for her date, and the tension began to ease. Yet, in the back of his mind, Aston couldn't shake the image of Alex from the supermarket, a man who seemed to spark something in his mother.

He resolved to try be supportive. For his mom's sake, but knew it would be tough. With a deep breath, he allowed himself to focus on his meal, taking a forkful and chewing it as he sat alone at the table, staring at his reflection in the stainless steel toaster sitting on the counter.

Chapter Seven

The salty breeze rustled the leaves of the palm trees lining the marina, carrying with it the sounds of waves lapping against the hulls of boats bobbing gently in the water. Aston stood in front of the small, weather-beaten office where his new job awaited him. He had spent the last few weeks trying to settle into Clearwater, a place that was supposed to offer him and his mom a fresh start. Now, it felt like stepping further into the unknown, the weight of his past still clinging to him like a shadow.

"Come on, Aston! Don't dawdle," his mother, Laura, called from the truck, breaking his moment of hesitation. Her voice was cheerful, a contrast to the uncertainty gnawing at him. She waved him over with a bright smile that only made him feel more anxious.

Taking a deep breath, the familiar scent of the sea filled his lungs and he took a first tentative step forward.

As he approached the office, he could see the weathered sign that read "Taylor Charters," peeling slightly from years of exposure to the elements.

Inside, the atmosphere was quiet. In the distance, a few tools clanked, and the smell of fish hung heavily in the air. The walls were adorned with pictures of boats and families grinning on the decks of charters, capturing moments of sun-soaked joy. Aston felt a flicker of excitement, but it was quickly dampened by his nerves.

"Hey, kid!" A burly man with brown hair and a friendly face approached, extending a hand. "I'm Samuel Taylor. You must be Aston? Welcome aboard!"

"Yes, thanks," Aston replied, shaking his hand firmly. "I'm excited to be here."

"Good to hear! We've been needing an extra set of hands for some time. Boats don't fix themselves, you know!"

"I'm sure, yeah. Thanks for the opportunity. I'll do my best," Aston replied, trying to sound more confident than he felt. He watched as Samuel moved toward a nearby boat, gesturing for Aston to follow.

"My son Eli is working on a couple of boats that need some attention. He knows the ins and outs of everything around here. I'll introduce you."

As Samuel led Aston through the narrow aisles filled with tools and equipment, he felt a mixture of curiosity and apprehension. He wondered what Eli would be like. Would he be welcoming, or would he make Aston's first day more challenging?

Samuel opened a door leading to a work area at the back of the building. Inside, the sounds of power tools hummed, and Aston spotted a lean figure hunched over a boat, focused on the task at hand.

"Eli! Come meet your new coworker!" Samuel called out.

Eli looked up, his blue-gray eyes widening slightly before he quickly glanced back down at the task in front of him. His hair was tousled from the day's work, and he wore a faded t-shirt that clung to his wiry frame.

"Hey," Aston said, stepping forward. "I'm Aston."

"Hi," Eli muttered, barely meeting his gaze. There was a hint of shyness in his voice, an introverted quality that made Aston instinctively want to draw him out. Eli stood up. He was slightly shorter than Aston.

"Eli's our boat guru," Samuel said with a proud grin. "He knows his way around just about everything in this marina. You'll be learning a lot from him."

"Nice," Aston replied, trying to keep the conversation going. "I've always wanted to learn about boats. I'm pretty handy with tools, too."

Eli glanced up briefly, a flicker of interest in his eyes before his gaze dropped again. "Cool," he said, his tone flat but not unfriendly.

"Don't worry if you're not familiar with everything," Samuel encouraged, clapping Eli on the shoulder. "Aston's here to learn, Eli, and I know you'll show him the ropes."

Aston felt a twinge of hope at the prospect of working alongside Eli. As they stood there, the air thick with unspoken words, Aston sensed the walls around Eli. He was cautious, unsure, and Aston could relate, since moving here. It reminded him of the vulnerability he carried within himself, a shared experience he hoped they could navigate together.

"Alright, you guys get started," Samuel said, breaking the tension. "Aston, why don't you help Eli with that motor? He's been working on it for a while."

Aston nodded and stepped closer to the boat, his heart racing with anticipation. "What do you need help with?"

Eli hesitated, his hands fidgeting with a wrench. "Just… trying to fix this engine. It's been acting up."

"Okay, show me what to do," Aston said, his enthusiasm bubbling beneath the surface. Eli was quiet, still cautious, but Aston was determined to break through.

They worked side by side, Aston mimicking Eli's movements and asking questions that seemed to bring him out of his shell, little by little. "So, how long have you been working here?" Aston asked, trying to keep the conversation flowing.

"Since I was a kid," Eli replied, glancing at Aston with a mix of surprise and wariness. "My parents own the place."

"That's cool. Do you enjoy it?"

Eli shrugged, his eyes darting to the tools before him. "It's alright. I guess. I love the boats. Don't really enjoy the tourists much."

Aston sensed the reluctance in Eli's words and decided to probe a little deeper. "You don't sound too enthusiastic. Is there something else you want to do?"

Eli paused, chewing on his bottom lip. "I don't know. I just… feel pressured sometimes."

"Pressured?" Aston's curiosity was piqued.

"Yeah," Eli said, his voice barely above a whisper. "I mean, I like boats and all, but…" He trailed off, his gaze fixed on the motor.

Aston felt a pang of empathy. "I get it. Moving here was supposed to be a fresh start for me, but it's hard to shake off the past."

Eli looked at him, "When did you move here?"

"Just a few weeks back," Aston admitted. "My mom wanted a change. It feels… different. I'm still figuring things out."

Eli nodded slowly, the tension easing from his shoulders just a fraction. "Yeah. Different."

Changing the subject suddenly, Eli gestured to the boats lined up along the docks.

"This one here is our main charter boat, the Sea Whisperer. She's a beauty, but she needs a little work on the engine before the in-season starts. The one next to it is a local guy's fishing boat—we're fixing it up for him. And over there," Eli pointed toward a battered old boat that looked like it had seen better days, "is my dad's pride and joy. He says it's a classic, but it's a wreck if you ask me."

Aston was surprised at the change of course, but went with it.

"Wow, you've got your work cut out for you… Well, we have," Aston remarked, taking in the sights. "How do you know what to do with all of this?"

"I just learned over the years," he said and then continued working.

They worked in a comfortable silence for a while, Aston's presence starting to chip away at Eli's initial wariness. The engine was stubborn, but they tackled it together, and Aston found himself enjoying the camaraderie that was beginning to blossom.

"Do you ever get tired of this?" Aston asked, surprising Eli with the question.

"Tired of what?"

"Of the same routine, I guess. The boats, the fishing…"

"Sometimes," Eli admitted, feeling the truth of Aston's words resonate within him. "But I don't know what else to do."

Aston shrugged, a flicker of uncertainty crossing his features. "Yeah. I really do get that. I don't know. Life has a way of throwing us into stuff and we just have to go with it."

"Yeah, I don't know anything else."

"Well, maybe it's time to start exploring," Aston said, a smile creeping onto his face. "Life's too short to just do what's expected, right?"

Eli met Aston's gaze, a mixture of caution and intrigue in his eyes. For the first time, he seemed to consider the idea.

"Maybe," he replied softly, a hint of a smile playing at the corners of his lips.

Aston felt a bit of encouragement. His first day had gone well.

And maybe working alongside Eli would not only teach him about boats but also allow him to forge a connection that could help them both navigate their individual struggles.

In the midst of engines and fishing nets, Aston sensed the potential for friendship. As they continued to work side by side, the shadows of their pasts began to fade, leaving room for the promise of new beginnings.

Chapter Eight

The soft glow of candlelight flickered across the intimate setting of the seaside restaurant, casting dancing shadows on the walls. The sound of gentle waves crashing against the shore filled the air, mingling with the laughter of diners enjoying their evening. Laura sat across from Alex at a small table for two, her heart fluttering with a mix of excitement and nerves as she caught her breath from laughing.

"I'm having such a good time," she said, her eyes sparkling.

"I'm glad, Laura. So am I. It's been a while," he smiled. Their eyes locked and then Alex leaned back in his chair, his warm blue eyes sparkling with curiosity as he studied her. "So, tell me more about why you moved to Clearwater."

Laura smiled, grateful for his genuine interest. "Well, after my husband passed away, I needed a fresh start. We were both born and raised in the same town, and everything there just felt… too familiar, too heavy with memories. Clearwater offered a chance to start anew, away from all those reminders."

Alex's expression softened, the lightness in his demeanor shifting to something more serious. "That must have been incredibly tough for you and Aston," he said quietly.

"It was," Laura replied, her voice steady but tinged with sadness. "Aston took it hard. He was only seventeen when his father died, and he's still grappling with it. He can be prone to getting down sometimes, especially since we moved here. I worry about him."

"Of course," Alex said empathetically. "It's a lot to process at that age. Kids don't always know how to express what they're feeling. I know that firsthand."

Laura looked up, intrigued. "You do?"

"Yeah," he began, picking up a spoon from the table and fiddling with it. "I went through a divorce about three years ago. It was a tough time, especially for my daughters. They were only eight and ten at the time, and it was hard not being able to see them as much as I wanted."

"I can't imagine," Laura said softly. "How do they cope with it?"

"They've each handled it in their own way," Alex replied, a fond smile creeping onto his face. "Sometimes, I think kids are better at processing things than we give them credit for. They have their moments of sadness, but they also have this amazing resilience. We've worked hard to make sure they know they're loved, no matter what. We all go through ups and downs, but I try to remind them that it's okay to feel sad or confused sometimes."

Laura nodded, appreciating his insight. "That's so important. I've tried to communicate that to Aston, too. It's okay to talk about his feelings, to let it all out. I just wish he would. He is always so closed."

"Just be patient with him," Alex advised gently. "Sometimes, it takes time for kids to open up. He'll get there, especially with a mother like you who cares so much."

She smiled, feeling a warmth spread through her chest. "Thank you."

"Does he know you're on a date with me?"

"Yes," she replied.

"And?"

"Well… He seems to be okay with it. I sensed a little jealously and reservedness. But I expected more."

"I'm sure he hates me already," he smiled. "But I'll do my best to win him over."

"No, Aston isn't like that. Once he gets to know you, I'm sure he will warm up to the idea of you and I dating."

Alex smiled and took a sip of his wine, his gaze steady on Laura. "And what about you? How have you been handling everything?"

She sighed and hesitated before answering.

"I'm trying," she replied honestly, her eyes momentarily drifting to the candle flickering between them. "Some days are easier than others. I'm finding joy in small things, like cooking or discovering new places and crashing into people," she laughed and he joined her.

"But seriously, I am trying to move forward. For Aston's sake I have to. And I keep telling him that we will never forget his dad."

"That's a healthy approach," Alex said, admiration lacing his voice. "It's important to honor those we've lost while also living for ourselves. Life has a way of balancing the two, doesn't it?"

"It really does," Laura agreed, feeling a connection building between them, woven through shared experiences and understanding. "And I'm grateful for the chance to start anew here. Clearwater has its charm, and I think it's helping both of us heal."

The conversation flowed seamlessly, with each revelation bringing them closer. Alex spoke about his time in the military, his divorce, and his family. Laura found herself laughing at Alex's stories about his daughters—how they would dress up their dog in ridiculous costumes for photos and how he tried to keep up with their fast-paced lives.

In return, Laura shared tales of her life with husband and Aston, her laughter mingling with Alex's as they reminisced about their childhoods, their aspirations, and the challenges they had faced.

As the waitress cleared their plates, Alex leaned forward, his expression earnest. "I'm really glad we decided to do this. You're an incredible person, Laura, and I admire your strength."

Laura felt a warmth spread through her, a mix of appreciation and something deeper. "I feel the same about you. It's nice to connect with someone who understands. Thank you for being so easy to talk to."

"Anytime," he replied, his smile genuine. "I think we should do this again sometime."

Laura agreed.

They shared a moment of silence, the weight of unspoken emotions hanging in the air, feeling the possibility of moving forward. Laura could see the kindness in Alex's eyes, a comforting presence amidst the uncertainty of her life.

As the evening wore on, they finished their desserts, and laughter punctuated their conversation. Laura felt lighter, a sense of hope blossoming within her.

Chapter Nine

As days turned into weeks, the summer sun began to stretch across the sky with more warmth, casting a golden hue over the marina. Aston settled into his routine at Taylor Charters, working alongside Eli and gradually peeling back the layers of his quiet personality. Each day felt like a step forward, not just for Aston but for Eli, who seemed to become a little more comfortable in his skin with every shared experience.

One afternoon, while they were cleaning up after a long day of work, Aston noticed a canvas draped over something at the far end of the marina. Curiosity piqued, he wandered over to inspect it, lifting the edge of the canvas to reveal a small, weathered boat nestled beneath. The wood was faded, and patches of peeling paint clung stubbornly to its surface.

"Hey, Eli! What's this?" Aston called out, his voice laced with excitement.

Eli, who had been organizing tools nearby, looked up and followed Aston's gaze. A flicker of surprise crossed his face before it settled into a softer expression.

"Oh, that," he said, crossing his arms over his chest. "That's my personal project."

"Your personal project?" Aston asked, stepping closer to get a better look. "What do you mean?"

"She used to be a beaut," Eli explained, moving to stand beside him. "But time has taken its toll on her. She is falling apart. I thought I might restore it one day."

Aston ran his fingers along the worn wood, feeling the history in every groove. "It looks like it has potential. Why haven't you worked on it?"

Eli shrugged, his gaze shifting to the ground. "I haven't had the time. Working here, I just… I don't know. It feels like a lot sometimes. My parents have expectations about what I should be doing, and this…" He trailed off, glancing back at the boat. "It's just a small project that probably wouldn't mean much to them."

Aston noticed the weight in Eli's words, the way he seemed to carry the burden of others' expectations on his shoulders. "But it means something to you, right? This boat is yours. Do you want to restore it?"

Eli hesitated, his expression clouded with uncertainty. "Yeah, I do. I just—" He paused, looking back at the boat. "I guess I've always wanted to bring it back to life. It feels like a reflection of me, you know? Something that's been left behind."

Aston felt a spark of understanding ignite within him. "Then let's do it! We can work on it together in our spare time. I can help you."

Eli's eyes widened in surprise. "Really? You'd want to do that?"

"Of course."

"Don't you have better things to do than spend time with me?"

"No. I'm bored at home. And besides, spending time with you isn't a chore, you know... Even if you think it might be."

"Oh..."

"Oh? It sounds like a fun project. Plus, it'll be a great way to get to know each other even better," Aston replied, unable to resist a huge grin at the quirkiness of Eli.

A faint smile tugged at Eli's lips, a sign of the connection they were beginning to build. "Okay. I mean, I'd like that."

"It will be our personal project... We'll be sailing in her in no time!"

Eli smiled and looked genuinely touched and Aston couldn't help putting his arm around Eli's shoulder as they surveyed the small boat together.

Over the next few weeks, they dedicated their evenings and weekends to restoring the small boat. Each day, they would meet after finishing their regular work at the marina. They worked side by side, scrubbing away years of grime, sanding down rough edges, and discussing their plans for the boat's transformation.

As they worked, Aston encouraged Eli to share more about his vision. "What do you want it to look like when it's finished?" he asked one day, a paintbrush in hand as he dipped it into a can of bright blue paint.

"I want to make it look like it used to," Eli replied, staring intently at the boat. "It had this beautiful, vibrant color before. I want to restore it to its original glory. Maybe even add some personal touches."

"What kind of personal touches?" Aston prompted, curious about what lay behind Eli's quiet demeanor.

Eli hesitated, running his fingers along the boat's edge. "I've always liked the idea of painting a small mural on the side. Something that reflects the sea, or maybe something that inspires me."

"Yeah, I like that! What would you paint?" Aston encouraged, his excitement evident.

"I don't know yet. Something that reminds me of… freedom, I guess," Eli said, his voice trailing off. There was a flicker of vulnerability in his eyes, an opening that Aston sensed was significant.

"Freedom?" Aston echoed, sensing the deeper meaning behind Eli's words. "What does freedom look like to you?"

Eli looked away for a moment, contemplating the question. "It's not this… I don't know if I can break free from it," gesturing at the building

"Do you want to break free?" Aston asked gently, wanting to draw Eli out.

"Yeah," Eli admitted, his voice barely above a whisper. "But it's hard. They want me to take over the family business, find a girl, settle down."

Aston nodded, feeling a rush of empathy for Eli's situation. "That sounds tough. But you have to find what makes you happy, even if it's not what they want."

Eli looked at Aston, a mixture of appreciation and apprehension in his gaze. "You really think so?"

"Absolutely," Aston replied with conviction. "This boat is a start. You're pouring your heart into it. That's more than just a project; it's a way for you to express who you are."

Eli seemed to consider this, a flicker of determination sparking in his eyes. He gave a small contemplative nod.

As the weeks progressed, Aston watched Eli grow more confident in his decisions, finding joy in the restoration process. The small boat became a canvas for Eli's thoughts and feelings, each brushstroke representing a piece of himself he was beginning to reclaim.

One afternoon, as they took a break from painting, Aston leaned against the side of the boat, watching the sun dip low in the sky.

"You know, this boat is really something special," he said. "It's like a metaphor for us. You're taking something that was forgotten and giving it new life."

Eli chuckled softly, a genuine smile lighting up his face. "You're getting deep on me, Aston."

"I can't help it," Aston said, grinning back. "But seriously, we're doing an amazing job. I can't wait to see how it turns out."

"Agreed," Eli replied, his smile fading a bit as he looked back at the boat. "It feels good to work on it. Like I'm taking a step towards something better."

"Exactly! And you know what?" Aston leaned in closer, lowering his voice conspiratorially. "Once it's finished, we should take it out on the water. Just the two of us."

Eli's eyes widened, the invitation hanging in the air like a promise. "Really? You'll go with me."

"Of course! Try stop me! We can have our own little adventure. Just think about it: the two of us, out on the open water, away from all the noise."

Eli's expression softened as he considered the idea. "That sounds nice. I've always wanted to do that. Just… be free for a while."

"Then let's make it happen," Aston said, a thrill running through him at the thought of their shared adventure. "This boat can be our ticket to freedom."

As they resumed their work, the camaraderie between them deepened, each moment reinforcing the connection that was blossoming in the wake of their shared project. Aston could see the transformation happening in Eli—not just in the boat, but within himself.

Weeks passed, and with every brushstroke and every repaired plank, they not only brought the boat back to life but also helped each other navigate the complexities of their own lives. Eli began to share more about his struggles, his fears, and the weight of expectations that felt like a storm threatening to pull him under.

In those quiet moments between laughter and hard work, Aston learned to appreciate the strength it took for Eli to open up, even in small ways. It was as if the boat was more than just wood and paint—it was a vessel of hope, carrying their dreams and aspirations, a symbol of their journey towards self-discovery.

As they stood back to admire their progress one day, Eli stepped away from the boat, a newfound confidence radiating from him. "You know," he said, a hint of vulnerability in his voice, "I never thought I'd actually get to work on this. I always thought it was just a dream."

"Well, dreams can be built," Aston replied, a smile spreading across his face. "You just need to put in the work."

Eli nodded slowly, a flicker of realization crossing his features. "Maybe I can start building more than just boats. Maybe I can build a life that feels right for me."

"That's the spirit!" Aston said, feeling the warmth of encouragement surge between them.

As the sun dipped below the horizon, casting a warm glow over the marina, Aston couldn't shake the feeling that their friendship was becoming something more. It was in the laughter, the shared moments, and the unspoken understanding that blossomed amidst the restoration of that small boat.

Together, they were discovering more than just a passion for boats; they were uncovering the essence of who they were and what they wanted out of life, one brushstroke at a time.

Chapter Ten

Laura set the dining table for three. Soft music played in the background, creating an inviting atmosphere for the evening. Tonight was special; she had invited Alex over for dinner to formally introduce him to Aston, something that she felt strongly about. Laura felt a mix of excitement and anxiety—she hoped this evening would be a positive step forward for both of them.

As she placed the last fork down, she glanced at the clock. Alex was due to arrive any minute. She smoothed her hair, a flutter of nerves stirring in her stomach. "This is going to be great," she reassured herself, hoping her enthusiasm would translate to Aston.

When the doorbell rang, she nearly jumped. "Aston!" she called out, her voice bright. "Can you get that?"

From the living room, she heard a muffled reply. "Yeah, sure."

Laura stood in the kitchen, closed her eyes momentarily and took a deep breath to try and relax her nerves. She so wanted Alex and Aston to get along well.

Aston appeared at the door, hesitating for a moment before pulling it open. Alex stood there, holding a bouquet of flowers, a bottle of wine and a warm smile. "Hey Aston, I hope I'm not too early!" he said, his friendly demeanor putting Aston slightly at ease.

"Not at all," Laura chimed in, stepping forward to greet him. "Those are beautiful! Thank you."

"I thought they might brighten up the evening," Alex replied, handing the bouquet to her.

Laura placed the flowers in a vase, and they made their way to the dining table. As they settled in, Aston remained somewhat stiff, his brow furrowed as he observed Alex from across the table. The initial warmth of the room began to feel constricting, the air thick with unspoken tension.

"Thanks for having me over," Alex said, looking at Aston, trying to make him feel at ease, his voice light and casual. "I've been looking forward to this." Aston sensed a tinge of nervousness in Alex as well.

"Yeah, sure," Aston muttered, his tone betraying a lack of enthusiasm. He picked at his food, glancing up occasionally to gauge Alex's reactions.

"So, Aston," Alex began, attempting to break the ice. "Laura's told me a bit about you. I hear you're quite the athlete?"

Aston shrugged, feeling a flush of embarrassment. "I was at school. I played some sports. It's nothing special."

"Nothing special? You're modest," Alex chuckled, his smile genuine. "What sports do you play?"

"Soccer and swimming," Aston replied, his voice barely above a whisper. He noticed Alex's genuine interest, but it only made him more uneasy. He couldn't shake the feeling that he was being scrutinized, like a specimen under a microscope.

"Those are great! I used to swim a bit when I was younger. Always loved being in the water," Alex continued, trying to engage Aston further. "Do you compete?"

Aston's stomach churned. "No," he replied, focusing on his plate.

The conversation meandered as Laura attempted to draw them both out, sharing light stories and laughter.
But the more they talked, the more Aston felt like a third wheel.

As the evening wore on, he could sense the chemistry between his mother and Alex, the way they exchanged glances and laughter, and it left a sour taste in his mouth.

Once dinner was finished and dessert was served, Aston excused himself. "I think I'm going to go to my room, if you don't mind," he announced, standing up too quickly.

"Are you sure?" Laura asked, concern etched across her face. "You're missing out!"

"Nah, it's fine. I'm just tired," he mumbled, avoiding her gaze as he walked away, leaving the adults to continue their conversation.

Once in his room, Aston plopped down on his bed, frustration bubbling inside him. He heard Laura's footsteps approaching, and a soft knock on the door interrupted his thoughts.

"Aston, can I come in?" she asked gently.

"Yeah," he replied, trying to sound nonchalant.

Laura entered, closing the door behind her.
"How are you feeling?" she asked, her expression warm but searching.

"Fine," he muttered, crossing his arms defensively.

"Just fine?" she pressed, settling on the edge of his bed. "What do you think of Alex?"

"I don't know," Aston replied, his voice low. "He seems… nice, I guess. But it feels weird."

"To be expected, I suppose. It's all new," Laura said, her tone encouraging.

"I just don't know if I like him," he admitted, the words spilling out before he could contain them. "I mean, is he really going to fit in? Like, does he really get us?"

Laura sighed, her eyes softening. "Aston, again, I promise he will never replace your father. He can never be your father. No one could ever do that. This is just a chance for us to maybe have someone we can rely on in our lives again."

"Yeah, but…" Aston hesitated, the weight of his insecurities pressing down on him. "Does he know about me? About… you know?"

"Yes," Laura said gently. "I told him you're gay. He's supportive, Aston. He understands."

Aston felt a flicker of relief, but it was quickly overshadowed by doubt. "You're sure he's fine with it?" His voice trailed off, the implication hanging in the air.

"Yes. He is more than fine with it," Laura reassured him, sensing his discomfort. "Aston, you don't have to feel threatened by him in any way, shape or form. He wants to get to know us both, and he cares about me. That doesn't change anything between you and me. I want you to try to give him a chance. For me."

"I just don't want him to think I'm weird," Aston confessed, his voice barely a whisper.

"You're not weird," Laura said firmly. "You're my son, and I love you just the way you are. You have nothing to prove to him or anyone else."

Aston met her gaze, searching for reassurance in her eyes.

"If he ever causes any issues between us, I'll kick him to the curb," she replied, her expression earnest. "You're my number one guy, remember? That's never going to change. You're the only priority in my life."
He felt a warmth spread through him, though uncertainty lingered like a shadow. "Okay," he said, feeling slightly more at ease. "I guess I'll give him a chance."

"Thank you," Laura said, her smile brightening. "That means a lot to me, Aston. Let's see where this goes together, okay?"

"Yeah, alright," Aston replied, a hesitant smile breaking through.

"You want to come down for dessert?"

"I suppose," he smiled. "Your dessert is always good."

Laura smiled and gave him a hug. Then they both made their way back down the stairs to join Alex.

After dessert, Aston shook Alex's hand, hugged Laura and thanked her for the great meal and retreated to bed.

As Laura stood at the front door with Alex, the evening's warmth lingered in the air, the stars twinkling above like tiny diamonds. She smiled up at him, feeling a flutter of excitement. Alex's expression, however, seemed to hold a hint of uncertainty.

"So, Aston hates me, right?" he said, attempting to keep the mood light, but the underlying worry was clear in his voice.

Laura chuckled softly, shaking her head. "No, not at all! He's just… adjusting. I think it's a great start, honestly. He'll come around. You just have to give him some time."

Alex's eyes searched hers, and a flicker of doubt crossed his face. "You really think so?" he asked, his voice tinged with vulnerability.

"I know so," Laura replied earnestly, reaching out to squeeze his hand. "You're a good guy, Alex. He'll see that, just like I have."

With a shared smile, they leaned in, and Alex pressed a gentle kiss to her lips—a sweet, tender moment that felt like magic. When they pulled away, a warmth spread through Laura, making her feel giddy and alive. "Goodnight, Laura," he said softly, his gaze lingering on her.

"Goodnight, Alex," she replied, her heart soaring as she watched him drive away, feeling as though she was walking on clouds.

She stepped inside and shut the door and stood there for a moment. The house was quiet. She couldn't help but grin and did a little silent dance.

Laura's heart swelled with hope and happiness, thinking of the connection she was building with Alex, while also believing that her son would eventually come to accept him. It felt like a new beginning for them all, a fragile yet promising step into a future she had dared to hope for.

Chapter Eleven

The morning sun was just starting to burn off the fog hanging over the marina, casting a soft golden light across the rows of boats bobbing gently in the water. The place was still waking up, the salty air heavy with the scent of seaweed and damp wood. Eli had already been at the dock for an hour, quietly inspecting a few fishing boats that had come in needing repairs. His hands moved methodically, tracing the lines of the hulls, checking for cracks and wear, but his mind was far away.

He barely registered the rumble of an approaching truck until the sound of tires crunching over gravel snapped him out of his thoughts. Eli glanced up, squinting through the morning light to see a large pickup truck pulling an expensive, but battered boat on a trailer into the yard.

The truck came to a halt with a screech, and the driver's door swung open, revealing Mark Benson. He stepped out, his tall, broad frame casting a shadow across the boat as he slammed the door shut behind him. His movements were sharp, impatient, like he had somewhere more important to be. Eli felt his stomach tighten at the sight of him.

Mark was hard to miss around town—he was one of those guys who seemed to take up too much space, with his loud voice, bigger-than-life attitude, and the constant need to throw his weight around.

Aston was across the yard, stacking some crates by the dock, still new to the job and watching everything with a keen eye, but staying out of the way. He had noticed Eli's shift in demeanor as soon as Mark pulled up. Eli's usual calm seemed to fade, replaced by a tense, guarded expression. Aston kept to his task but stayed close enough to observe.

"Hey!" Mark called out, his voice sharp as he gestured to the boat. "I need this piece of junk fixed *now*."

Eli wiped his hands on his rag and approached, his expression carefully neutral as he stepped toward the trailer. The boat looked like it had been through hell—gashes along the side, the hull dented and scraped, and a large crack near the bow.

"What happened?" Eli asked, kneeling to examine the damage more closely.

Mark snorted, leaning against his truck. "Hit some rocks near the reef. These damn maps are all wrong. Not my fault they don't mark everything properly."

Eli's lips pressed into a thin line. He'd heard that excuse more times than he could count. "It's pretty bad," he said, standing up and wiping his hands again. "This is going to take some time. At least a few weeks to get it seaworthy again."

Mark's face immediately twisted in annoyance. "A *few weeks*? Are you kidding me? I need this thing back by the weekend. I've got people waiting to take a spin in it."

Eli met his gaze steadily. "I understand, but there's a lot of structural damage. If you want it done right, it'll take time. I can't rush a repair like this."

"Done right?" Mark's voice rose, his temper flaring. "I've been bringing my boat here for years, and I've never had to wait this long for a repair. What kind of service is this? You guys slowing down or something?"

Eli's jaw tightened, but he kept his voice calm. "We're not slowing down. You hit a reef. This isn't a quick patch job, Mark. If you want the boat safe, I need time to do it properly."

Mark pushed off his truck, taking a step closer to Eli, looming over him with his usual aggressive posture.

"I don't think you get it. I need this boat *this weekend.* I'm not asking for much—just for you to do your damn job."

Eli's eyes flickered, but he didn't back down. "I'm doing my job. You want it done fast, or do you want it done right? Because I can't do both. And fast is dangerous. I won't do that."

A tense silence hung in the air. Mark's fists clenched at his sides, his face flushed with anger. For a moment, Aston thought Mark might swing at Eli, the way he was glaring at him. Aston had stopped stacking crates and now stood a few yards away, watching carefully, unsure if he should step in.

But Mark seemed to catch himself. He exhaled sharply, muttering something under his breath as he turned and stormed back toward his truck. "Fine. But it better be done before the end of the month," he snapped, turning and he unhitching the trailer.

Without another word, he yanked the door open and climbing inside, revved the engine and sped out of the marina, leaving a cloud of dust in his wake. The trailer with the boat stayed behind, sitting abandoned in the yard.

Eli stood there for a moment, staring at the boat as the tension slowly ebbed from his shoulders.

He let out a long breath, shaking his head before turning back to his workbench. Aston approached cautiously, watching Eli with curiosity.

"That guy's a real piece of work," Aston commented, trying to gauge Eli's mood.

Eli shrugged, his hands busy again as he picked up a tool and started to tinker with something on the bench. "He's a tourist," he said simply, as if that explained everything. "They can be difficult."

"Doesn't seem like he was here for sightseeing," Aston said, still frowning in the direction Mark had disappeared. "You get people like that a lot?"

Eli glanced at him briefly, then back to his tools. "More than I'd like. They come in, mess up their boats, and expect miracles in a couple of days." He let out a quiet sigh, his fingers working methodically. "You get used to it."

Aston didn't say anything for a moment, watching Eli's focused, almost mechanical movements. There was something about the way Eli had brushed off the encounter that bothered him. It was like Eli was used to swallowing his frustration, used to people pushing him around.

Aston had seen the flash of defiance in Eli's eyes during the argument with Mark, but it had been fleeting—just a moment before Eli had pulled back, retreating into himself.

"You shouldn't have to deal with that," Aston said finally, his voice quieter now. "People like him… they think they own the place."

Eli gave a small, humorless chuckle. "They do, in a way. They're the ones who keep the business running. Without them, we wouldn't have much of a job."

Aston wanted to argue, to tell Eli that no one had the right to treat him like that, but he could see that Eli didn't want to dwell on it. The wall was already back up, and Aston knew enough about Eli by now to understand when not to push.

"Still," Aston said, giving a half-smile, "if that guy gives you any more trouble, you let me know. I'll take care of it."

Eli glanced at him, a faint smile tugging at the corners of his mouth. "I appreciate that," he said softly before turning back to his work.

Aston stood there for a moment longer, feeling a strange mix of frustration and admiration for Eli's calm resilience.

It was clear that Eli had dealt with people like Mark his whole life, but it still didn't sit right with him. As he walked back to his crates, he couldn't shake the feeling that there was more going on beneath Eli's surface than he was letting on.

Chapter Twelve

Over the past few weeks, they had spent countless hours together at the marina, often working late into the night, the sound of waves lapping against the dock providing a soothing backdrop to their efforts. The boat, once a forgotten piece of driftwood, was slowly but surely regaining its former glory, and their friendship was blossoming.

Aston loved how the nighttime atmosphere enveloped them in a blanket of quiet intimacy. As they worked, the world faded away, leaving only the two of them and the task at hand. The stars began to twinkle overhead, and a gentle breeze carried the salty scent of the ocean.

"Can you believe how far we've come?" Aston said, stepping back to admire their handiwork. The boat's blue hue glimmered under the soft light, and the fresh paint made it look like a completely different vessel.

Eli stood beside him, a hint of pride in his eyes. "Yeah, it's hard to believe. It feels good to see her come together."

Aston glanced sideways at Eli, noting how the moonlight illuminated his features, casting shadows across his face.

It was the first time that he felt something more towards Eli. Something more than just friendship.

A smile tugged at the corners of Eli's lips and then it dropped, and he looked away, clearly lost in thought. "I've always loved sailing. My parents used to take us out when I was very young. I loved feeling the wind in my hair and the salt on my skin. I've never felt as free as when I'm out on the ocean."

Aston asked, intrigued. "That sounds amazing."

Eli nodded slowly, his gaze still fixed on the boat. "Yeah. We would go on these long trips, just the four of us—me, my mom, my dad, and my sister. We'd explore the coastline, find hidden coves, and fish. Those trips were some of my favorite memories."

Aston leaned against the side of the boat, wanting to encourage Eli to share more. "You've got a sister! I didn't know."

Eli hesitated, his brow furrowing. "Had one. She died."

The bluntness of the statement took Aston by surprise, him stumbling to find the right words.

But Eli continued without hesitation. "She died in a sailing accident a few years ago. We were out on the water, and it was supposed to be a nice day out. But things went wrong. Very wrong." His voice trailed off, and he looked away, the pain evident in his expression.

Aston felt a chill run through him at Eli's words. "Ah shit, Eli. I'm so sorry, man," he said softly. "That must have been devastating for you… and your parents."

Eli nodded, swallowing hard. "After that, my parents became overly protective. They don't let me go out on my own anymore, not like I used to. I can't just sail around freely anymore." He picked at a small pebble, his frustration palpable.

"That's really tough," Aston said, feeling the weight of Eli's loss. "It must be hard not being able to do something you love because of it."

Eli sighed, his shoulders slumping. "I get it—they're just trying to keep me safe. But I miss the ocean. I miss the feeling of being out there whenever I want to be, away from everything. It feels like I'm trapped, like I can't escape this cycle of work and responsibility."

Aston felt a swell of empathy for Eli, understanding the weight of family expectations all too well. "You should take that feeling back. Once we finish the boat, we will go out. Just you and me. You won't be alone."

Eli's gaze snapped to Aston.

"I promise," Aston said, his voice filled with conviction. "I want you to experience that freedom again, to feel the wind and the waves. It's important."

Eli's expression softened, and he nodded slowly, as if considering the idea. "It would be nice to get back out there, just… I don't know if I can handle it, you know?"

Aston leaned in closer, reaching out to place a comforting hand on Eli's shoulder. "You're not trapped, Eli. You have the power to change your course, just like this boat. You're rebuilding it, just like you can rebuild your own path. You're not a kid anymore. They have to let you go sometime."

Eli took a deep breath, the tension in his shoulders easing slightly. "Thanks, Aston. It helps to talk about it. I've never spoken to anyone about it."

Aston looked solemnly, feeling a rush of warmth at their shared moment.

"I'm glad you did. I'm here for you, you know? You don't have to go through that alone anymore. You speak whenever you want to."

In that moment, as they sat side by side under the blanket of stars, Aston felt the connection between them deepen. It was a bond forged through shared experiences, vulnerabilities, and the promise of something more.

Eli's eyes softened, and for a heartbeat, the world around them faded away. "I appreciate that. It's nice to have someone who understands."

"I moved here against my will. My dad died a couple of years ago. Cancer. So yeah, I do understand. I think we're both learning from each other. And it feels like we were meant to meet. To help each other," Aston replied, his heart racing. "And that's a good thing."

"I'm not good with words. But I'm sorry about your dad," said Eli.

"Thanks Eli," said Aston.

All of a sudden, Eli reached over and hugged Aston. Aston hugged him back. And just as quickly, Eli sat back.

Aston was surprised at the moment of vulnerability, but understood and appreciated the hug more than words could say. So he said nothing.

As they resumed work, the weight of Eli's past lingered, but so did the possibility of a brighter future. Together, they were not just restoring a boat; they were building a foundation for their friendship, one that was filled with hope, dreams, and the promise of new adventures on the horizon.

Each moment of connection brought them closer, revealing layers of each other's lives, fears, and aspirations. The boat, once a mere project, had become a symbol of their ever growing bond—a reminder that even amidst uncertainty, they had each other to lean on.

In the stillness of the night, under the vast expanse of the stars, Aston felt a sense of belonging he hadn't experienced in a long time. It was as if the universe was aligning, guiding him toward something beautiful—a friendship that was true, a connection that felt genuine and real. And for the first time in a long while, he dared to believe in the possibilities that lay ahead.

Chapter Thirteen

The air was thick with the sweet smell of cotton candy and popcorn as Aston led Eli through the vibrant crowd at the annual beach festival. Colorful lights strung between palm trees blinked like stars, illuminating the festivities. Music floated through the air, a lively tune that seemed to echo the rhythm of the waves crashing against the shore.

Eli hesitated, glancing around at the throngs of people, the laughter and excitement swirling around them. The openness of this small-town community felt both welcoming and overwhelming. "Are you sure this is a good idea?" he asked, his voice nearly drowned out by the sounds of merriment.

"Come on, Eli! It's just a little fun," Aston replied, grinning ear to ear. His enthusiasm was infectious, and Eli couldn't help but feel a flicker of excitement despite his nerves. "I promise I'll look out for you. It'll be great!"

"Okay, but I don't really do crowds," Eli admitted, shifting his weight from one foot to the other.

"Trust me," Aston said, placing a reassuring hand on Eli's shoulder. "We'll stick together, I won't let anything happen to you. Besides, there's so much to do! Games, food, music… and I hear the fireworks are amazing."

Eli took a deep breath, a mixture of anticipation and apprehension swirling inside him. He nodded slowly, allowing Aston to lead him deeper into the festival. They grabbed a couple of beers and decided to have some fun.

As they wandered through the festival, Aston's excitement was palpable. He pulled Eli from one booth to the next, their laughter ringing out amidst the festival's chatter. They played games together, throwing rings over bottles, tossing darts at balloons, and Eli found himself smiling more than he thought possible. Aston's playful nature drew him out, and for the first time in a while, he felt a sense of freedom—like he could just be himself without the weight of expectations pressing down on him.

"Look! Cotton candy!" Aston exclaimed, dragging Eli toward the booth where the fluffy, sugary treat was being spun before their eyes. "You want some? I haven't had in ages!"

"With beer?"

"Oh come on! Live a little. Two please!" called Aston to the vendor.

They each got a large stick of cotton candy, and as they turned away from the booth, Aston took a huge bite, his face lighting up in delight. Eli couldn't help but laugh at the sight, and for a moment, all his worries faded away.

"This is way better than working at the marina," Aston said, his voice muffled by the sweet fluff.

"I guess," Eli agreed hesitantly, his gaze drifting to the crowd.

As they continued to explore, they stumbled upon a small area where families gathered to watch a local band perform. The energy of the crowd surged as people danced along to the upbeat tunes.

As the night wore on, Eli found himself relaxing more and more. They shared stories and laughter, their connection deepening with each passing moment. Aston was effortlessly charming, making him feel at ease, as if he had known him forever.

"You good?" Aston asked, nudging him gently as they walked past the game booths.

Eli gave a small smile, but it didn't reach his eyes. "Yeah… I'm surprised that I'm actually enjoying myself."

Before Aston could say anything, a loud, grating voice cut through the air behind them.

"Well, look who we got here."

Aston turned, his eyes narrowing as he recognized the figure standing a few feet away, reeking from booze. Mark Benson, the local tourist jock and overall troublemaker, swaggered toward them, with a smirk plastered across his face. He was taller than both Aston and Eli, broad-shouldered and intimidating, with short dark hair and eyes that always seemed to be sizing people up. The guy that had brought the speedboat in to be fixed a few weeks ago and had caused an altercation down at the docks.

Eli stiffened immediately, his body going rigid as Mark approached.

"Who's this?" Mark's gaze shifted to Aston, sizing him up in that smug, dismissive way he did with everyone. "Your boyfriend, Eli? You a faggot, huh?"

Aston felt a surge of anger rise in his chest, but before he could say anything, Eli spoke, his voice tight. "Mark, just leave us alone. You're drunk."

Mark snorted, his eyes gleaming with malicious amusement. "Leave you alone? I'm just asking a question. What, you too good to hang out with people like me now, Eli? You've been taking your sweet time with my boat. Got some extra 'distractions' these days, huh?"

Aston clenched his fists at his sides, struggling to keep his temper in check. He could see the tension radiating off Eli, his friend's usual quiet composure cracking under the pressure of Mark's words.

"You know the boat's not ready," Eli said, his voice strained. "It's structural damage. You crashed into the reef, Mark. Like I said, it's not a quick fix."

"Yeah, yeah, excuses," Mark growled, stepping closer to Eli. "I need that boat back on the water. You've had it for weeks, and all I hear are your lame-ass excuses. Maybe you're spending too much time with your little *boyfriend* here." He poked Aston in the chest with a finger.

Aston couldn't hold back anymore.

"Get your fucken hands off me," He said as he stepped between Eli and Mark, shoving Mark's hand away, his heart racing but his voice steady.

"Well, well... The faggot has some fight in him."

"He said it's structural damage. You crashed it because you don't know how to handle your boat. And now, you need to back off."

Mark's smirk faded, and his eyes narrowed dangerously as he sized Aston up. "Who the hell do you think you are, stepping into this? You don't know a damn thing about boats, and you sure as hell don't know how this works. Eli works for *me*. I'm the customer... so I think I'll say whatever the hell I want."

Aston met his gaze without flinching. "You need to leave him alone. He's doing his job. You're the one who can't drive a boat."

Mark's hands twitched at his sides. His face flushed with anger, his breathing heavy.

"Stay out of this," Mark growled, his voice low and menacing. "You think you can just come into town and tell me what to do? You don't even know what's going on here."

Aston didn't back down, his jaw clenched tight. "I know enough. You want your boat fixed? Then stop acting like a jackass and give Eli the time he needs to do it right. Or keep talking, and it'll take even longer."

There was a tense silence. Mark's face contorted with anger, his fists clenched so tight his knuckles turned white. For a brief moment, Aston thought he might actually take a swing and prepared for an evasive side-step. But then Mark scoffed, stepping back with a sneer.

"Whatever," Mark spat, his gaze flicking to Eli one last time. "You better get that boat done soon, or you'll regret it, Eli."

With that, he turned and stalked off into the crowd, shoving past festival-goers as he went. The tension in the air lingered for a moment longer before finally dissolving.

Eli let out a shaky breath, his shoulders slumping as the adrenaline drained from him. Aston turned to him, concern written all over his face.

"You okay?"

Eli nodded, but his expression was tight, his gaze fixed on the ground. "Yeah… I'm fine. This is why I hate crowds and people."

"Yeah, I hear you."

Seeing Eli like this—so clearly upset and trying to hold it together—made Aston angry.

"That guy's a prick," Aston muttered, shaking his head. "Don't let him get to you."

Eli glanced up, a faint, bitter smile tugging at the corners of his mouth. "You get used to it. There are a lot of pricks in this town. Tourists with money."

"Well, you shouldn't have to get used to it," Aston said, his voice firm. "He's got no right to talk to you like that."

Eli didn't say anything, his gaze distant as they continued walking through the festival. He hated that Eli had to deal with people like Mark, and he hated even more that it was getting to him.

"Let's get to someplace quieter," said Aston, seeing that Eli was no longer enjoying himself.

He pulled Eli away from the crowd, leading him down to the beach and the water's edge. The moon hung low in the sky, casting a silvery glow over the ocean, the waves shimmering as they lapped gently at the shore.

They sat down on the sand, the cool grains beneath them, and for a moment, the world felt still. Eli could hear the distant sound of laughter and music, but it felt like a lifetime away.

"This is more my style," Eli said, glancing at Aston, who was gazing out at the ocean.

"Yeah, it is nice," Aston replied, his tone quieter now. "I'm glad you came with me. I know it's not easy for you. And I'm sorry we had to bump into that dick."

Eli shifted, feeling a rush of warmth at Aston's words. "Forget about him. Thanks for inviting me. I didn't think I would enjoy it as much as I did, until that point. But it's because you are here."

Aston turned to face him, their eyes locking for a brief moment. "I think you're a lot more fun than you give yourself credit for."

Eli felt his cheeks flush at the compliment, a mix of shyness and something deeper stirring inside him. "I guess I just don't let loose as much as I should."

Aston leaned closer, his voice dropping to a whisper. "You should. Life is too short to hold back." There was an intensity in Aston's gaze, a sincerity that sent a thrill down Eli's spine.

Eli looked away, biting his lip as he tried to process the shift in the air between them. It felt charged, like an electric current. "I just... I don't know *how* to let go sometimes."

"Just be yourself," Aston said, reaching out to brush a stray piece of hair from Eli's forehead. The gentle touch sent a jolt of warmth through Eli, and he leaned into it instinctively. "You're safe with me."

As the moment lingered, Eli's heart raced. He could feel the weight of Aston's gaze on him, the atmosphere thick with unspoken words. "Aston, I..."

Before he could finish, Aston leaned in slightly, as if caught in the same moment of hesitation. Eli's breath caught in his throat, the world around them fading away. There was a magnetic pull, an urge to close the gap, but a flicker of doubt held him back.

"Maybe we should get back to the festival," Eli blurted out, the words tumbling out in a rush.

"Yeah, okay," Aston replied, his voice a mixture of disappointment and understanding. He pulled back, a soft smile lingering on his lips, but the intensity in his eyes remained.

As they stood up and brushed the sand from their clothes, Eli's heart was still racing. The chemistry between them had ignited, and it was a thrill that left him both exhilarated and nervous. Eli couldn't shake the feeling of what almost happened, the thrill of the moment lingering in the air.

They walked back toward the festival, the laughter and music washing over them once again, but the moment by the water remained etched in Eli's mind. Aston's presence felt like a safe harbor amidst the storm of his emotions, and as they rejoined the festivities, Eli couldn't help but wonder about what lay ahead for them.

The night was still young, but the connection they had forged felt more profound than ever. Eli felt alive like he had never felt before.

Chapter Fourteen

The festival's joyful atmosphere lingered in Aston's mind long after they returned home. Yet, as he lay in bed, he couldn't shake the feeling that something had shifted within Eli. The vibrant laughter and excitement from earlier had given way to a quiet tension that Aston sensed but couldn't quite understand.

The next day, he decided to check on Eli. It was a Saturday, and the sun shone brightly, casting a golden hue over the coastal town. Aston paced around his room, contemplating how to approach the subject. He wanted to help Eli feel better but feared pushing too hard. After some deliberation, he sent a quick text.

Hey, want to come over for a movie night? Just us. My mom is going out on another damn date with some guy she drove into.

Eli's reply came shortly after, a simple, hesitant

LOL. Sure.

Aston felt a flutter of hope. He wanted to create a space for Eli to feel safe, to open up without the pressure of the world outside pressing in on him.

When Eli arrived that evening, Aston greeted him with a bright smile, trying to mask his own nervousness. "Hey! I've got popcorn, candy, and a bunch of movies. We can do whatever you want."

"Sounds good," Eli replied, but Aston noticed the way his eyes seemed to drift, his smile a touch more subdued than usual.

As they settled onto the couch, Aston grabbed the remote and flicked through the options, ultimately landing on a light-hearted comedy. The room was cozy, the glow of the TV casting flickering shadows against the walls. Aston could feel the warmth of Eli's presence beside him, but the air was heavy with unspoken words.

"Is this okay?" Aston asked, nudging Eli gently as their shoulders brushed.

"Yeah," Eli said softly, though his gaze remained fixed on the screen.

They started watching, but the movie felt like background noise. Aston sneaked glances at Eli, who seemed lost in thought. He longed to reach out, to break the tension, but he didn't want to overwhelm Eli.

As the film progressed, laughter occasionally erupted from the characters on screen, but it felt distant. Finally, Aston paused the movie. "Eli, you seem… different today. Is everything okay?"

Eli looked at him, a mix of surprise and hesitation crossing his features. "I'm fine. Just tired, I guess."

"Really? Because you don't seem fine," Aston pressed gently. "You can tell me if something's bothering you."

A heavy silence filled the room, and Eli sighed, and scratched his arm. "I don't want to drag you down with my problems."

"Eli," Aston said, his voice steady. "I want to know. We're friends, right? I care about you."

Eli shifted on the couch, visibly wrestling with his thoughts. "It's just… my mom has been really pressuring me lately. She wants me to start dating. She has this idea of what my life should look like, and it's suffocating me. A lot."

Aston nodded, trying to understand. "What does she want you to do?"

Eli hesitated, his voice dropping to a whisper. "She has set me up on a couple of dates with her friend's daughter, Ava. And she is a lovely person, don't get me wrong. I get along very well with her. But my mom wants me to date her. She thinks that if I settle down with someone like her, it'll solve everything."

"Doesn't sound like it'd make you happy," Aston replied, keeping his tone gentle.

"It wouldn't. It would make her happy, and that's what matters… to her," Eli admitted, his gaze dropping to his hands. "I don't even know if I'm ready for all that. I mean, I don't even know how to tell her that I'm not... I think…"

His words stuttered and he couldn't get them out.

"It's okay. Speak your mind. It's just me."

Eli glanced at Aston and then looked down, feeling very self conscious, "You have to promise to keep it a secret."

"Of course. What is it?" said Aston, instinctively knowing what was coming next.

"I'm scared to tell you."

"Don't be. Just say it. It's not going to change anything between us, I promise."

"I'm… I don't think I'm interested in girls."

The weight of Eli's confession hung in the air, and Aston felt a swell of empathy. "Nothing wrong with that."

"You're not mad?"

"Why would I be mad? You shouldn't have to hide who you are, Eli. None of us should."

Eli let out a long sigh, as if telling someone enabled him to exhale the burden he felt he had carried all these years.

"I know, but it's complicated. My parents… they're so set in their ways," Eli said, his voice trembling slightly. "After my sister died, everything changed.

My mom would never understand. She has become a hard person. She would never accept me being gay."

Aston's heart ached for Eli. "I can't imagine how hard that must be for you."

Eli looked up, his eyes shimmering with unshed tears. "It's just that I see so many people living their truth, and I want that too. But I don't know how to get there. I feel like I'm letting them down."

"You're not letting anyone down by being yourself," Aston said, his voice firm. "Your happiness matters. It's your life, Eli, not theirs."

A silence fell between them, and Aston could feel the intensity of the moment. He leaned in slightly, wanting to bridge the gap between them. "What do you want, Eli?"

Eli's breath hitched as he considered the question. "I want to be free. Free to explore who I am without judgment, without fear of disappointing my parents."

The vulnerability in Eli's voice struck Aston deeply. He wanted to reach out, to comfort him, to show him that he wasn't alone. "You deserve that, Eli. You really do."

Eli nodded.

"What makes you happy?" Aston asked, his heart racing as he watched Eli's expression soften, the barriers he had built slowly beginning to crumble. "You do. You make me feel safe, Aston," Eli confessed, his voice barely above a whisper. "I haven't felt that since my sister died."

Aston's heart swelled at the admission. "I'm glad. I want you to feel safe with me. You make me happy too, Eli."

In that moment, everything felt charged between them. The space narrowed, their proximity igniting a longing that had been brewing beneath the surface. Eli's eyes flicked to Aston's lips, a question lingering in the air. Aston felt the pull as he leaned closer, his heart pounding.

But then Eli pulled back slightly, uncertainty clouding his gaze. "We shouldn't," he said, his voice laced with both fear and desire.

"Why not?"

"I don't know if I'm ready," admitted Eli.

"Okay. No pressure," Aston replied, his voice barely a whisper. He wanted to reach out, to pull Eli closer, but the weight of their circumstances loomed heavily over them.

Eli sighed, running a hand through his hair again, frustration flickering in his eyes. "I just don't want to ruin what we have."

Aston felt a pang in his chest at the thought. "You won't. Whatever this is between us… it's real."

"I know, but… I'm scared," Eli admitted, vulnerability spilling over. "What if it doesn't work out? What if my parents find out? What if—"

"Eli," Aston interrupted gently, "we can take this slow. We don't have to rush anything. Just being here with you feels right."

Eli nodded, though uncertainty still clouded his eyes. "I just don't want to mess things up."

"Stop beating yourself up. You won't," Aston reassured him. "I'll help you get there. I promise."

They sat in silence, the air thick with unspoken feelings and possibilities.

The movie played softly in the background, but neither of them paid it any mind. Instead, they focused on each other, their breaths mingling as they navigated the delicate territory of their growing connection.

After a few moments, Aston leaned back slightly, trying to break the spell and let Eli feel more comfortable. "Let's watch the movie, okay?"

Eli nodded, though a flicker of disappointment crossed his features. They settled back into their positions, but the atmosphere had shifted, charged with the weight of their conversation.

Throughout the remainder of the movie, Aston could feel the unbreakable bond forming between them, the shared vulnerability stitching their hearts together. They didn't need to rush into anything; the emotional intimacy they had built in that small space was more than enough. There was an understanding now.

And as they sat side by side, their fingers brushing occasionally, both Aston and Eli knew that whatever lay ahead, the future would happen and they would face it together.

Chapter Fifteen

The sun had dipped low on the horizon, casting a warm golden glow over the marina as Aston made his way to the docks. The familiar scent of salt and sea air filled his lungs, bringing with it a wave of anticipation. He had been looking forward to diving into the shared project that had become a sanctuary for him and Eli.

As Aston approached the small boat they had been working on, he saw Eli already there, bent over the hull, his brow furrowed in concentration. The sight of him made Aston's heart race, a familiar flutter igniting in his chest.

"Hey, Eli!" Aston called out, breaking the tranquil silence.

Eli looked up, his eyes meeting Aston's with a flicker of warmth. "Hey! You're early."

"Just couldn't wait to get started," Aston replied, grinning as he grabbed a rag and moved to join Eli. "What are we working on today?"

"Just some final touches on the hull," Eli said, gesturing toward the boat. "I think we're almost there."

"I can't wait for the maiden voyage," smiled Aston, genuinely excited.

As they worked side by side, the sun began to slip behind the clouds, casting long shadows across the marina. Their hands brushed against each other more frequently than usual, each touch sending a jolt of warmth through Aston. The laughter they shared felt lighter today, laced with an undertone of something deeper. It was as if the world outside had faded away, leaving just the two of them, caught in a bubble of connection.

They talked easily, moving from the boat to snippets of their lives. Aston found himself hanging onto Eli's every word, mesmerized by the way his face lit up when he spoke about sailing and the ocean. Eli was coming into his own. He seemed more confident to Aston. Yet, beneath Eli's stronger exterior and passion lay an undercurrent of uncertainty that Aston couldn't ignore.

"I love the water," Eli said, his voice softer now as he ran a hand over the boat's surface. "But sometimes it feels like it's the only thing I can count on.

"You can always count on me," replied Aston.

"I know... I just don't know why, but everything else feels... unstable."

Aston paused, sensing the vulnerability in Eli's admission. "What do you mean?"

Eli hesitated, glancing down. "It's just... with my parents. I feel like I'm drowning in their dreams for me, and I can't breathe."

"Eli," Aston said gently, stepping closer. "Remember, you're not alone in this anymore."

Eli looked up, and their eyes locked for a moment that felt like eternity. Aston could see the turmoil behind Eli's gaze, the struggle between what he wanted and what was expected of him.

The air shifted. A dark cloud had rolled in, blocking the sun and casting a shadow over the marina. Aston felt the first droplets of rain hit his skin, a soft patter that quickly turned into a downpour.

"Great timing!" Eli exclaimed, laughing as he grabbed his tools. "We should find cover!"

Aston couldn't help but smile and followed him.

They dashed toward the nearest boat, laughter echoing above the sound of the rain pounding against the wooden dock. As they scrambled up the ladder and jumped inside, Eli closed the door behind them, and they were enveloped in the smell of wet wood and the sound of the rain drumming overhead.

The intimacy of the small space heightened the atmosphere. Water cascaded down the sides of the boat, the world outside fading into a blurred backdrop. Aston's heart raced, the tension between them palpable in the close quarters.

"Looks like we're stuck for a bit," Eli said, his voice a mix of amusement and something else—something deeper that resonated between them.

"Guess we'll have to wait it out," Aston replied, shifting slightly closer, feeling the warmth radiating from Eli's body.

They settled onto the small bench inside the boat, their shoulders brushing against one another. Aston could feel his pulse quicken as he caught Eli glancing at him, the storm outside amplifying the feelings swirling in the air.

"Do you think it will let up soon?" Eli asked, his voice barely audible over the rain.

Aston shook his head. "Not for a while, I think. But I'm okay with it. I'd rather be here with you than anywhere else."

Eli's breath caught at Aston's words, and the air grew thick with unspoken emotions. Time seemed to stand still, and the world outside faded further away as they leaned in closer.

"Eli," Aston murmured, his voice low and filled with intent. "I… I really like spending time with you."

"I like it too," Eli replied, his voice trembling slightly as he leaned in even closer, their faces inches apart.

In that moment, everything around them seemed to fade even further. The rain drummed a steady rhythm, a backdrop to the heartbeat echoing in Aston's ears. Eli's gaze flickered to Aston's lips once more, the question again lingering in the air.

With a swift, almost instinctual movement, Aston leaned forward, and their lips met—tentative at first, as if both were testing the waters. The kiss was sweet and soft, filled with a warmth that enveloped them both. Aston felt a rush of emotions surging through him, a mix of exhilaration and tenderness that ignited something deep within.

But just as quickly as it had begun, Eli pulled away, his eyes wide with shock. "Aston, we can't—"

"Why not?" Aston asked, breathless, a mix of confusion and longing filling the space between them. "I thought you wanted this too."

"I do," Eli admitted, his voice barely a whisper, "but what if someone sees us?"

"We're in a fucking boat, Eli… In a downpour. No-one's going to see us," smiled Aston, finding the statement humorous.

Eli was serious though. "No, I mean, what if my parents find out? I can't handle that kind of pressure."

The reality of Eli's fears crashed down around them like the storm outside, heavy and unyielding. Aston's heart sank at the realization. "Eli, I don't want to hide."

"I don't either," Eli said, his voice trembling with uncertainty. "But I'm scared. Scared of what it means, scared of how it will change everything."

Aston reached for Eli's hand, intertwining their fingers, hoping to bridge the gap between them. "I know. As I said, we don't have to rush into anything. Just being here with you feels right. And of course it will change things. But if it changes it for the better, that's not bad."

Eli glanced down at their joined hands, a flicker of hope crossing his features. "I just… I'm scared that you will leave me."

"What? I won't," Aston reassured him. "Whatever this is, it's worth exploring. We can take it slow, okay? Just don't freak out."

The rain continued to pour around them, a soothing backdrop to the tumult of their emotions. Eli's eyes searched Aston's, seeking reassurance in the depths of his gaze. "Okay," he said finally, a tentative smile breaking through his worry. "Let's take it slow then. I'm sorry. I'm not used to this type of thing. Never been good at… Stuff like this."

"No kidding," smiled Aston, "You have nothing in the world to be sorry about… Nothing!"

As they sat together, fingers still intertwined, the storm outside felt like a distant memory.

In that small boat, with the rain cascading around them, they had crossed a threshold into something new and beautiful— a connection deeper than either had felt before.

And as the storm raged on, Aston knew they had embarked on a journey filled with the sweet thrill of discovery.

They chatted for ages and eventually decided to head back, realizing the the storm was not going to let up anytime soon. They ran and laughed together through the heavy rain and parting ways at the end of the road, each going their separate direction, back to their respective homes.

Chapter Sixteen

Aston came walking in a fresh pair of clothes, warmed up from the hot shower he had just taken. The clattering of dishes and the warm, inviting aroma of roasted chicken filled Aston's small kitchen. His mother hummed softly as she moved about, setting the table with care. The rain continued pattering on the window outside, with less intensity now, as the sun began to set. As Aston watched her bustle around, a wave of affection washed over him.

"Dinner is almost ready, sweetheart!" Laura called out, glancing over her shoulder. Her warm brown eyes sparkled with the kind of love that had always made him feel safe.

Aston felt a knot tighten in his stomach. Tonight, he had something important to share, something that felt both thrilling and terrifying and he needed his mother's opinion.

"Can we sit down for a minute before we eat?" he asked, his voice slightly shaky.

"Of course! What's on your mind?" she replied, setting down the platter of chicken and joining him at the small dining table.

Aston took a deep breath, steeling himself for the conversation ahead. "I wanted to tell you that I've met someone," he began, his heart racing.

Laura's eyes widened in surprise, then softened with warmth. "Oh, Aston! That's wonderful! I knew you would!" She reached across the table, her hand covering his. "I'm so happy for you. Who is he?"

"It's—well, I'm still figuring things out, but it's a guy I work with," Aston stammered, glancing down at their hands.

"Oooh… a work relationship. Be careful, love. You don't want to make things awkward," she warned.

"No, that's not the issue. I mean, I really like him, but he's still in the closet." The words hung in the air between them, heavy with the weight of his admission.

"Being in the closet is perfectly okay, sweetheart. You'll just have to take your time with him then," Laura reassured him, her voice gentle yet encouraging. "But I hope he knows how important it is to be happy and open in your relationships. Hiding who you are can create a lot of pressure. I remember how unhappy you were before you came out to your dad and I."

Aston nodded, feeling a mixture of excitement and apprehension. "Yeah, I know. But he's not ready to come out yet, and I don't want to push him. He is kind of an introvert."

His mother leaned back, her expression thoughtful. "You know, sometimes it can be helpful to encourage the person you care about to be more open. It might lead to a stronger bond between you two."

Aston hesitated, his heart racing. "I guess, but I just don't want to overwhelm him. He is different. But not in a bad way. He is very guarded."

"Just be supportive then," Laura said with a smile. "Show him that you're there for him, and let him know how much he means to you. It might make him feel safer to open up."

"Yeah, I'll try," Aston replied, a mix of excitement and concern swirling in his mind. He felt grateful for his mother's support, but the thought of encouraging Eli to come out weighed heavily on him, knowing it would not be easy with his parent's beliefs.

"It's just that he lives with very conservative parents. Especially his mother. She is one of my bosses," winced Aston. "I get the feeling she is gonna not accept it."

"Oh… You know how to complicate things, don't you, son? Going out with your conservative boss's, in the closet son," she smiled.

"Yeah…" smiled Aston.

"Look, when you came out to us, we were surprised, but got over it. I'm sure there is the possibility of that happening there too."

"I don't know," said Aston, shaking his head. "She is not an easy woman."

"I suppose I could always talk to her, mother to mo—"

"NO!" Definitely not. Eli would not like that," snapped Aston.

"Quite the strong response. Just trying to help, my boy. I mean, when and if you guys come out to her. If she has an issue with it, that is. But I would never get involved unless you both wanted me to," she reassured.

"Thanks mom. But no. I'll handle it. Just wanted to let you know."

"Well I'm happy for you. Just be careful. It seems like a potentially thorny situation. But thanks for telling me. I'm so happy for you. For you both."

"I will be. Thank you."

"Eli, hey? Okay. Well, Eli is a very lucky guy," she smiled, touching Aston's cheek.

"I think I'm the lucky one," smiled Aston.

After a moment of silence, she stood up and said "Well, let's celebrate with some chicken!"

After dinner, Aston decided to text Eli, wanting to share the news of their conversation. He hoped it would reassure Eli, that they could lean on each other during this confusing time.

"Hey Eli. Told my mom about us. She's really supportive. Excited for us."

A few moments later, his phone buzzed with a response. *"Why would you tell her???"*

The sudden edge in Eli's message sent a chill down Aston's spine as he remembered telling Eli he would keep it secret.

"It's just my mom, don't stress. I thought it would be okay. She won't say anything, I promise. She said she wouldn't."

"So did you! You have no idea how this could affect me. I don't want people knowing!"

Eli's response was sharp, and the tension was palpable through the screen.

Aston's heart sank as he realized how much pressure Eli must be feeling and immediately regretted telling her.

"Eli, please. My mom is not like that. She cares about us. She just wants us to be happy."

"I don't want anyone else involved!" Eli replied quickly. *"I don't want to be the topic of conversation! You don't understand!"*

Aston felt a surge of frustration and fear and lowered the phone. "Eli," he murmured aloud to himself.
He had never intended to put Eli in such a vulnerable position. He picked up the phone, typing carefully.

"I'm sorry. I didn't mean to upset you. I just thought it might help. I do apologize..."

Eli's silence hung heavy in the air. Aston could feel his worry, the joy of their recent moments together dimming under the weight of fear and misunderstanding.

He remembered Eli's words about the pressure of expectations from his family. The last thing he wanted was to add to that burden.

"Can we talk about this? Can I meet you at the Marina in 30?" Aston typed, his heart racing as he sent the message.

The reply came slowly. *"Fine"*

As Aston walked there, the worry gnawed at him. He didn't want Eli to feel cornered or scared, yet he couldn't help but wonder if he had crossed a line by sharing their secret.

When he arrived, the rain had finally subsided, leaving a cool breeze that danced across the water's surface. Eli stood by the boat, his expression clouded with concern. Aston's heart ached at the sight of his friend looking so troubled.
"Hey," Aston said softly, moving closer.

"Hello," Eli replied, his voice flat.

"I'm really sorry that I told my mom. I didn't mean to put you in a tough spot," Aston began, his voice earnest.

Eli sighed, clearly struggling with his emotions. "I just... I don't want anyone knowing. Anyone! It's complicated for me, and I told you that I'm not ready for it."

"I get it. I didn't think it through. I have always been able to trust my mom. I've been out to her for a long time now." Aston said, stepping closer, desperate to convey his understanding. "I should've asked you first though. I know that now. It's your story, too."

Eli looked down, his shoulders tense. "It's not just about you. This is my life, my parents—"

"I know," Aston interrupted gently. "And I'm here to support you. I don't want you to feel like I'm pushing you into something you're not ready for. I won't tell a single other soul, I swear to you. And I know my mother won't repeat it."

Eli met Aston's gaze, and the vulnerability in his eyes made Aston feel terrible.
"I just don't want to be a subject of concern for my parents. They've already lost so much; I don't want to add to their worries. I can't handle that right now."

Aston nodded, understanding Eli's fears all too well. "I promise I won't say anything more. You can trust me. Our secret is safe, you have my word."

"I know I can," Eli said, his voice barely above a whisper. "It's just… hard."

"I'm here, Eli," Aston replied, stepping closer, closing the distance between them. "We'll take this at your pace. Whatever that looks like, I'm with you."

Eli looked up, his expression softening slightly. "My pace might be a very long time, Aston. And I just don't want this to ruin everything we have."

"Again, stop stressing. Nothing can ruin what we have," Aston reassured him. "You mean too much to me."

As they stood there, the weight of their fears slowly began to lift. Aston reached out, brushing his fingers against Eli's hand, a simple gesture of support and connection.

Eli glanced down at their hands, the tension in his shoulders easing just a fraction. "I appreciate you being here. It means a lot. I was stressing out like you cannot believe when you told me."

"I'll always be here for you," Aston promised, his heart swelling with a fierce determination to protect Eli. "No matter what."

They stood side by side in comfortable silence, with the waves lapping against the shore.

Chapter Seventeen

Eli was sitting in front of the TV. His mother, Rebecca, stood at the kitchen counter, as she busied herself with the last touches for dinner.

"Eli, honey," Rebecca's voice broke the silence, laced with a certain calculated sweetness that made his stomach tighten. "Just thought I'd let you know that I invited Ava over for dinner tonight. Isn't that nice?"

Eli turned his head in a swift snapping motion. He swallowed hard, his throat suddenly dry. "Ava?" he repeated, hoping he had misheard.

"Yes, Ava. It's been ages since you've spent any real time together. You are spending so much time working with Aston that you're neglecting her. So I invited her around. She seemed quite excited." Rebecca stepped into the lounge, her sharp blue eyes narrowing slightly. "She's such a lovely young woman, don't you think? A perfect match for you."

Eli's heart raced as he tried to compose himself. He felt trapped, as though the walls of the house were closing in around him. He had known this moment was coming.

And she let him know just before dinner, on purpose. So he couldn't get out of it. His mother had always been keen on pushing him toward Ava, subtly at first, and now more blatantly.

"She's… nice," he muttered, his voice barely audible.

Rebecca flashed him a smile, as if she hadn't detected the hesitation in his voice. "I'm glad you agree. It's important to have someone like her in your life. In all these years and you've never had a serious girlfriend."

His heart sank further. Girlfriend? The idea felt foreign and suffocating all at once. He couldn't even think about dating Ava, let alone spending his life with her. And that's what he knew his mother wanted. Marriage and kids. His mind drifted, unbidden, to Aston—the way his laugh filled the quiet spaces between them, the comfortable silence they shared when words weren't needed, and how, when they touched, even in the smallest of ways, it felt like everything in the world made sense.

But his mother didn't know about Aston. She didn't know about the life he hid, the pieces of himself he kept carefully tucked away, out of sight, where they wouldn't disappoint or shame the family.

"I don't know, Mom," Eli said, forcing himself to speak. "Ava's great, but I'm not sure I'm ready for all that."

Rebecca's expression faltered for a moment before she quickly masked it with a smile. "Nonsense, Eli. You're just being shy. Ava is perfect for you, and it's time you gave her a chance. Your father and I think highly of her, and I know you'll make a great couple."

The pressure weighed on him like a physical force, crushing his chest. He wanted to scream, to tell her that he didn't want to date Ava—that he couldn't date her. But instead, he remained silent, as he always did, his fear of disappointing her binding his voice. It was as if no matter what he said or did, he couldn't escape the expectations his mother had for him.

Just then, the doorbell rang, and Eli's heart sank. Ava was here. He wasn't ready for this. He wouldn't ever be ready for this.

Rebecca hurried to answer the door, her heels clicking against the floor. Eli forced himself to stand, every step feeling like it took monumental effort. When Rebecca returned, Ava was with her, all smiles and bright eyes, wearing a floral dress that fluttered as she walked.

"Hi, Eli," Ava greeted him cheerfully, her green eyes sparkling. "It's been a while."

"Hello Ava. Yeah, it has," Eli replied, his voice tight as he managed a forced smile.

Rebecca beamed as she ushered Ava into the living room. "You two sit and catch up while I finish up in the kitchen."

Eli sat stiffly on the couch as Ava settled next to him, the space between them feeling like a chasm despite their close proximity. He could feel her eyes on him, but he couldn't bring himself to meet her gaze. His mind was a mess, tangled with thoughts of Aston and the impossible situation he was in. He felt like he was betraying himself, betraying the growing feelings he had been trying to navigate.

"So, how's work at the marina?" Ava asked, her voice light and conversational.

Eli cleared his throat, trying to push the heaviness in his chest away. "It's fine. Just the usual stuff—fixing up boats, helping out around the docks."

"That sounds fun," she said with a smile. "I've never been much of a boat person, but I'm sure you're great at it."

The awkwardness between them felt unbearable, and Eli's mind raced for a way to deflect the conversation, to keep it from becoming more personal. But it was futile. He knew what his mother was trying to orchestrate—knew that this dinner was more than just a friendly meal. It was a step toward something he wasn't ready for, something he didn't even want.

"Maybe we could hang out sometime," Ava continued, oblivious to Eli's inner turmoil. "You know, outside of your boat duties."

Eli nodded, not trusting himself to speak. She was a lovely person and he had always gotten along well with her. But she was just a friend. Since his mother got involved, it felt more awkward. His stomach churned as the pressure mounted, the weight of his mother's expectations pressing down on him from all sides.

Dinner was a blur. His mother chatted animatedly with Ava, dropping subtle hints about how nice it would be to have Ava around more often. His father, Samuel, was quieter, but even his presence added to the invisible force pushing Eli toward a future he wasn't sure he could survive. Eli barely tasted the food, his mind too consumed with thoughts of escape.

After dinner, Rebecca walked Ava to the door, giving Eli a knowing look over her shoulder. "You should say goodnight properly, Eli," she said softly.

Eli clenched his jaw, feeling like a puppet on strings. He followed Ava to the door, his hands shoved deep in his pockets, his heart heavy with dread. As Ava turned to face him, she smiled up at him, clearly unaware of the turmoil inside him.

"Thanks for having me over," she said, her voice light. "It was nice to catch up. I was thinking that maybe we could go to the beach tomorrow? Maybe get some ice cream or something?"

"Um, yeah, okay," Eli replied, though the words felt hollow.

"Great. I'll meet you there and we can walk together. Maybe at 10? Would that be fine?"

Rebecca smiled at her and looked at Eli.

"That will be fine," he said, meeting his mother's gaze.

Ava hesitated for a moment, then stepped forward, pressing a quick, soft kiss to his cheek. Eli froze, the action sending a wave of panic through him.

He hadn't expected it, hadn't wanted it, but there it was—a small, innocent gesture that felt like a betrayal of everything he held inside.

"Goodnight, Eli," Ava said with a smile before walking down the steps and disappearing into the waiting car running outside.

Eli stood there, his body rigid, his mind racing. When he finally turned back inside, his mother was waiting for him in the living room, her eyes alight with satisfaction.

"That was nice, wasn't it?" Rebecca asked, her tone as smooth as silk. "She's a wonderful girl, Eli. You two would be perfect together. You should go to the movies with her on Saturday too."

Eli's stomach twisted. He felt the unspoken demand that he follow the path she had laid out for him. The path that didn't include Aston.

"I'm tired, Mom," he said, his voice quiet and strained. "I'm going to bed."

Rebecca frowned slightly, but she didn't press. "Alright. Goodnight, sweetheart."

As Eli climbed the stairs to his room, the weight in his chest became unbearable. He closed the door behind him and leaned against it, trying to breathe, trying to find a way to reconcile the person he was expected to be with the person he knew he was.

He didn't know what to do.

His phone buzzed in his pocket, and he pulled it out, seeing a message from Aston.

"Missed you today. How have you been?"

Eli stared at the screen, his heart aching as he typed out a response.

"It was awful. I wish I could've spent the night with you. But mom insisted I stay home".

The reply came quickly.

"I'm here whenever you need me. Just say the word."

Eli let out a shaky breath, the knot in his chest loosening slightly. He wanted nothing more than to run to Aston, to be in his presence, where everything felt right.

But the fear—the fear of what his family would think, of what they would say—kept him rooted in place.

He was trapped between two worlds, and he wasn't sure how much longer he could survive the pull of both.

Chapter Eighteen

The day began with the sun shining brightly over the coastal town, promising warmth and a sense of possibility. Eli had suggested to Aston that they take a day off from their usual routines, as Ava was coming by for day. Aston felt a mix of anticipation and unease. He didn't know Ava, and her presence represented the expectations Eli faced from his family. Ava, the "family approved girlfriend". The thought made him feel uncomfortable. Still, he told himself that it was important for Eli to have friends outside their circle, so he agreed to join.

As they stood at the marina, Aston tried to shake off his nerves. He paced slowly at the edge of the dock, watching the boats sway gently in the water. He could feel the breeze in his light brown hair, a reminder that change was in the air. He glanced up when he heard laughter approaching, spotting Eli and Ava walking toward him.

"Hey, you must be Aston, Eli's friend," Ava greeted, her voice bright and cheerful. She wore a flowing sundress that danced around her knees, her dark curls bouncing with each step. Eli walked beside her, his usual calm demeanor shining through with a warm smile.

"Hey," Aston replied, trying to sound enthusiastic. He offered a small wave as they approached.

"Ava thought we could grab some ice cream and maybe check out the beach," Eli smiled, his excitement reserved but clearly there.

"Cool," Aston said, forcing a smile as he fell in step beside them.

As they walked, Aston observed how Eli and Ava interacted. Their occasional laughter rang out as they shared stories and exchanged playful banter. Eli's laughter was light, and the sight of him with Ava sparked a strange pang of jealousy within him.

"Have you guys been to the new ice cream shop?" Ava asked, her green eyes sparkling. "I heard they have the best flavors."

"Not yet," Eli replied. "But I'm all for trying new things." He glanced at Aston.

Aston remained quiet, lost in thought. He couldn't help but feel a little overshadowed by Ava's lively personality.

As they approached the ice cream shop, he watched as Ava animatedly described her favorite flavors, her passion infectious. Eli noted that she was a lot less awkward now that his parents weren't around. Eli listened, nodding along with an occasional smile.

As they stepped inside, the shop was bustling with people, the air thick with the sweet aroma of waffle cones and freshly scooped ice cream. They each ordered their treats, and Aston chose a classic chocolate fudge.

"Really?" Ava teased, raising an eyebrow. "Living on the edge with the chocolate?"

Aston chuckled, his guard lowering a fraction. "Hey, you can't go wrong with chocolate."

"I agree, you can't beat a classic," smiled Eli.

They found a small table outside, and as they dug into their ice cream, Ava entertained them with tales of her summer adventures. Aston listened, both enjoying her enthusiasm and wishing for a moment that he could be as carefree with Eli. He glanced at Eli, who seemed interested in Ava's stories, a soft smile on his face. Aston couldn't help but feel a twinge of insecurity as well.

Aston thought that Eli was so involved at keeping his sexuality a secret that he seemed to overdo it when he was with Ava. But when around him, he was more reserved. In public anyway. When it was just the two of them, Eli was the true Eli, the one he knew well.

"So, Aston?" Ava asked, breaking his train of thought. "What's the craziest thing you did this summer?"

Aston hesitated, unsure of how to respond. "Not much, really. Just been working on some stuff."

Eli shot him a look, clearly sensing his discomfort. "He's been helping me with my projects," he said, trying to steer the conversation in a more comfortable direction.

Ava perked up. "Oh, that sounds fun! What kind of projects?"

Aston felt himself relax a little. "Just some repairs to boats and things around the marina," he replied. "Nothing too exciting."

"You're too humble," Eli interjected, his tone teasing. "He's been a lifesaver." He glanced at Aston again. Aston smiled at him.

Ava grinned at them both, her admiration evident. "That's awesome! You're a good friend, Aston."

Aston felt a warm flush creep up his cheeks at her words. "Thanks," he managed to say, his voice barely above a whisper.

Friend.

As they continued their outing, they wandered along the beach, the sound of waves crashing against the shore filling the air. Ava collected seashells, and Eli snapped pictures of her at her request, as she posed with her finds, laughter echoing around them. Aston trailed behind, an observer in their cheerful exchange.

"Come on, Aston! Join us!" Eli called, motioning and willing him to come closer.

"Yeah, don't be shy!" Ava added, waving him over with a seashell in her hand.

With a reluctant smile, Aston stepped forward while trying to shake off the jealousy that clung to him like sea mist.

"Look at this one!" Ava exclaimed, holding up a beautifully spiraled shell.

"It's pretty cool," Eli said, leaning in to admire it. Aston felt a flicker of envy at her having Eli so close to her.

After a while, as the sun began to dip lower in the sky, Ava ran a bit down the beach, exploring and looking for more. Aston couldn't hold back any longer. He turned to Eli, his voice low but firm. "You know, Ava seems great and all, but I just—"

"What is it?" Eli asked, sensing the tension in his tone.

"I don't want you to feel like you have to fit into some kind of mold for your family," Aston confessed, the words spilling out before he could stop himself. "I know she's your parents' choice. I just—"

Eli raised an eyebrow, surprise flickering across his face. "What? You think I'm into her?"

"I don't know, maybe?" Aston replied, the frustration evident in his voice. "You two look good together."

Eli shook his head, a smirk tugging at his lips. "Aston, she's a friend. That's all."

"But what if—"

"Aston," Eli interrupted, his tone serious. "You don't have to worry about that."

The weight of Eli's words hung in the air, and Aston's heart raced. "But what if—"

"No 'what ifs'," Eli insisted, stepping closer. "I care about you, and I want to be with you."

Aston felt a mixture of relief and lingering doubt. "But your family… they want you to settle down, and she's the perfect choice for them."

Eli sighed, running a hand through his hair. "I know. But that doesn't change that I want to be with you, Aston. That's what matters to me."

As Aston absorbed Eli's words, he could see the sincerity in his eyes. "Okay," Aston said finally, his voice softer. "I just needed to know where you stand."

"Always with you," Eli promised, a gentle smile spreading across his face.

As they continued their walk along the beach, Aston felt slightly better.

But he knew that even though Eli was saying the words, following through with them, especially due to the pressure he felt from his family, would be difficult. Although the path ahead was uncertain, he felt a little more reassured by Eli's words. What Eli felt was what mattered.

Ava joined them a moment later, her hands full of seashells. "What were you two talking about?" she asked, her curiosity evident.

"Just stuff," Eli replied casually, shooting Aston a reassuring glance.

"Serious?" Asked Ava, raising an eyebrow.

"No, just...life stuff," Aston said, trying to steer the conversation away from the tension.

"Life stuff? Sounds serious," Ava smiled, her voice playful.

As they strolled along the shore, Ava collecting shells and laughing at the waves that lapped at their feet, Aston felt a flicker of contentment.

Chapter Nineteen

Later that afternoon, Eli stood alone on the dock, staring blankly at the water lapping against the boats. The warmth of the afternoon did little to settle his unease. He felt like he was drowning in an invisible sea of expectations—his mother's unspoken demands, Ava's sweet, unassuming presence, and Aston's nervous frustration.

A few feet behind him, Eli's father, Samuel, watched his son with a quiet, concerned gaze. He had always been a man of few words, someone who believed more in doing than talking, but lately, he had been watching Eli more closely. He had always known that since Eli's sister passed away, Eli was a different person. Withdrawn, quiet, reserved, anxious. It had hurt him to see a part of his son die along with his daughter. Eli was never the same since that day.

But today, he could see that something else was bothering Eli. Something was wrong, and while Samuel didn't know exactly what it was, he felt it in his bones. Eli had grown even more distant, even quieter than usual, and the easy rhythm of the work day they once shared had been replaced by a tension Samuel couldn't quite place.

Samuel leaned against the railing of the dock, pretending to check one of the fishing lines while keeping an eye on his son. He thought back to the days when Eli had been a carefree kid, running along the beach with a wide smile, asking a million questions about the boats and the sea. That version of Eli seemed so far away now, replaced by a young man burdened by grief. And now something else that Samuel couldn't understand. He wished he could reach out, offer some kind of help, but Eli had grown good at keeping his emotions locked away, especially from his parents. Eli was a closed book to most people.

"You look like you've got the weight of the world on your shoulders, son," Samuel finally said, his voice low and steady, breaking the silence between them.

Eli blinked, snapping out of his daze, and glanced over at his father. "Just tired," he muttered, not meeting Samuel's eyes.

Samuel nodded, though he didn't believe it for a second. He knew Eli too well. "Granted, you've been working hard," he said carefully. "But it's more than that, isn't it?"

For a moment, Eli hesitated, his hands fidgeting in his pockets.

The weight of his father's words hung in the air, and for the briefest moment, Samuel thought Eli might actually open up. But then, just as quickly, Eli's defenses went up again, and he shrugged.

"I guess," Eli said, his voice clipped. "It's just a lot, with Mom pushing me about Ava and everything."

Samuel winced at the mention of his wife. Rebecca had always been the more vocal one in their marriage, the one with stronger opinions about how things should be. Lately, she had been pushing Eli much harder, especially when it came to Ava. She believed that if Eli settled down with someone like Ava, it would help heal some of the wounds their family had endured over the years. Losing Eli's sister in that sailing accident had broken something in Rebecca, something Samuel wasn't sure would ever fully heal. He understood her desire to protect Eli, to push him toward a life that seemed safe and predictable, but he wasn't sure she understood how much pressure it was putting on their son.

"Ava's a good girl," Samuel said slowly, watching Eli's face for any reaction. "But you know, it's okay if you don't feel the same way Mom does about her. You don't have to—"

"I know," Eli interrupted, a trace of frustration creeping into his voice.

He looked down at his feet, scuffing his shoe against the wooden dock. "It's just… hard, Dad. Mom doesn't listen. She wants me to be someone I'm not."

Samuel's heart ached at the quiet admission, surprised that Eli was even saying anything. This was as close as Eli had come to telling him what was really going on, and it confirmed what he had feared. Eli was trapped between what his mother wanted and what he wanted, and that was a burden no young man should have to bear.

"I can talk to her," Samuel offered gently, though he knew it wasn't a perfect solution. He wished he could do more, wished he could lift the weight off Eli's shoulders. But he wasn't sure if a conversation with Rebecca would really change anything.

Eli shook his head, a bitter smile tugging at his lips. "She's not going to change her mind, Dad. You know she's not."

Samuel sighed, rubbing a hand over his face. He wasn't sure what else to say, and the silence that followed felt heavy, like there was something much larger looming between them. He glanced back at Eli, noticing the tension in his posture, the way he seemed to be holding something back, something much deeper than the issue with Ava.

"You know," Samuel said, his voice softer now. "I just have to say, that whatever it is… What's chewing at you… you can talk to me. I might not have all the answers, but I'll listen."

Eli's shoulders stiffened, and for a long moment, he didn't respond. Then, with a deep breath, he finally looked at his father, meeting his gaze for the first time in days. "I know," he said quietly, though the words felt like they were laced with hesitation.

Samuel nodded slowly, though he felt frustrated at the distance between them. He wanted to reach out, to pull his son into a hug and tell him that everything would be okay, but he knew Eli didn't like that kind of thing.

Eli's phone buzzed in his pocket, cutting through the quiet moment, and he pulled it out, glancing at the screen. His expression shifted, a flicker of something—guilt? Anxiety?—crossing his face before he quickly shoved the phone back into his pocket.

"I've gotta go, dad," Eli mumbled, his voice tight.

Samuel watched him walk away, his heart heavy with the knowledge that something was slipping through his fingers.

He wished he could do more, but as Eli disappeared down the dock, Samuel realized that this was one of those times where his son needed to find his own way—even if it meant struggling along the path.

Later that evening, Eli found himself sitting alone in his room, the weight of the day pressing down on him. He stared at his reflection in the small mirror above his dresser, his thoughts spinning in a tangled mess of emotions. His father's words from earlier echoed in his mind, but they didn't bring the comfort he had hoped for.

Eli knew his dad cared, but even if he wanted to confide in him, how could he? How could he tell him about Aston, about the way his heart raced every time they were near each other, about the stolen moments that felt more real than anything else in his life? His dad wouldn't understand. And his mom… she would lose it. Not to mention the idea of disappointing her felt like a betrayal he simply couldn't bear.

But the pressure was suffocating. Eli felt torn in so many directions—toward his parents, toward Ava, and most of all, toward Aston. Aston, with his easy smile and carefree attitude, had become Eli's anchor in a sea of confusion. But even that felt like there was the possibility of it slipping away. The more time Eli spent trying to live up to his mother's expectations, the further he drifted from Aston.

And the jealousy—the way Aston's eyes hardened every time Eli mentioned Ava—only made it worse.

The truth was, Eli didn't know what to do. He loved Aston. He hadn't said it out loud yet, but he knew it deep down. But that love was tangled in so much fear—fear of being discovered, fear of losing his family, fear of hurting Aston by not being enough.

He glanced at his phone, hesitating before sending a text to Aston.

Can we talk tomorrow?

The reply came almost instantly.

Yeah. Same place?

Eli's heart twisted. He knew they couldn't keep going like this, circling around each other, pretending that everything was fine when it wasn't. He had to make a decision, but the very thought of choosing—between his family, his sense of duty, and his feelings for Aston—was paralyzing.

The next day, Eli arrived at the marina, his heart pounding as he spotted Aston waiting by their usual spot near the boat they had been working on together.

Aston looked up as Eli approached, his face guarded, the same slight tension between them that had been building for weeks now.

"Hey," Aston said, his voice calm but distant.

"Hello, Aston," Eli replied, his hands shoved deep into his pockets, as they always were, the weight of what he needed to say hanging between them.

They stood in awkward silence for a moment before Aston broke it. "You said you wanted to talk?"

Eli nodded, his throat dry and scratchy. He didn't know how to start, how to put into words everything that had been gnawing at him. But he had to try.

"I'm sorry," Eli said quietly, his voice barely above a whisper. "I know I've been pulling away, and I know you hate me for it"

Aston's expression softened, but there was still a hint of frustration in his eyes. "I don't hate you, Eli. I love you."

"I... ," Eli breathed out, his eyes dropping to the ground. Aston knew how difficult speaking about this type of thing was for Eli.

He didn't blame him for not being able to say the words yet. Not now. Not with all the pressure he was feeling.

Aston sighed, "You might be what she wants, but you don't want her. Not like that. But you're *exactly* what I want, Eli. You're all I want. And need you to see that and be able to somehow figure it out. I don't know how much longer I can watch you hurting yourself like this. If you're choosing her, I'd rather not be around you. Cause it makes it worse for you and for me."

The words hung in the air, heavy and painful. Eli wanted to say something, to reassure Aston, but the truth was, he wasn't sure how much longer he could wait either.

Because the more he waited, the more everything felt like it was slipping away.

Chapter Twenty

The next day at the marina, the rhythmic sound of hammers and sanders filled the air, blending with the distant cry of seagulls and the gentle lapping of water against the docks. The whole scene felt peaceful, idyllic even—except for a growing tension between Eli and Aston.

Eli moved with a familiar ease, his hands working deftly as he patched up an old wooden hull. His fingers, rough and skilled from years of working with his father, moved with muscle memory, but today, his heart wasn't in it. His mind was elsewhere, weighed down by the events of the past days. The dinner, Ava's kiss on his cheek, his mother's constant, subtle pressure—it was too much. And then, there was Aston.

Aston stood a few feet away, focusing on his own task. He was sanding down the worn edges of a boat, but every so often, he'd glance over at Eli. Something was off. Eli was quieter than usual, his movements more tense, like he was on edge. Aston could feel it, that unspoken heaviness in the air between them, and it gnawed at him.

Finally, unable to take the silence any longer, Aston set down the sander and wiped his hands on a rag. He approached Eli cautiously, his eyes searching the other boy's face for any sign of what was bothering him.

"Hey," Aston said, trying to keep his tone light. "You seem kind of out of it today. You okay? What you thinking?"

Eli paused, not looking up, just running his hand along the hull of the boat as if the wood could give him some kind of answer. His jaw clenched, and for a moment, Aston thought he might not respond at all. Then, with a sigh, Eli straightened and turned to face him, his eyes dark with something deeper—something he hadn't let Aston see until now.

"No, not really," Eli finally said, his voice low, almost as if he were speaking to himself. "The other night… It was bad for me. It was a lot. Dinner with Ava around. They are all pressuring me, Aston. And Ava even kissed me on the cheek when she said goodnight."

Aston's heart quickened. He had a feeling this conversation was going to be heavier than he had anticipated and he was right. Eli was freaking out. Aston stepped closer, closing the gap between them, the concern evident in his gaze.

"Do you want to talk about it?" Aston asked gently.

Eli looked down at his hands, his fingers still stained with the grit and sawdust of their work. The words he wanted to say lodged somewhere deep, hard to pull out, hard to articulate. But he couldn't keep holding it all in. The weight of it was suffocating him.

"She…" Eli began, his voice faltering. "It was just… She keeps pushing, Aston. Pushing so damn hard. And I know she won't stop."

Aston stayed quiet, letting Eli speak at his own pace, even though a frustration was building. He knew it shouldn't be about himself, but the emotion danced inside him regardless. He didn't say anything. This was about Eli.

"I hate it," Eli continued, his words becoming more strained. "I hate how they all expect me to just be this person… this version of myself that I can't be. I can't tell them about you, about us. It would… it would ruin everything."

Aston's stomach dropped. *Us.* The word lingered in the air, heavy with meaning. For a moment, he felt a surge of hope. But then Eli's next words hit him like a punch to the gut. "I don't know if we should keep doing this," Eli said, his voice barely above a whisper, his eyes fixed on the ground.

"It's so complicated. Maybe… maybe it would be easier if we just stayed friends… coworkers."

The world seemed to tilt on its axis for Aston. He blinked, trying to process what Eli had just said. Stay friends? The thought felt like a knife twisting in his chest. He had been so sure they were moving forward, that they were on the same page. But now Eli was pulling away, retreating behind his walls of fear and uncertainty.

"Eli," Aston began, his voice strained, "I don't want to just be your friend."

Eli looked up, his blue-gray eyes filled with turmoil. "I know. But this… us… it's getting too hard. I hate lying to my parents. But I'm terrified of what will happen if I tell them. I am absolutely not ready for that, Aston. I have been thinking and I doubt I'll ever be. I'm not strong enough to face them like that."

Aston swallowed hard, his own emotions swirling in a mess of frustration, sadness, and fear. He wanted to understand, to be patient, but it was difficult. He had been open with his mom about Eli, about his feelings. Sure, his mother was supportive, but he had taken that risk when he came out, hoping that telling Eli would help him follow.

But now, Eli was talking about pulling back, and Aston didn't know how to handle that.

"Fuck," Aston murmured, his voice laced with tension. "Eli… you can't live your life like this forever, hiding, pretending to be something you're not. It's eating you up inside. I can see it. Every time you talk about your mom or Ava, it's like you're suffocating. Look at you, you're shaking. You shouldn't have to live like that."

Eli clenched his fists at his sides, frustration bubbling up. "You think I don't know that? You think I don't feel that every single day? But it's not that simple. It is not just up to me. My family… they wouldn't accept it. I know she won't. My mom—she would cut me off. My dad… I don't know how he'd react. But he won't go against my mom. And Ava… she's a good person. She doesn't deserve to get caught up in all this. Giving her false hopes of being with me. It's not fair."

Aston's heart broke for Eli, but at the same time, he couldn't help the anger that was building inside him. "So what? You're just going to keep living this lie, pretending to be someone you're not? What about you, Eli? What about what you want? Doesn't that matter?"

"I'm good at being on my own. I can handle it."

"And what about me?" Said Aston, raising his voice slightly in frustration. "Don't I have a say in this? I don't want to lose you. Act like you're just a friend. No!"

Eli's eyes flashed with emotion, a mix of fear, anger, and sadness all rolled into one. "It's my life, Aston, not yours. You have it easy with your mom accepting you."

"Easy? You don't think I've struggled like you are doing now? I know exactly what you're feeling," said Aston, getting really flustered now.

"I don't know what I want anymore!" he shouted, the words spilling out before he could stop them. "I don't know how to live this. I don't know how to make things right."

Aston stepped forward, his hand reaching out to rest gently on Eli's arm. The touch was meant to be comforting, but it only made Eli flinch, pulling away as if the contact burned him. Aston's heart sank.

"I want to be with you, Eli," Aston said softly, his voice shaking. "I care about you. But I can't do this if you're not willing to be honest with yourself. It's not fair to either of us. I'm not saying you have to do it soon. Take your time. Take as much time as you need. I'll be here. But don't push me away."

Eli's breath hitched, his chest heaving with the weight of his emotions. He wanted to scream, to tell Aston that he did care, that he wanted him more than anything. But the fear—the crippling, all-consuming fear—held him back.

"I'm terrified," Eli finally admitted, his voice breaking. "I'm scared of what will happen if I come out. I'm scared of losing everything. And I know I'm not strong enough to face that."

Aston's hand fell to his side, the rejection stinging more than he wanted to admit. "I get that you're scared," he said, his voice tight. "But you *are* strong enough. Regardless, you don't have to face anything alone. I'm here. I'm with you. I just need you to meet me halfway."

Eli's eyes filled with tears, but he blinked them away, turning his back to Aston as he fought to keep his emotions in check. The silence between them stretched, heavy and suffocating. Aston wanted to reach out, but something momentarily held him back—maybe it was the fear that Eli might push him away again.

"I don't know if I can," Eli whispered, his voice trembling.

Aston's heart clenched, the ache of those words almost too much to bear.

He stepped forward now, closing the distance between them despite the walls Eli was putting up fast. Gently, he turned Eli around to face him, his hands resting on Eli's shoulders.

"I know it feels like a lot, cause it is," Aston said quietly, his eyes searching Eli's face. "But please… don't shut me out. I'm begging you. Don't push me away because of your fear. We can figure this out together. Please don't push me away. I need you more than you know."

For a moment, Eli's resolve wavered. He looked into Aston's eyes, seeing the genuine care, the love that was there. He wanted to believe that they could make it work—that somehow, things would be okay. But the weight of his predicament loomed large, and he wasn't sure if he had the strength to move forward.

Eli finally spoke, his voice barely above a whisper. "I don't know if I can be what you need me to be. I'll try, but I won't promise anything."

Aston's heart swelled with a mixture of fear and hope. He nodded, knowing that for now, that was all he was going to get from Eli.

"Okay," he said softly, pulling Eli into a hug. "We'll figure it out. Stop stressing. Just be how you are."

Eli let himself sink into the embrace, his arms wrapping around Aston as he buried his face in Aston's shoulder. The weight of the confession, of the fear, and of the uncertainty hung between them.

Chapter Twenty One

The marina was bustling with its usual activity, tourists walking the docks, boats being loaded for afternoon trips, and the scent of saltwater mingling with the sun-baked wood. Aston had become familiar with these sights and sounds, but today, none of it registered. His attention was locked on Eli.

Eli was standing near the office, laughing softly with Ava. His body language was relaxed, maybe too relaxed, and that infectious laugh—the one Aston had come to cherish—was directed at her now. Eli didn't laugh often. He was too reserved, but when he did, it melted Aston. But not when he heard it directed towards Ava. Ava, with her bright floral dresses and cheerful smile, looked effortlessly comfortable by his side, like she belonged there. Aston felt the knot in his stomach tighten as he watched them. This was becoming a pattern. Eli was spending more and more time with Ava, more time conforming to his family's expectations, and less time with Aston.

Aston turned back to the boat he was supposed to be working on, his hands gripping the wrench tighter than necessary.

The metal bit into his palm, grounding him momentarily, but it didn't help much. He was angry—angry at Eli for drifting away, angry at himself for feeling this way, and angry at the whole situation. It wasn't supposed to be like this.

Eli had been distant for the past couple of weeks, ever since their conversation. Aston thought they had made progress, that they were moving toward something real, but now… now it felt like they were back at square one. The quiet nights working on the boat together had been replaced by Eli's growing absence. When Eli wasn't with Ava, he was with his family, being pulled deeper into their expectations of who they wanted him to be.

Ava was sweet, kind even, but every time Aston saw her with Eli, it felt like a punch to the gut. The overwhelming jealousy gnawed at him, making everything seem darker, heavier. He knew Eli wasn't in love with her—that was clear enough—but it didn't change the fact that Eli was trying to be someone else when he was around her. Someone that his mother would approve of. And that realization hurt more than anything, because he could see Eli struggling with it.

The sound of footsteps approaching brought Aston back to the present. He looked up and saw Eli walking toward him, his hands shoved into his pockets, his expression cautious.

Aston tried to school his features, to push down the jealousy that was clawing at him, but he knew it was no use. Eli could see through him. And he felt bad for it.

"Hey," Eli said quietly, stopping a few feet away from where Aston was working.

Aston put the wrench down and straightened up, his eyes meeting Eli's. "Hey."

The tension between them was palpable, thick and suffocating. Eli shifted uncomfortably, glancing over his shoulder as if to make sure no one was watching. Aston's jaw tightened at the sight—Eli was still afraid of being seen, of being caught.

"How's Ava," Aston said, unable to keep the bitterness out of his voice.

Eli's face fell slightly, a hint of guilt flashing in his eyes. "She's fine. My mom wanted us to have lunch together. You know how it is."

Aston snorted, turning away and picking up his wrench again. "Yeah, I know *exactly* how it is, Eli."

Eli's shoulders slumped, and he stepped closer, lowering his voice. "Aston, come on. Lighten up. It's not like that."

"Then what *is* it like, Eli?" Aston asked, spinning around to face him, the frustration finally bubbling over. "Because from where I'm standing, it sure looks like you're doing exactly what your mom wants—spending time with Ava, acting like the perfect son, the perfect boyfriend. And where does that leave us?"

Eli flinched at Aston's words, but he showed little emotion. "You know I'm trying."

"Are you?" Aston shot back, his voice sharper than he intended. "Because it doesn't feel like it. It feels like you're pulling away, like you're choosing them over me. You are choosing *her* over me!"

Eli took a step back, his mouth opening and closing as if he was searching for the right words. "I'm not choosing them or her over you. I'm just... I'm trying to keep everything together. It's not Ava's fault. She's just caught in the middle. I don't want to hurt her. But I don't want to lose you either."

Aston clenched his teeth, trying to keep his anger in check, but it was hard. The jealousy, the confusion, the feeling of being sidelined—it was too much.

"But you *are* losing me, Eli. Every time you go along with what your mom wants, every time you spend more time with Ava, you push me further away. I don't know how much more of this I can take. You're killing me here!"

Eli's face crumpled, and he looked down at the ground, his hands clenching into fists. "I don't want to lose you, Aston," he whispered, his voice trembling. "I just don't know how to make this work. It's a lose-lose situation for me. Like no matter what I do, I'm going to disappoint someone."

Aston's heart twisted at the sight of Eli's anguish. He wanted to reach out, to comfort him, but the hurt was still too raw. "What about what you want? What about what you really want, Eli?" Aston pleaded, his voice tense now, but the anger ebbing away. "What about what *we* want? Doesn't that matter to you?"

Eli looked up, his eyes hard. "Of course it matters," he said, his voice barely audible. "My parents… They've already lost so much with my sister. I don't want to be another disappointment to add to their worries."

Aston's heart sank. He understood the fear, the pressure, but it didn't make the situation any easier.

Unable to stop himself, he reached out, placing a hand on Eli's arm, feeling the tension in his muscles. "You can't keep living your life for other people. You deserve to be happy too. We do. And right now, you're a fucking miserable person… And so am I!"

Eli's breath hitched, and for a moment, Aston thought he might break down. But then, just as quickly, Eli pulled back, retreating behind the walls he had built around himself. "I need time," Eli said quietly. "You promised you'd give me that."

Aston nodded, though the answer felt hollow. *Time*. That was all he ever seemed to need. But how much time could he give before it all became too much?

"Yes, I did, but not for you to start building your walls again and planning your future with someone else."

"I got work to do. So do you. I'll chat to you later," said Eli, and turned and walked off.

Days passed, and the distance between Aston and Eli grew, an invisible barrier that neither of them seemed able to cross.

They still worked side by side at the marina, still shared conversations, but the easy connection that had once flowed between them had been replaced by tension, by unspoken words and uncertain glances.

Eli was still seeing Ava—more than Aston could handle—and every time he saw them together, it was like a slow knife being pushed further into his stomach.

One evening, after a long day of work, Aston found himself at the edge of the docks, staring out at the sunset. The golden light shimmered across the water, but instead of bringing the usual sense of calm, it only amplified the turmoil inside him. He couldn't shake the feeling that he was fast losing Eli, that no matter how much he tried to pull him closer, Eli was slipping further away. He was beginning to lose hope.

The sound of footsteps behind him made him turn, and there was Eli, standing a few feet away, his expression unreadable.

"I saw you with Ava again today," Aston said, not bothering to hide the disdain in his voice.

Eli sighed, but said nothing. He just bit his lip.

Aston clenched his jaw, the frustration boiling over once again.

"You're just going along with this fake life with her. And throwing me aside."

Eli's face twisted with frustration. "What do you want me to do, Aston? My mom… she's holding onto me like I'm the last piece of the family that's still intact. I can't just tear that apart."

Aston stepped closer, his heart pounding. "Well, you're tearing me apart. You can't just keep stringing me along while you play the part your damn mom wants."

"I'm not stringing you along," Eli snapped, his voice rising. "I'm trying to figure this out, but it's not easy. You'll never understand what it's like being me, Aston."

Aston's eyes flashed with anger. "I don't understand? I'm the one standing here, watching you slip away. Don't you feel it? This gap between us now? I'm the one who has to pretend like it doesn't hurt every time I see you with her."

Eli's expression softened, the anger fading into something more fragile. "I really don't want to hurt you, Aston. I care about you more than you know. But I'm stuck here and I don't think I can get out."

Aston took a deep breath, his heart aching for both of them. But he struggled to not let the anger and hurt he was feeling say what he was thinking.

"You have to make a choice, Eli. You can't keep living like this, torn between what your family wants and what you feel. Eventually, you're going to have to decide who you want to be. And it's simple… me or her."

Eli looked away, his eyes fixed on the horizon. The silence stretched between them, heavy and uncertain. Finally, he spoke, his voice barely above a whisper.

"I don't know if I'll ever be ready to make that choice."

The words cutting deeper than he expected. He nodded slowly, the reality settling in.

"I can't wait forever, Eli. One day the choice will be made for you. I thought I could keep this up, but I'm struggling."

Eli didn't respond, and for a long moment, they just stood there, two people caught in the in-between, neither willing to move forward or let go.

Suddenly Eli shouted, "Stop pressuring me!" He turned and stormed off, leaving Aston in shock and all alone.

Chapter Twenty Two

Aston, sitting at the desk in his bedroom with his chin propped on his hand, a barely touched sandwich in front of him. His thoughts swirled with frustration, tension bubbling under the surface. Eli had been distant again—more than usual—and it was starting to wear him down.

Laura, sensing her son's quiet mood, knocked on the door quietly and entered. She could always read him so easily, a skill honed from years of raising him alone after his father's death.

"Something's bothering you," she said softly, her voice filled with concern. "Tell your mom."

Aston turned around and looked up, meeting her gaze. His mother had always been his rock, his confidante, and the one person he could talk to about anything. But talking about Eli, especially with things going the way they were, felt heavy. Still, he couldn't keep it bottled up any longer.

"It's Eli," Aston muttered. "Things aren't good."

Laura's brows furrowed in concern as she came to sit across from him on the edge of the bed. "What's going on?"

Aston exhaled slowly, looking down again. "It's… complicated. He's still not ready to come out, and it's putting a strain on everything. I don't know what to do. I thought, maybe, over time, he'd feel more comfortable, but… I don't know. He's so scared, and I'm starting to feel like I'm waiting for something that might never happen."

"I'm sorry, honey. That sounds really hard. But you know, coming out isn't easy for everyone. Eli's probably dealing with a lot of fear—of his family, of how people will react. It's not about you."

Aston nodded, "I get that. But he's pulling away. That's what's getting me. If he just stayed like he was, I could deal with that. But he is actually retreating now and I don't know how much longer I can stay around him and watch it happen. I don't want to push him. I really don't. But I also don't want him to keep hiding. I just don't want to lose him, and I think him coming out would ease his concerns. Like we could handle it together then. It's like I'm stuck in this middle space, and I'm really getting tired of it."

Laura shifted. "Have you talked to him about how you feel? I know you don't want to pressure him, but maybe he needs to understand that this is affecting you too. Relationships are about both people."

He sighed, leaning back in his chair. "I've tried. He just shuts down whenever I bring it up. He's under so much pressure from his family—especially his mom. But I can't keep pretending that it doesn't hurt me. Cause it does."

Laura's eyes softened as she regarded her son. "I know, sweetheart. It's hard when you love someone and want them to be free, but they're not ready. But maybe… maybe if you made a plan, something concrete, it might help him feel less overwhelmed. Take small steps. Suggest a day, or even just a moment, where the two of you can talk about what it would look like for him to come out. You can't rush him, but you can let him know that you're ready when he is."

Aston thought about it for a moment. His mother's words made sense—giving Eli something to focus on, rather than just the vague fear of the unknown, might help ease his anxiety. Maybe if they planned a date to come out together, Eli would feel more supported. It wouldn't just be some looming, terrifying event, but something they could face together.

"Yeah… maybe," Aston murmured, the idea slowly taking root in his mind. "It might help to make it feel less… chaotic. Like, if we both know when and how we're going to do it, he'll feel more in control."

Laura smiled gently. "It's worth a try, darling. Just make sure you're patient with him. He's lucky to have you, and I'm sure he knows that. But fear can be paralyzing, especially when it comes to something as personal as this."

Aston nodded, feeling a glimmer of hope that maybe this was a possible step in the right direction. He stood up, giving his mother a small, grateful smile. "Thanks, Mom. I'll talk to him about it."

Laura returned the smile, watching as her son headed toward the door. "You'll figure it out, Aston. You always do. Just be patient with each other."

Later that evening, Aston arrived at the marina. The smell of saltwater and the rhythmic sound of the waves hitting the docks greeted him as he made his way toward the boatyard. Eli was there, bent over a toolbox, his focus trained on the boat they had been restoring together. Aston was surprised to see him working on it.

The sight of him—his hair catching the fading sunlight, his body tense with concentration—caused a familiar flutter in Aston's chest. But tonight, that flutter was mixed with a knot of anxiety.

Aston approached quietly, stopping a few feet away before speaking. "Hey."

Eli looked up, his eyes meeting Aston's with a hint of surprise. He straightened up. "Hey. Didn't know you'd be here this late."

Aston shrugged, trying to keep his tone casual. "I wanted to talk. If that's okay."

Eli hesitated, his gaze flickering to the boat before he nodded.

Aston stepped closer, leaning against the side of the boat. He could feel the weight of the conversation pressing down on him, but he knew it had to be done. They couldn't keep avoiding it.

"I've been thinking," Aston began, watching Eli's reaction carefully. "About us. And everything going on."

Eli's posture stiffened slightly, his hands fidgeting with a screwdriver. "Okay…"

"I know you're scared," Aston said softly. "About coming out. About what your family will think. But I've been thinking that maybe… maybe we should set a date. A day where we can just do it together. We don't have to keep hiding, Eli. I'll be right there with you. We set a date of your freedom. Our freedom. And work towards it."

Eli's eyes widened, a look of panic flashing across his face. He took a step back, shaking his head quickly. "What the hell are you saying?"

Aston felt his heart sink at the immediate rejection. He had hoped that framing it as something they could do together would make it easier, but clearly, he had miscalculated. Still, he wasn't ready to give up. "I know it's scary, but we can take it slow. We'll pick a day when you feel comfortable. It can be far in the distance. It doesn't have to be right now, but just something we can work towards. Get your mind around it a bit. Make it more concrete."

Eli's breathing quickened, "You promised me you wouldn't pressure me, Aston. You promised… And I asked you not to," he muttered, his voice and hands shaking. "I can't just… I'm so not ready."

Frustration bubbled up inside Aston, and before he could stop himself, the words tumbled out. "It's not about being ready or not. It's about the fact that while you're uncertain, you're busy preparing for a life without me in it. Preparing to do whatever your mother says. Do you really want to live the rest of your life with someone you don't love? And throw me away in the process. Cause you haven't said it yet, and that's fine… But I know you love me too. It's obvious."

Eli's eyes flashed with something between anger and fear. "Just stop!" he snapped, his voice rising. "I don't know what to say…"

Aston took a deep breath, trying to calm himself, realizing that getting angry again was not helping. "Don't you want this, Eli? Aren't you going crazy like I am, not being able to be together?"

Eli's gaze dropped to the ground, his chest heaving with the weight of his emotions. He didn't answer right away, and the silence stretched between them like a chasm. Finally, he looked up, his expression pained.

"I want to be with you, Aston, you know that," Eli whispered, his voice barely audible.

Aston's heart ached at the vulnerability in Eli's voice, "Then be with me! Please choose me... Choose us," begged Aston.

Eli shook his head, his eyes glistening with unshed tears. He had no words.

Aston clenched his jaw. He knew Eli was struggling, but he couldn't help but feel like he was being left in limbo, stuck in a secret relationship that couldn't move forward.

"I love you, but I need to know that we at least have a future. Cause if we don't, then I need to leave. It's too painful being around you and not knowing," said Aston, his voice trembling.

Eli's breath hitched, and he wiped at his eyes with the back of his hand. "I so badly want to say yes," he whispered, his voice breaking. "I just don't think I can."

Aston's stepped forward, throwing caution to the wind and just speaking his mind, "No. I'm not accepting that. I'm not going to let you fuck your life up without at least trying to help. I'm not asking you to do it alone," he said softly. "I'll be right there with you. But if you're ever going to be happy, you have to at least take that first step. I'm not saying come out. What I'm saying is be open to the possibility. I feel like you've shut that down completely."

Eli's eyes met Aston's, and for a moment, the fear in his expression was replaced by something softer—something closer to hope. But it was oh so slight, and soon the weight of his fears came crashing back down and he took a deep breath.

"You can be happy again, Eli. And I'm giving you fucking permission to be open to at least acknowledging that fact. Say it. Say I can be happy again."

Eli stood, trembling.

"Eli, when we first met, you felt it. You know it's there for the taking. You just have to be open to reaching out for it. Say it."

Eli wiped wiped a tear that had formed in the corner of his eye and whispered, "I can…"

Aston nodded, "Come on, Eli! Say the words. All the words! Don't condemn yourself to this bullshit. It's your life. Say them!"

"I can… I can be happy again," he struggled, but said the words.

It was all Aston needed to hear and he immediately grabbed Eli, pulling him into a solid, tight embrace, holding him as close as he could as the silence of the night wrapped around them.

Eli began to cry into his shoulder and Aston held him tight.

"Please don't abandon me, Aston. Please don't leave me while I work through this," sobbed Eli. The tears flowed freely, wetting Aston's neck and shirt.

"As long as I know you're open to the idea of us, I'll never leave you," Aston murmured into Eli's hair, tears welling in his eyes, as his heart ached seeing the man he loved in so much turmoil. "And I'll wait as long as you need."

"I love you too, Aston. I'm sorry for all of this."

"No, you don't be sorry. I understand it. I'm here," Aston whispered, taking a deep breath as a tear escaped the corner of his eye.

Then Eli said something Aston was not expecting in the slightest.

"I'll set a date… I can't promise anything, but I'll at least set a date."

Chapter Twenty Three

The following day, Aston was standing beside the boat they had been working on for what felt like an eternity. When he saw Eli approach, he gave him a smile, something soft and patient. Eli had always admired that about him—Aston's ability to make things feel manageable, even when everything else felt impossible.

"Hey," Eli greeted, a small smile tugging at the corners of his mouth.

Aston grinned, motioning for Eli to come closer. "I've been thinking about something," he said, his voice almost a whisper against the quiet of the morning. "You know how we've been talking about finishing touches on our boat project? I think she's there. We've done it."

Eli nodded, glancing at the vessel. Over the months, the boat was a project that had come to mean more than just hours of labor; it was a piece of them now, their friendship, their understanding. "Yeah, what about it?"

"Well, every boat needs a name." Aston's gaze shifted from the boat to Eli, his eyes filled with something gentle and steady. "I've been thinking… maybe we should name her after someone who means a lot to you."

Eli looked at him, caught off guard by the suggestion. "You want me to name it?"

Aston nodded, watching him closely. "I was thinking about your sister… if it feels right to you, we could name the boat after her."

Eli swallowed, a lump forming in his throat. No one had ever asked him that before—no one had ever thought to honor her memory in such a way. It was always something that hovered in the background, a shadow he carried, rarely mentioned but always present.

"Her," Eli said, his voice low. "Her name was Joy."

Aston's eyes softened, and he took a moment, letting the name sink in, letting its meaning linger in the air between them. "Joy," he repeated, almost reverently. "It's perfect."

Eli managed a small smile, glancing away to hide the emotion that was surfacing.

"I… I've never really talked about her much with anyone," he admitted, his hands gripping the edge of the boat as he tried to steady himself.

Aston's hand found his shoulder, grounding him, giving him permission to continue.

"Tell me about her," Aston said softly, breaking the silence.

Eli looked at him, his expression unreadable at first, as if he was still deciding whether to share. But then, after a moment, a small, almost wistful smile tugged at his lips. "Joy…" he began, his voice filled with the gentle warmth of memory. "She was… everything to me? The kind of person you couldn't help but admire."

Aston settled in, leaning back slightly, listening with his full attention as Eli's expression softened, the weight of his usual reserve easing in the golden light of late afternoon.

"There was this one day… it was summer, and we'd been planning this little sailing trip for weeks." Eli's voice softened as he leaned forward, elbows on his knees, his gaze unfocused as he let himself fall back into the memory. "I was maybe thirteen, and she was fifteen. She had just gotten her own little skiff—not much bigger than a rowboat with a sail, really—but to her, it was like a yacht.

She had saved up for it, little by little, from odd jobs and chores around the house. She used to joke that she was going to sail us around the world on it one day."

Aston couldn't help but smile at the image of a younger Eli, slightly awkward and shy, being pulled along by an older sister with such a big heart and an even bigger sense of adventure.

"That day was perfect," Eli continued, his eyes brightening as he remembered. "We woke up before dawn, sneaked out of the house, and she steered us down to the marina with that boat. I remember the sky was this pale, soft pink, and she kept saying how lucky we were, how the ocean was going to be calm just for us."

Eli chuckled, a low, nostalgic sound. "She was always full of things like that—she used to say the world was hers to explore and that I was her first mate, no matter what. I remember sitting there, holding the sail ropes while she guided us out past the breakwaters. The whole world felt like ours, just for that morning."

Aston's gaze didn't waver, and he could almost see it—Eli as a kid, nervous but thrilled, his sister's enthusiasm pulling him out of his shell, even then.

Eli paused, the expression on his face a strange blend of joy and sadness. "It was just the two of us out there, miles from shore. She'd pack these peanut butter sandwiches and a flask of orange juice, and we'd sit there, watching the sun come up over the water. She had this laugh…" He trailed off, a soft smile breaking through as he looked down, trying to find the words. "It was like music. She'd laugh and it would feel like the whole ocean was laughing with her, like even the world itself couldn't help but be happy with her around."

Aston felt his heart ache with a bittersweet empathy. "She sounds incredible," he murmured, not wanting to interrupt the memory but needing Eli to know he understood.

"She was." Eli's voice was a whisper now, filled with a longing that reached across time. "That day, she told me something I'll never forget. She said, 'Life is too short to be scared of it, Eli. Even if it feels like a storm sometimes, you have to ride the waves it creates. You have to feel everything, even the hard stuff, because that's how you find the good stuff, too.'"

Aston could see how deeply those words had sunk into Eli, how they'd stayed with him even after all these years, hidden beneath layers of his own reserve and fear.
She had tried to prepare him for the harsh realities of this world.

"She believed in everything so fiercely," Eli continued, his gaze distant, as if he was seeing Joy's face again. "She didn't let anything hold her back. And I guess… after she died, I couldn't find that same courage. It was like… like she took all of it with her. She was the complete opposite of me. I felt lost after she…"

Aston felt a tightness in his chest as he watched Eli's expression soften into something vulnerable, something raw. He rubbed Eli's back, to let him know he was there, but he held back from saying anything, sensing that Eli needed to speak, to let the words flow unburdened.

Eli's voice grew softer. "I remember that after she died, I couldn't look at the ocean the same way. I kept thinking about all the things she'd wanted to see, all the places she'd wanted to go. It felt like an open wound every time I went back to the marina, like I was betraying her memory by being afraid of everything."

"I think she'd be proud of you, Eli. For remembering her like this. For honoring her by still doing this, by still loving being on the water," Aston said, his voice barely above a whisper.

Eli's gaze met Aston's, something vulnerable and grateful in his eyes.

"Maybe," he murmured. "Sometimes I feel like… like if I can just hold on to these memories, I won't forget her. I won't forget the way she looked at the world, how she made me feel like I could be brave, even if I was terrified inside."

"She'd be proud, Eli. I know she would. You're still that brave person, even if you can't see it yet."

They stood in silence for a moment, the quiet filled with an understanding that words couldn't quite capture. The golden light of the setting sun cast a warm glow around them, the memories of Joy alive in the air between them.

After a long pause, Eli gave a small, almost sheepish smile, glancing at Aston. "Thanks for listening. I don't really… talk about her. It feels too big sometimes. But with you, I feel like it's okay."

Aston felt a warmth spread through him at those words, a quiet pride at being trusted with something so sacred. "I'm glad you shared her with me," he said softly. "She sounds like she was as amazing person, and I'm glad I get to know her a little bit through you."

Eli's smile widened, and for a moment, Aston could see a different version of him—the young boy he must have been, carefree and light-hearted, his spirit unburdened by the weight of incredible loss.

They sat together until the sun dipped below the horizon, the world around them growing dark and still. In the silence, Aston could feel Joy's spirit, a quiet, comforting presence that lingered around them, woven into the air, into the sound of the waves, and into the unspoken bond between them.

For the first time in a long time, Eli felt a sense of peace, of something shifting deep within him. He had shared his sister with Aston, and somehow, it made the weight of her memory lighter, something that he could carry forward without it holding him back.

It allowed him to continue to share, even the worst parts of it all. His voice grew softer, edged with pain. "The waves were rough that morning, and I asked her if we should turn back. But she just laughed, said we'd done this a hundred times, that we were fine. And then… everything happened so fast. One minute, we were together, and the next… she was gone."

Aston's grip on Eli's shoulder tightened, a steady presence in the midst of the memories threatening to overwhelm him. "I'm so sorry, Eli," he whispered.

Eli closed his eyes, feeling the sting. "After that, my parents changed. They stopped seeing me the same way. They started seeing her ghost in me, the son they couldn't lose because they'd already lost a daughter. And it was like I lost a part of myself that day too. Like the part of me that was brave enough to be who I was went with her."

Aston nodded, his expression filled with understanding. "You didn't lose her, Eli. She's still with you. And you'll carry her memory in every moment you spend on this boat, in every sunrise you watch over the water."

Eli looked at him, his chest tight with emotion. "Maybe that's why it's been so hard to let anyone in. She was the only one who knew me, who really saw me. And I guess I'm afraid that if I let anyone else get close, it'll make me forget her somehow."

Aston shook his head, his eyes shining.

"You won't forget her, Eli. She's a part of you, always. And if you let me in… if you let anyone in, that doesn't take away from what you had with her. It just means you're carrying her memory forward, sharing the best parts of her with the people who care about you."

Eli smiled and said nothing.

After a moment, Aston spoke again, his voice soft but resolute, "Let's name the boat *Joy*," he said, a small smile breaking through the sadness. Aston nodded. "I think it would be an honor. She'd want you to remember her like this, don't you think? With something you built, something that brings you peace."

A wave of emotion washed over Eli, but it felt different this time—lighter, almost cleansing. He gave Aston a small nod, his voice choked but determined. "Yeah. She would. And we built it. Not just me."

Aston smiled and went to retrieve a can of paint and a small brush from the dock, and they worked together in silence, preparing the space on the bow for the name. Eli dipped the brush into the paint, his hand trembling as he carefully formed each letter, as if this act were a tribute, a promise to his sister's memory.

When he was finished, he stepped back, looking at the name scrawled in careful strokes across the bow. *Joy*. There it was, a tangible reminder of her spirit, something he could carry forward, even if it hurt. Aston stood beside him.

Eli swallowed, his voice barely above a whisper. "I think… I think this is what she would have wanted."

Aston smiled, nodding in agreement. "I think so too."

They stood there for a long time, watching the paint dry. It was a quiet moment, but one filled with meaning, with memories that Eli was finally able to face, maybe for the first time.

"I never thought I'd be able to talk about her like this," Eli murmured, his gaze fixed on the boat, on the name that now felt like a piece of him.

"You don't have to hold it all in, Eli," Aston said gently. "You don't have to carry it alone."

Eli nodded, feeling a warmth settle in his chest that hadn't been there for years. For the first time, he felt like he was honoring Joy's memory, not by clinging to the past, but by allowing himself to let go, even just a little.

"Thank you, Aston," he whispered, his voice filled with a quiet gratitude that went beyond words.

Aston smiled, his hand still resting on Eli's back, grounding him, reminding him that he was always there.

"Anytime," Aston replied, his voice soft but full of understanding.

As they watched the sun set over the water, Eli felt a sense of peace settle over him. For the first time in years, he could breathe, he could remember without pain, and he could feel Joy's spirit with him, not as a weight, but as a light guiding him forward.

They had named the boat together, and in that simple act, Eli felt a part of himself come back to life.

Chapter Twenty Four

Set a date… I can't promise, but I'll set a date.

Eli was having conflicting thoughts about those words. But it was too late. He had made the promise.

The air was thick with an unspoken tension that Eli could feel creeping up on him the entire day. Ever since he and Aston had agreed to have dinner with both of their families together, he had been filled with a dull sense of dread. The idea had seemed reasonable enough at the time—a small step toward the future, where maybe things would feel less suffocating. A chance for his parents to meet Aston's mother and for everything to seem…normal. Even if only for a while.

But now, as Eli stood at the door of his house, waiting for Aston, his mother, and her new boyfriend, Alex, to arrive, his nerves felt raw. His own mother, Rebecca, had been in a mood all afternoon, fluttering around the kitchen, making sure everything was perfect. His father was calm, as usual, sitting at the dining table and reading the newspaper, but Eli knew he was also keeping an eye on things.

That was just how it always was—his father, silently present but not involved in the family dynamics, and his mother, tightly wound and in control of every detail.

He wiped his palms on his pants for the tenth time when the knock on the door finally came. Taking a breath, Eli opened it to see Aston standing there, his usual confident smile on his face, but there was a softness in his eyes—a quiet reassurance. Beside him, Laura Carter, Aston's mother, stood with a warm smile, holding a bottle of wine. Next to her, Alex.

"Hi! You must be Eli. I'm pleased to meet you. Aston has told me a lot about you," she greeted, her voice soothing. "This is Alex. Thanks for inviting us."

Aston had repeatedly told his mom and Alex to not bring up the fact that he was gay and not mention anything along those lines. He felt confident that they wouldn't.

Eli managed a small smile in return, feeling his cheeks flush and getting uncomfortable already. He stepped aside to let them in.

"Relax," Aston mouthed silently, giving Eli a reassuring smile.

"It's no problem," Eli said to Laura, trying to keep his tone casual as he smiled to Alex, who firmly shook his hand. Then Eli's eyes flickered back to Aston, another silent exchange passing between them. Aston gave him a nod, as if to say, *It'll be okay.*

In the living room, Eli's mother, Rebecca, greeted them all with the same crisp politeness she always had. Her eyes, however, were watchful, like a hawk surveying the territory. Eli could tell she was already evaluating Laura, trying to figure out where she stood, who she was, and most importantly, whether she fit into Rebecca's narrow vision of what was acceptable.

"Mrs. Carter," Rebecca said with a tight smile. "So good to finally meet you. Aston is a good employee and it's lovely to finally meet his mother. Hi Aston. Hello, Alex."

"Hi Mrs. Taylor," replied Laura.

"Hello there. Pleased to meet you. Thanks for having us!" said Alex, confidently.

"Please, call me Laura," Aston's mother said warmly, stepping forward to shake her hand. "I've heard wonderful things about your family as well."

"Rebecca, please… and thank you," said Eli's mom in return.

Eli shifted uncomfortably as his father, Samuel, rose from the table to shake hands with their guests. He could sense his parents slipping into their roles—the friendly, conservative family, polite but guarded. And yet, under the surface, he knew his mother was already looking for ways to control the conversation. It was inevitable. She couldn't help herself.

As they all sat down for dinner, the conversation was light at first—talking about the town, the marina, the summer rush of tourists. Eli tried to focus on the food, even though his appetite had disappeared the moment the evening started. He glanced at Aston every now and then, grateful for his presence. Even just having him here made things feel more bearable. He'd told Aston time and again that his mother was pushy about everything, but Aston had promised it would be fine. That they would handle it.

Eli had only agreed to this dinner if there was no chance that it would lead to them talking about themselves or their relationship. It was purely just an introductory dinner.

The night went on in the usual slightly uncomfortable and awkward manner that always seems to happen when people don't really know each other and don't have too much in common and are forced to spend an evening together. Alex's casual demeanor took a lot of the pressure off though, as he chatted to Samuel about the boating industry. It slowly got easier as the evening went on.

But Eli's unease never left. He could feel the pressure mounting with every passing minute, and eventually, his mother's usual grace began to crack and turned the attention onto him, much to his annoyance.

"So, Eli," Rebecca said suddenly, setting down her fork and turning toward him. "I was just speaking to Ava the other day. She mentioned you've been seeing more of her at the marina recently. She's been asking about you… a lot. It warms my heart to see you two getting closer."

Eli froze. His fingers clenched tightly around his glass of water as he forced a polite smile. "Yeah, the marina's been busy," he replied, hoping to keep the conversation away from Ava.

"Busy is good, but you shouldn't forget about your social life," his mother pressed, her voice full of suggestion.

"Ava's such a lovely girl, and she's been wanting to spend more time with you. It wouldn't hurt to take a break from work, to nurture that budding relationship. Maybe you two could catch up again soon."

Eli's stomach twisted. He shot a quick glance at Aston, who had gone still beside him. Laura noticed the shift in tone but remained silent, her eyes flicking between Eli and Rebecca, sensing the tension. She glanced at Aston occasionally too, but she knew the score and wasn't about to rock the boat.

"I've been pretty tied up. Lots of work, as you know. That's why she is coming down there," Eli mumbled, wishing the conversation would shift.

"Oh, but Ava's very understanding," his mother insisted. "She knows how important your work is, but she's always had a soft spot for you, hasn't she? Besides, now you have Aston. Aston, you should take over some of Eli's duties in order to allow him to explore more with Ava."

Aston, forced a smile and took a sip of the wine, without saying anything.

Eli could feel the weight of expectation pressing down on him like a vice. His skin felt hot, his heart pounding in his chest.

He wanted to shout, to tell his mother to stop, to tell her that he wasn't interested in Ava—or any girl for that matter—but he knew without a doubt that he wouldn't. Especially not tonight.

Aston, sensing Eli's discomfort, leaned forward slightly, his voice calm but firm. "We've been working really hard at the marina. Eli's been doing a great job teaching me about everything regarding the boats. He is a great teacher."

Rebecca's eyes narrowed slightly, her polite façade thinning. "Of course, Aston. But he shouldn't lose sight of other important things in life."

"You're right. You're very right," said Aston, glancing over at Eli.

The tension at the table became unbearable. Eli couldn't take it anymore. His mother's constant pushing, the pressure to be someone he wasn't—it was too much. Three people around the table knowing he was gay. He could feel himself unraveling, and before he knew it, he was on his feet, the chair scraping loudly against the floor as he stood.

"I'm sorry," Eli muttered, his voice strained. "I need some air."

Without waiting for a response from anyone, he turned and walked out of the dining room, the suffocating atmosphere of the house closing in on him. The door to the porch banged behind him as he stepped outside, breathing deeply of the cool evening air.

Behind him, he heard footsteps, and then Aston's voice, soft but steady. "Eli."

Eli didn't turn around. His hands gripped the porch railing as he stared out at the darkening sky, his chest tight with frustration and fear. "I don't know why we're even doing this dinner," he whispered. "I don't know how I'll ever be able to tell them."

Aston stepped closer, placing a gentle hand on Eli's shoulder. "We're not saying anything tonight. Relax," he said softly. "I know you're stressing, but you're doing great."

Eli shook his head, his voice trembling. "I thought maybe tonight would be a step in the right direction. That if they got to know your mom, if things felt more normal, it would help. But it's just—everything's so much harder than I thought it would be. My mom…she's never going to understand."

Aston squeezed Eli's shoulder, his voice filled with quiet reassurance. Eli shrugged his arm away and whispered "Don't do that here."

"Okay, calm down. I'm sorry. It was a step, Eli. Just organizing this dinner, that was a huge step. I'm proud of you for that."

Eli's eyes stung, his throat tight. He wasn't sure if Aston understood just how much the pressure was crushing him. But he appreciated that Aston was here, standing by him, not pushing him further than he could handle.

"I just…I wish things were different," Eli murmured, his voice barely above a whisper.

Aston sighed softly, "So do I," he said, his voice filled with quiet sympathy. "They will be, one day."

Eli turned then, meeting Aston's eyes for the first time since leaving the dinner table. For a moment, the weight of the world seemed to lift just slightly, the knot in his chest loosening.

"I'm sorry I walked out," Eli said, his voice strained. "I didn't mean to… I made it awkward, didn't I?"

Aston shook his head. "You didn't. You did what you had to do. Don't apologize."

Eli looked at him and raised an eyebrow.

"Okay, maybe you made it a little awkward. But it's fine. Just say you felt sick or something," smiled Aston, finding a little humor in a tough situation.

Eli force a smiled.

The porch light flickered above them, casting long shadows across the yard. For a moment, they stood there in silence, the distant sound of waves crashing against the shore providing a small sense of peace in the midst of the chaos.

Inside the house, Eli could hear the murmur of everyone's voices, no doubt wondering what had happened, but continuing the discussion. But for now, he didn't care. For now, he was grateful for this moment, for Aston's steady presence beside him, and for the small but important step he had taken tonight.

It wasn't perfect, and it wasn't easy—but it was a start.

Chapter Twenty Five

The sky was an endless expanse of blue, the sun warm as it rose, casting gentle, shimmering light over the marina. Aston took in the scene with a smile as he approached the docks, spotting Eli near the boat they'd so lovingly restored together. Eli was securing a few ropes, lost in his own world as he prepared another boat for a round of sanding, painting—whatever that day's work would call for. But Aston had a different plan.

"Good morning, Eli," Aston called out, grinning.

Eli looked up, surprised by the brightness in Aston's voice. "Morning," he replied, a hint of a smile tugging at his lips. "What's got you so cheerful?"

Aston walked over to their boat, letting his hand rest on the gleaming surface of the bow, right where they'd painted her name: *Joy*. "I was thinking," he said, almost daring Eli to guess what he had in mind, "we could take her out today."

Eli's eyes widened. "Out…? You mean, on the water?"

"Yep. She is a boat after all," Aston said, his eyes dancing. "Let's take her out and live a little. Just you, me, and Joy. You can show me the ropes. Isn't that why we did all this, to finally see her in her element? And after last night's dinner, I think we owe it to ourselves to take today and just enjoy it. Whadaya say?"

Eli's expression wavered between excitement and apprehension, but there was a sparkle in his eyes that hadn't been there since the kiss. He glanced out to the open water, longing flickering across his face. He seemed to struggle with a silent question, and then, with a slow exhale, he nodded.

"All right," he said, unable to hide his smile. "Let's do it."

With Eli guiding the way, they prepared the boat, and soon they were drifting out of the marina, leaving behind the bobbing hulls of the docked boats and the echo of quiet conversations between other boaters. Eli took to the helm, his eyes bright, his shoulders relaxed, as if he'd been waiting for this day without even knowing it. He watched the horizon with a rare ease that Aston hadn't seen before.

Aston sat beside him, letting the sun warm his face, the salt breeze filling his lungs as they sailed.

"You look like you're home," he said, breaking the gentle silence. Eli looked at him, his face softened by the sunlight, and chuckled.

"Guess I am, in a way," Eli said, his voice barely above a whisper, as if speaking too loudly would break the spell. "It's been a long time since I've been out like this. It's strange but... Good."

Aston's heart filled with a warmth he could hardly describe. He watched Eli—truly watched him—as he guided *Joy* with caring, strong hands and a focused gaze, the gentle breeze flapping the sails, as if he were one with the wind and water. Every time Eli's eyes brightened as the boat caught a new breeze, or his grin widened as they cut through a wave, Aston felt his own happiness swell. There was something so pure about seeing Eli this way, unburdened and alive.

After a while, Aston joined Eli at the bow, both of them leaning into the wind, feeling the spray as they soared over the waves. They were quiet, simply soaking in the experience together, but it was a silence filled with understanding and warmth. Aston felt like he was seeing a side of Eli that had been hidden, protected, for way too long.

"I don't think I've ever felt this free," Eli finally admitted, his voice thoughtful. He glanced at Aston, his eyes filled with gratitude, his usual guarded expression gone. "I… I never thought I'd be out here like this again, not really. And with you… it feels… right."

Aston's throat tightened, touched by the vulnerability in Eli's voice. "That makes me so happy to hear, Eli," he said softly.

Eli's gaze softened, and he reached out, gripping Aston's shoulder, his touch firm and reassuring. "Thank you," he said, his voice thick with emotion. "For everything."

They sailed for hours, the boat cutting through the water in graceful arcs, each moment brighter, freer. They were like two kids, laughing and joking, letting go of the expectations and weight they'd been carrying for so long. And for a little while, it was only them, *Joy*, and the open ocean.

As they returned to the marina later that afternoon, laughter still echoing between them, they didn't notice Rebecca watching from a distance, her arms folded, a wary expression on her face. She noticed the joy on Eli's face, the ease in his movements, but to her, it seemed reckless. Too carefree.

Later that evening, in the quiet of their kitchen, Rebecca approached her husband, her eyes still narrowed with worry. "Did you know they took the small boat out today?"

Samuel looked up from his plate, a flicker of surprise crossing his face. "No, I didn't know. I saw they called the boat Joy. I thought it was quite a nice gesture. I'm glad he is finally allowing himself to have some light-hearted fun."

Rebecca stood in silence, reflecting for a moment.

"Light-hearted or irresponsible?" Rebecca snapped, her tone sharper than intended. "Ever since Aston showed up, Eli's… changing. He's been so much harder to reach, and now he's running off, breaking who knows how many rules. This isn't him, Samuel. It's not like Eli."

Samuel sighed, folding the paper and setting it aside. "Maybe it's exactly what Eli needs. Yes, he is still struggling, some days more than others. But overall, he seems happier, Rebecca. Don't you see that?"

She looked at him, uncertain, her mouth drawn in a line. "I don't want some… some bad influence derailing Eli. He has been through a lot. He needs stability."

"He needs to live again. Be a young man and enjoy himself. It's been too long since… And Aston's not a bad influence," Samuel said gently. "He's a good kid.
He is giving Eli a chance to find himself again. They're good friends. That's what's important. I really think it's good for them both."

Rebecca's mouth tightened, and she looked away, unwilling to admit that her husband might be right, but considering it. The image of Eli, bright-eyed and laughing beside Aston on the boat, flickered in her mind, filling her with both a pang of nostalgia, a flicker of happiness and the cold stab of fear. She had been there for his grief, had seen how fragile he'd become after Joy's death. She wasn't sure she could step back and give him space.

But despite her fears, she couldn't deny the happiness she'd seen on Eli's face, a happiness she hadn't witnessed in years.

Chapter Twenty Six

The sun had barely begun its descent, casting soft golden rays across the marina, as Aston and Eli steered *Joy* gently into the shallows. They eased her onto the sand, securing her just beyond the waterline. After hours out on the open water, they were both flushed from the sun, windblown, and full of a quiet contentment that didn't need words.

Eli had been different all day, lighter somehow, and Aston noticed. There was a calm confidence in his movements, a relaxed way he smiled and laughed, that hinted at something deeper. Like maybe he had finally laid down a heavy weight, allowing himself to step out from under it. Aston couldn't stop watching him, reveling in the subtle transformation that he hoped would last.

They started to cover the boat for the evening, working side-by-side, silent but comfortably close. As Aston leaned in to tuck the last corner of canvas, a hidden nail scraped his arm. He flinched, pulling back and cradling his hand as blood began to well up along a jagged scratch.

"Oh, shit," Aston muttered, inspecting the cut.

Eli turned immediately, his gaze falling to Aston's arm. "Let me see," he said softly, guiding Aston's hand up for a better look. The concern in his eyes was warm, protective. "Don't want an infection. Hang on a sec. Follow me."

Eli led him toward one of the boats that were in the storage area behind the workshop, where a tall wall housed all the boats that were in various phases of repair. The latest one to be brought in, and closest, was Mark's. Aston realized with a slight twinge of unease, remembering the ridiculousness of the angry man. But Eli's presence kept him calm. Eli climbed up onto it and lifted the cover on the storage compartment near the helm, retrieving a small first aid kit. He helped Aston climb into the boat, still perched on its trailer. Gently, he took Aston's hand and led him to sit on one of the cushioned seats in the shade, holding Aston's gaze for a moment before kneeling down to tend to the wound.

As Eli carefully wiped the cut clean, Aston felt a surge of something he couldn't quite name. The closeness, the quiet intimacy of Eli's hands on his arm, the gentleness in his touch… it left Aston feeling open, vulnerable.

Eli bandaged up Aston's wound with tenderness and care.

When Eli looked up, his gaze soft and deep, their faces were only inches apart. For a second, neither of them moved.

Then, almost instinctively, Eli leaned forward, brushing his lips against Aston's. The touch was tentative at first, hesitant, as if seeking permission. But as Aston responded, leaning into the kiss with equal softness, the moment deepened. The world around them faded, leaving only the warmth of their connection and the steady beat of their hearts.

The kiss grew more assured, each movement unspoken yet perfectly understood. They were gentle, savoring the closeness, the safe space they'd created in each other's arms. Eli's hands slipped up Aston's shoulders, tracing the line of his neck, and Aston felt a thrill of sensation with each delicate touch. Their breaths mingled, the rhythm of their connection slow and peaceful, each kiss a quiet promise.

They lay down on the cushioned seat, curling into each other like it was the most natural thing in the world. There, in the cocoon of their shared warmth, the tenderness between them filled the air, surrounding them with a feeling so serene it was almost unreal.

Without hesitation, without worry and without all the heavy thoughts that had burdened him for so long, Eli pulled off Aston's shirt. One by one, each piece of clothing dropped to the floor until they were naked.

They made love in the quiet and secluded spot in the workshop's yard, on Mark's comfortable and luxurious boat, as though they were the only two people in the world.

Afterwards, Aston stroked Eli's hair, feeling the softness beneath his fingers as Eli rested his head on Aston's chest. They stayed like that, their breathing evening out, their hearts beating in gentle unison. The world outside was quiet, as they fell into a drowsy peace.

The evening was warm and comforting and as the minutes passed, sleep began to take them both, sending them drifting off in the quiet embrace of each other's presence. For the first time in a long while, everything was perfect. The chaos, the uncertainty, the heaviness—all of it melted away, leaving only this moment, this shared peace.

Chapter Twenty Seven

The late night air was soft and cool, accompanied by a gentle breeze that kissed their naked bodies. Aston and Eli lay together on the comfortable sun deck cushions of the boat. They were wrapped in a light sheet and shared silence that carried more weight than any words could. The distant sound of water lapping against the dock outside soothed them, a rhythmic lullaby against the backdrop of a wide-open sky. Stars twinkled above, and for a moment, it felt as if they were the only two people in the world. Just them, the boat, and the quiet hum of possibility between them.

Eli shifted slightly beside Aston, his bare shoulder brushing against Aston's arm, pulling him out of his thoughts. After their second round of lovemaking earlier, they lay there, spent and comfortable in each other's presence, not needing to fill the space with anything other than their closeness. But something was stirring in both of them—an unspoken yearning to dream, to imagine a life that, for a long time, had seemed impossible.

Eli was the first to speak, his voice soft but tinged with the excitement of a fantasy shared for the first time. "What do you think it would be like?" he asked, his gaze focused on the stars as if the answer might be written there.

Aston turned to him, studying his profile in the dim light. "What do you mean?" he asked, though he already had a feeling.

"Us," Eli said, his voice barely above a whisper. "What would it be like if we could just... be together. For real."

Aston swallowed, his heart skipping a beat. He had thought about this, dreamt about it in quiet moments when the world was too much and all he wanted was to escape with Eli. But to talk about it now, with Eli right there, felt both exhilarating and terrifying.

"Firstly, it's not a crazy idea. We can be. And secondly, I think it would be... amazing," Aston finally said, his voice steady but filled with emotion. "No more hiding, no more pretending. Just us."

Eli smiled, a small, hopeful curve of his lips. "Where would we go?"

Aston thought for a moment, letting the fantasy take hold. "France," he said, surprising himself with the certainty in his voice. "I've always wanted to go there. Somewhere by the coast, maybe a little cottage near the sea."

Eli laughed softly. "France, huh? Why France?"

Aston grinned. "Because it feels far enough away to start over. Somewhere no one knows us. We could be anyone we wanted to be. And besides, it's beautiful. You would fit right in with the scenery."

Eli smiled, as his eyes sparkled, considering it, the idea of France painting a picture in his mind. "I like that," he said. "A little place by the sea. We could walk along the beach every morning, go into town to buy fresh bread… it sounds so idyllic."

Aston nodded, feeling a warmth spread through him at the thought. "And no one would care. We'd just be two guys, living together, loving each other. No pressure, no expectations. Just us."

Eli shifted closer, resting his head on Aston's chest once more. "Do you think that could really happen?" he asked, his voice quieter now, as if afraid to let the hope grow too large.

Aston scratched Eli's back gently, sighing softly, "I want to believe it could. Maybe not now, but one day. We could save up, plan it out. And when we're ready… we leave. Just like that!"

Eli closed his eyes, letting the idea settle in his mind. "I want that so much," he whispered. "Just to be with you, without all this… mess."

The weight of Eli's words hung between them, a reflection of the struggle they both knew too well—the pressure from Eli's family, the fear of being discovered, the constant hiding. But tonight, they allowed themselves to dream, to imagine a life where none of that mattered.

"Maybe we'd open a little café," Aston mused, letting the fantasy expand. "A cozy place by the water, with mismatched chairs and those old-fashioned chalkboards for the menu."

Eli chuckled, the sound vibrating against Aston's chest. "You'd want to run a café?"

"Why not?" Aston shrugged. "You could bake, I could serve. We'd make it our own little place. People would come from all over the world just for your cakes."

Eli tilted his head up, smirking. "You think I can bake? I do boats, not breads."

Aston laughed, the sound echoing softly in the stillness. "You'd learn. Or maybe we'd just hire someone who knows how."

"Definitely the second option," Eli teased, his smile growing. "I'd burn the place down if I tried."

"We could always open our own boat repair business. You've taught me well," Aston replied, pulling him closer.

"Now you're talking," replied Eli. "But how about we add a small coffee shop with bagels for the customers. The best of both worlds."

"Yes! That sounds like it," smiled Aston, picturing it already.

For a while, they continued to build this perfect world together—this dream of their future, where they could live without fear or judgment. They talked about the little things—the kind of house they'd have, how they'd decorate it, the lazy Sundays they'd spend together reading in their study. It felt like they were weaving a tapestry of hope, something tangible they could hold onto when reality threatened to pull them apart.

As the conversation lulled, Eli looked up at Aston, his eyes soft but serious. "Do you ever worry… about what will happen if we stay here?"

Aston's chest tightened at the question. "Yeah," he admitted, his voice barely above a whisper. "I do. It feels complicated."

Eli sighed, resting his head against Aston's shoulder, keeping eye contact. "I agree. Knowing that… as much as we want this, we're always going to have to fight for it. Especially with my family. It makes me anxious."

Aston's heart ached at the thought. He knew how much Eli struggled with that. And while Aston understood that Eli loved him, there was always a small part of him that feared the weight of that pressure might be too much for him and they would never realise their dreams. Although the fact that they were together like this, gave him a huge sense of hope.

"I don't blame you," Aston said quietly, his voice heavy with emotion. "I get it, Eli. I know it's not easy, and I'm worried too."

Eli lifted his head, his eyes searching Aston's. "I don't want my troubles to worry you, Aston."

Aston smiled, a soft, grateful smile. "I know," he whispered. "But in a relationship, your worries are my worries. I'll carry half of them for you. All of them, if you'd let me."

Eli smiled as Aston continued, "I just… sometimes I wonder how this will work, here… in Clearwater."

Eli was quiet for a moment, his gaze drifting back to the stars. "Yeah," he said finally. "Maybe not right now. Maybe we have to wait a little longer, figure things out. But I maybe we can get there. One day."

Aston nodded, letting the hope Eli's words offered sink in. "Yeah. One day." He couldn't help thinking that one day was a very long time away though.

They lay there in silence for a while, their bodies warm against the cool night air, their hands roaming, gently and tenderly touching each other, running soft fingertips over cool, moist skin. The future felt uncertain, but for the first time, it didn't feel impossible.

"France, huh?" Eli said after a while, a small smile playing on his lips. "I agree… We'd look good in France."

Aston laughed softly, pressing a kiss to Eli's temple and embracing him, pulling his body into his. "Yeah, we would.

But then, anyone would look good next to your handsomeness."

Eli wrapped his arms tightly around Aston in return.

"Promise me we'll make it happen someday," whispered Eli.

"I promise," replied Aston.

In each other's arms, they felt a rare, precious kind of belonging, one that they both knew would last beyond the dusk settling over the water. And in that stillness, with nothing but the quiet marina around them, they drifted off to sleep, their shared dream of living in France together, fresh in their minds. Both Aston and Eli felt, if only for tonight, like everything was perfect.

And it would have been, had it not been for the unseen Go-Pro camera that Mark used for his adventures on the water, perched in the cockpit of the boat, staring directly at their sleeping bodies.

Chapter Twenty Eight

The warmth of the early morning sun trickled onto the boat, casting a soft golden glow over where Aston and Eli lay tangled in the light sheet. Everything was calm—whispered promises in the dark, stolen touches, a few hours of peace. But that peace was shattered by the unmistakable sound of angry footsteps pounding on the dock, heading directly towards them.

"Shit," Aston muttered, shooting upright. His heart raced as he yanked the covers off and scrambled for his clothes, pulling on his board shorts.

Eli stirred groggily beside him, rubbing his eyes. "What's—?"

Before he could finish, someone climbed the small ladder and the imposing figure was in front of him—Mark. He stood seething, his face flushed with fury, panting from the fast and determined walk.

"You two have got some nerve!" Mark's voice thundered, sending a jolt of fear straight through Eli's chest.

Aston froze mid-pulling his shirt over his head, eyes wide. Eli, still shirtless, stumbled off the small bed and fumbled with his short jeans, his face turning pale.

"I saw everything!" Mark snarled, stepping into the cabin with an imposing presence. "Every. Fucking. Thing."

"What are you talking about?" Aston's voice was calm, but his hands trembled slightly as he finished pulling his shirt on. Eli scrambled behind him, getting his clothes on.

Mark scoffed, pulling out his phone and tapping at the screen. "The camera footage. You fucking idiots! The security system uploaded it all to the cloud. I've got it. I've got all the footage of you two having faggot sex on my boat. And now everyone will see it."

Eli's stomach dropped, and he turned white as a ghost, standing up next to Aston. "No—no, no, please," he stammered, his breath coming in short, panicked bursts. "You can't—"

"I can," Mark spat back, eyes blazing. "And I will. I'll make sure every single person in this shitty town of yours sees what you two did on *my* fucking boat."

"Look, just calm down—" Aston started, stepping forward to put himself between Mark and Eli.

"Calm down?" Mark cut him off, voice rising even higher. "You're both done. When this gets out, no one will want to do business with you again. Your shitty little boat rental will go under. And I'll be the one to shut it all down. You hear me? I'll destroy you."

Eli's legs gave out, and he slumped onto the edge of the bed, hands shaking. "Please, Mark… don't. We didn't mean any harm. It was a mistake."

"A mistake?" Mark's laugh was cruel. "You two fucked by mistake, huh? Well, it's a mistake that's going to cost you everything unless you hand over the completely fixed boat by Friday at the absolute latest. And I ain't paying shit for it! You hear me?"

Aston's eyes narrowed. "Friday? That's impossible. The repairs won't be done by then, we told you that."

"Make it happen," Mark snapped. "Or else."

Eli looked up, eyes wide with desperation. "Mark, we can't—"

"I don't give two flying fucks, Eli!" Mark shouted, jabbing a finger toward Eli, his face twisted with contempt. "You fucked on my boat, and now you're gonna pay for it. If you don't hand it over by Friday, I'll go postal on both of you. I'll release the footage to the internet and send the link to everyone, and you'll be ruined. Are we clear?"

Aston clenched his fists, but forced his voice to stay level. "We'll figure it out."

Mark snorted. "You better. Or it's game over for both of you, fuckers." He turned on his heel climbed down the ladder and stormed off. Aston dropped on the subbed next to Eli.

The echo of Mark's footsteps faded as the two of them sat in stunned silence.

Eli's hands shook uncontrollably as he buried his face in them. "Aston… what are we gonna do? We can't finish by Friday… We're screwed. We're fucking screwed!"

Aston ran a hand through his messy hair and let out a long, slow breath. "We'll figure it out, Eli," he repeated, though his voice sounded less certain now.

The boat was silent once more, the only sound in the heavy, suffocating quiet that followed Mark's threat was the sound of their beating hearts and labored breaths.

Eli looked at Aston, eyes filled with dread. "And if we can't?"

Aston swallowed hard, not wanting to answer that. He moved his hand and rested it on the small of Eli's back. "Let's just… Let's just take it one step at a time. We'll find a way. We have to. Let's just think. Stay calm."

But even as he said it, the sinking feeling in his chest told him that it was probably just the calm before the storm.

Chapter Twenty Nine

Aston could tell from the look in Eli's eyes that he was spiraling. Mark had left the marina not five minutes ago, but his threats lingered in the air, heavy and suffocating. Eli stood in the empty dock, his hands clenched tightly around the worn edge of the workbench, his knuckles white. The crackling tension seemed to spill over everything—sticking to the air, thickening it.

"Aston, he's going to do it. He will. They are gonna find out. Everyone is," Eli whispered, almost to himself. His voice was raw, a tremor betraying the fear lodged deep inside.

Aston's heart twisted as he watched Eli fight to keep his composure. Mark had done enough damage for one day, hurling his threats like weapons and demanding an impossible timeline for the boat repairs. Aston wanted nothing more than to find a way to protect Eli, to shield him from the cruelty that seemed to shadow his every step. And he knew there was only one way to do it.

"Eli," Aston said quietly, resting his hand on Eli's. Eli looked down, his face taut with worry and frustration. "If we want to stop Mark… then we have to neutralize his threat."

"What do you mean?" Eli looked up, hoping for a solution, but Aston could see he already knew where this was going.

"Let's tell your parents about us," Aston said firmly. "It's time. Before he does. You take control, you get to tell them your truth—your way. Not his. You won't have it hanging over your head anymore."

Eli's face paled as Aston's words sank in, his breaths coming faster. "No! I can't… I can't just… It's not that simple."

"I know it terrifies you," Aston said, his voice steady but gentle. "But if he goes through with his threat, they're gonna find out in a really shitty way. This is it, Eli. We can't keep letting him hold this over us. You've been living under this pressure for so long. I'm not going to let him do this to you. I won't let him fuck you up like this. It's not coming out… You're not coming out by way of a fucking sex tape!"

Eli pulled his hand away, taking a step back. "What you're asking—it's too much, Aston." His voice broke, and he clenched his fists to steady himself. "You don't know what it's like for me. You don't know what my parents will say, how they'll react."

"But I do know you can't keep living like this anymore. You know that too!" Aston pressed, feeling an urgency he couldn't ignore. "Look, I said I'd be here for you, right? No matter what happens. I'll protect you, Eli. I promise you."

Eli stared at him, his eyes flickering with conflict, desperation mixing with fear. "Don't make promises like that," he said in a low voice. "You can't protect me from everything."

"I will," Aston insisted, feeling his own voice harden as he met Eli's gaze. "And you have to trust me. You know I wouldn't push you into this unless I thought it was the only way."

Eli's jaw tightened, and he looked away, a storm of emotion roiling under the surface. His entire life was crashing down around him, and he was feeling the weight of everyone's expectations, their judgments, and now, the fear of disappointing Aston too.

"Eli," Aston said, his voice softening, "I'm scared too. But what other option do we have? We can't fucking kill him!"

For a long moment, they stood there in silence, the marina eerily quiet in the fading light.

Aston watched as Eli's eyes slowly met his, a hesitant acceptance in them, albeit trembling.

"Fine," Eli whispered, voice barely audible. "But if this all falls apart…"

"It won't," Aston interrupted, his words coming out more sharply than he'd intended. "Because I'll be right there beside you. I swear, Eli. I'm not going to let anything happen to you."

As Eli took in Aston's words, a painful silence stretched between them. The enormity of what Aston was asking rippled through him, the weight nearly unbearable. Eli's breath quickened as he tried to process it, but panic clawed at him, tightening his chest, making the world feel small and constricted.

"Oh, fuck," Eli finally managed, his voice hoarse and breaking, each word catching on the raw edge of fear. "If I tell them… If I tell them, Aston, everything changes. Everything."

Aston reached for his hand, but Eli pulled away again, stepping back, shaking his head. "I can't believe this."

He turned away, scrubbing a hand over his face, trying to find some anchor in the turmoil. "You don't have to live with… with people looking at you and thinking you're someone you're not. I don't know if I can lose my parents too, Aston."

Aston felt his heart twist, his own frustration simmering under the surface. "Eli, that's exactly why we have to do this. You can't keep living with Mark threatening to ruin everything. With them controlling your life. This isn't about me or anyone else anymore—it's about you finally being free."

"Free?" Eli scoffed, the word heavy with bitter disbelief. "Free from what? You don't know what they're like when it comes to this. My mom… God, she's always talking about Ava, about the kind of girl she wants for me. And my dad just looks at me like… like I'm some stranger."

"I'm not saying it won't be hard, Eli," Aston replied, his voice softer now, trying to cut through the storm of emotions in Eli's eyes. "But you can't keep pretending. It's tearing you apart, and I can't just stand by and watch you get crushed under this anymore. And I won't let Mark have this kind of power over you. He doesn't get to decide your life."

Eli's hands were shaking. "It's not that simple! You don't have any idea what it's like to feel trapped in every direction."

"I'm on the fucking recording with you, Eli!"

Eli's voice broke, his eyes reflecting a deep, haunting anguish, "My mother will hate me."

"Fuck her!" Aston shouted, and immediately regretted saying it. "I'm sorry. I'm stressed too."

Aston reached for Eli again, this time more firmly, his grip steady and grounding on his shoulders. "You don't know that for sure. You're assuming she'll hate you, but has she ever even had the chance to understand? You're keeping everything locked inside. And what about us, Eli? If we're ever going to have a real shot… you need to be free."

Eli's breathing grew shallow, almost frantic, his chest rising and falling as he struggled against the suffocating anxiety threatening to overwhelm him. He could feel Aston's hands on him, steady and warm, grounding him. But it also made everything sharper, more real. It wasn't just his life he was risking now; it was theirs.

"What if I lose them, Aston?" Eli whispered, his voice hollow. "What if I lose everything?"

Aston's expression softened. "Then you'll still have me. I know it'll be different, but you have to trust me on this. This is about reclaiming your life. It's coming out on Friday, regardless. And I know it feels like the end. But just remember that it could be the beginning. It probably is."

Eli shook his head, his eyes shining with unshed tears. "I'm terrified, Aston. Terrified for the second I say it out loud. I'll be left with nothing."

"Then let me be your safety net," Aston said, his voice thick with emotion. "I'll say it again. You have my word. I promise I'll be right there with you, no matter what. Trust me."

The promise hung heavy in the air, a lifeline and a tether. Eli's fear gnawed at him, and he wasn't sure if he could let go of it, wasn't sure if he could trust Aston's promise to be enough. But what choice did he have?

"Okay… okay, then let's do it," said Eli, nodding. "Fuck Mark."

"Yeah. Fuck him!"

The sun was setting when they finally reached Eli's parents' house. The quiet residential street was bathed in a golden glow, the last warmth of the day spilling across the front yard.

Eli stood at the edge of the lawn, his feet planted as if rooted to the ground. Aston watched him, letting him take a moment, his presence a steady force at Eli's side.

"I don't know if I can do this," Eli whispered, visibly shaking, his eyes fixed on the house, as if he were seeing it for the first time, like it was something foreign and strange.

"You can. You're stronger than you think," Aston murmured, squeezing his hand. Eli pulled his hand away, looking at the windows, still worried they would see.

Eli took a shaky breath, "This is going to be such a massive fuckup. Jesus, I can't breathe."

Aston turned him so they were face to face, meeting his eyes with unwavering steadiness. "Well, if it is a massive fuck up… Let's face it, it already is… then we'll pick up the pieces together, Eli."

And with that, they walked towards the house and up the steps, Eli's heart pounding with each step. By the time they reached the door, his hands were clammy, and he felt his breath come faster, shallow and sharp. But Aston's hand was a steady anchor at his back, his presence a quiet strength that lent him just enough courage.

With one last glance at Aston, returned with a confident nod, Eli reached for the door.

Chapter Thirty

As Aston and Eli stepped into the house, the air felt charged, thick with an unease. The walls seemed to press in on them, and a silence heavier than stone filled the space between them and Eli's parents. Rebecca was in the living room, a cup of tea poised mid-air as her gaze snapped toward the door. Her eyes narrowed when she saw the two of them standing there together.

"Eli?" Her voice was a mixture of surprise and suspicion. "What's going on? Why are you so pale?" Samuel turned the TV off and looked across from his chair. He could see something was about to happen.

Aston shot Eli a reassuring, but uncomfortable and concerned look. Eli's hands were clammy, and he could feel his heart racing wildly. But seeing the concern in Aston's eyes calmed him, even as his mother's gaze bore into him like a spear. This was it. The moment he'd dreaded and tried to prepare for in equal measure. He was ready—at least he thought he was.

"Mom, Dad…" Eli's voice trembled, but he forced himself to continue. "There's something I need to tell you. Something I should have told you a long time ago."

His mother's expression shifted from suspicion to confusion. She set her cup down and rose slowly, crossing her arms tightly. "What is this about?"

Eli swallowed, glancing once more at Aston. He took a steadying breath and it finally just rolled out. "I'm gay, Mom. I'm in love with Aston."

For a moment, Rebecca's face remained blank, her eyes blinking as if she hadn't fully heard him. Then, as his words sank in, her expression twisted, a storm of emotions flashing through her eyes—shock, anger, disbelief.

"Gay?" She said it quietly at first, then shook her head, voice growing louder, sharper. "Gay? No. You're not, Eli. This isn't who you are. I raised you better than this."

Eli's heart dropped, but he forced himself to stand his ground. "Mom, I'm the same person. This is who I am. And Aston… Aston's been nothing but good to me. He's helped me be honest with myself."

Rebecca's gaze snapped to Aston, her eyes narrowing with fury, her voice cold, "You. You did this to him? I knew you were a bad influence since the first day I laid eyes on you. I told you, Samuel. Didn't I?"

Aston opened his mouth to protest, but Eli's father, Samuel, who had been silently watching with a furrowed brow, stood up and spoke, "Rebecca… maybe we should calm down and talk this through."

"Talk this through?" she scoffed, her voice rising with each word. "There's nothing to discuss! Eli, this is just… It's just wrong! The bible says so! You can't be serious. Tell me you're not serious."

Eli felt his chest tighten, his hands shaking as his mother's words tore through him. He'd feared she wouldn't accept him, but hearing the words cut far deeper than he'd expected.

"Mom. It's who I am and who I've always been, and you're just going to have to—"

"Have to what?" she interrupted, her voice ice-cold. "Accept this… this abomination of a relationship? No. Absolutely not. I won't have it." Her voice dropped, laden with anger.

"If you want to stay in this house, you'll never see or speak to Aston again. Not a single word, not a glance. Nothing. You'll forget about all of this nonsense."

"Rebecca, that's enough," Samuel interjected, his voice soft but firm, looking between his wife and Eli with a pained expression. "You're upset. We're both surprised, but… maybe with time…"

"Time? Oh, piss off, Samuel!" Rebecca's voice was a venomous hiss. "No amount of time will make me accept this." Her glare returned to Aston, her lips curling in disgust. "And you. You're no longer welcome here or anywhere near my family. You're fired, effective immediately."

The words hit Aston like a physical blow. Fired form his job. Banned from seeing the person he loved. But before he could process the sting of it, Eli spoke up, his voice barely holding back a tremor. "Mom, please—"

"If you don't want to respect me and my rules, then you'll leave." Rebecca's voice was cold and unyielding, her eyes locked onto Eli, unrelenting. "Either agree, or get out."

"Come on, Eli," Aston said quietly, taking Eli's wrist as the weight of the moment bore down on them both.

He could feel Eli's heart pounding under his grip, feel the tension vibrating through his entire body.

Eli's face was ghostly pale, his eyes wide with hurt and disbelief. Wordlessly, he wrenched his arm free and ran up the stairs, each step echoing in the silence left in his wake.

Aston stood there, helpless, torn between running after him and respecting his need for space. Rebecca turned back to Aston, her eyes flashing with anger and something deeper, a betrayal she could barely contain.

"Eli's made his decision. You won't be influencing him any longer. Now get out of my house," she said icily. Her words held no room for argument.

Aston looked at her, his heart pounding, the betrayal between them deeper than he could have imagined. Without another word, he turned and left, feeling her gaze on his back, burning like fire. As the door closed behind him, he felt the suffocating weight of failure settle over him. This was supposed to be the start of something hopeful, but it had turned into something shattered and broken, just as Eli had said.

Inside, Rebecca and Samuel sat in the silent aftermath, neither one knowing quite what to say. She was just about to walk up to Eli's room when Samuel stopped her.

"Rebecca," Samuel began quietly, "You need to calm down. You're gonna say something you're going to regret. Just give yourself some time. Drink your tea."

"Time won't change what I can and can't accept, Samuel. You remember, don't you?" Her voice wavered slightly, her lips pressed into a thin line.

Samuel watched her, a sense of unease flickering in his gaze. "Rebecca… that was years ago. You were a different person. And he wasn't Eli."

She shook her head, her face tightening. "No, but he broke my heart all the same. He lied, Samuel. I never would have… if I'd known…" She closed her eyes, memories of her younger self flooding back in painful waves. A relationship filled with love, only to end in betrayal when she discovered her boyfriend had hidden a truth about himself. Her suspicions had led her to leave him. And they were confirmed the day she found out that he marry a man a year later, his secrets spilling into her life like poison, leaving her bitter and broken.

"This is different," Samuel said softly, his voice hesitant. "Eli's our son. He needs us now, more than ever."

Rebecca's face hardened, the pain of her past twisting into anger. "He betrayed me too, Samuel. All this time, lying. Just like—"

"Stop," Samuel cut in, his tone firm but quiet. "He's our son. Not some ghost from your past."

She took a deep breath, her eyes dark and resolute. "You may be able to pretend it's okay. But I can't. This is wrong." She turned away, lost in the pain of her memories, unable or unwilling to let it go.

***

Meanwhile, in his room, Eli lay on his bed, his heart breaking into pieces. He'd tried, tried so hard to make her see who he really was. And now, he felt more alone than he'd ever imagined possible.

After a while, he couldn't stand the stifling confines of the room any longer. Quietly, he slipped out of the house, the cool night air hitting his face, offering a bitter reprieve from the suffocating heat inside.

As he walked down the empty street, he saw a familiar figure standing near the corner, pacing back and forth, waiting, just as he knew he would be.

Aston's face was etched with worry, his eyes softening when he saw Eli approaching. "Eli!" he began, jogging towards him. He wanted to say more, but the words stuck in his throat when he saw the raw hurt in Eli's expression.

Eli stopped a few feet away, his gaze filled with anguish. "I told you, Aston. I told you it would be a fuck up."

Aston took a step forward, but Eli held up a hand, stopping him. "No. This was a mistake. You pushed me into this, and now…"

"It was Mark, not me that forced this," said Aston sharply.

"No, but you're probably happy now, as you've been pushing me to come out for a long while now. So there, you got your way," said Eli, obviously still very emotional. Aston understood and tried to calm him.

"Eli, I just wanted you to be free. And although it might not feel like it right now, you finally are and can be," Aston said, his voice thick with emotion. "I wanted us to have a real chance. And now we can."

"A real chance?" Eli's voice was bitter, his hands clenching into fists. "At what cost, Aston? This is not reparable. Everything I feared… it's all real now. Broken and I can't put it back together. And I'm forbidden to see you again. How can that be a chance."

"You're choosing her? Really? I didn't say it wouldn't be complicated, but what other choice did we have here? I didn't ever mean to pressure you into anything. I'm sorry if that's how you felt. I truly am. But we will work through this. At least now we can—"

The words stung, but Aston couldn't bring himself to argue. The gravity of what he'd asked Eli to do settled heavily on him now. "I didn't mean for it to be like this," he whispered, his own voice breaking. "I thought… I thought maybe they'd understand, maybe it would all be okay."

"Well, they didn't. And I told you they wouldn't," Eli said sharply, wiping at his eyes. "I need some time. I need… space. Space from you. To figure out how to pick up the pieces."

Aston's heart sank, a feeling of helplessness wrapping around him.

"Eli, please. Don't shut me out. I promised I'd be here and I am. I'll always be here, no matter what. Just don't push me away again. We can leave. Together. What we chatted about. We cou—"

"How? Give me a plan! How, Aston?"

"I don't know how yet. But we'll figure something out."

But Eli's face was hard, guarded. "It's not negotiable. I'm taking some time away from you to figure stuff out. Don't push me anymore."

Without another word, he turned and walked away, each step feeling like a tear in Aston's heart.

Aston watched him head off, his own heart pounding with a desperation he couldn't name, knowing deep down that he was on the verge of losing something precious, something he might never get back. As Eli's figure disappeared into the night, Aston stood there, alone, realizing just how deeply, despite Mark's threat, he'd misjudged it all—and the awful finality of it hit him like a heavy blow to the gut.

But he also knew Eli loved him as much as he loved Eli. And that maybe some time for Eli to sort through his family issues would be necessary.

Aston wanted to be there and would be, but how could he be if Eli shut him out completely? Aston realized how much pressure loving Eli had put on the man. So he decided to give him the time he asked for. He had to. At least a couple of days to cool down. Maybe more.

Aston turned and dragged himself back home, shoulders slouched as he considered how quickly everything went from perfect to this disaster. They loved each other, and that was the bottom line. All he could hope for was that it would be enough to save what they had. Though, for now, it was up to Eli.

"Fuck sake," he muttered under his breath.

Aston felt hopeless.

Chapter Thirty One

The overcast morning was quiet, a stillness hanging over Eli's room like a heavy, oppressive blanket. He lay on his bed, unable to shake the gnawing ache in his chest. His mother's words from the night before played over and over in his mind, sharp and piercing, leaving a hollow numbness that seemed to settle into his bones. He couldn't face them—not after everything that had been said, after everything that had shattered. With a quiet resolve, Eli slipped out of bed, threw on his clothes, and slipped out of the house, careful not to make a sound.

He made his way through the deserted streets, the sound from his sneakers soft as he moved with purpose toward the marina. The air was cool and still. As he reached the docks, a familiar, comforting sight greeted him—the boat. Their boat, *Joy*, rocking gently against the pier.

Now, with everything in his life feeling so chaotic and painful, the idea of taking *Joy* out on the open water felt like the only escape he had left.

He climbed into the boat and untied the lines, his movements quick and practiced.

The water was calm and a sense of anticipation tingled through him as he pushed off from the dock. With practiced hands, he unfurled the sail, feeling the fabric catch the faint morning breeze. The boat slipped forward, gliding across the water as the marina disappeared behind him. Eli's chest eased and he felt like he could finally breathe again.

The sun rose higher, the light warming his skin as he steered the boat farther from shore. The gentle wind filled the sails, and the boat moved easily across the open water, cutting a smooth path through the glassy surface. Every inch he traveled away from land, from his parents, from all the turmoil, he felt a bit lighter. Out here, on the open water, he could just be himself—no expectations, no pressure. Just him and *Joy*.

As he sailed farther out, leaving the coastline as a hazy line in the distance, the wind softened, slowing the boat to a gentle drift. Eli pulled in the sails and let the boat float, rocking softly on the ocean's gentle rhythm. He slipped his shirt over his head and kicked off his shoes, letting the sun warm his bare skin as he lay back in the boat, crossing his legs in front of him, gazing up at the endless blue sky.

And then he closed his eyes. Memories began to flow through him—thoughts of his sister, Joy, whose name now graced the boat that held him.

She'd been the bright, fierce spirit in his life, her laughter filling every corner of his memory. He could still hear her voice, playful and teasing, urging him to take chances, to live boldly. She'd always been the one who'd encouraged him to be himself, even when he was too scared to say the words out loud. She would have been proud of him for confronting their parents. Even with all the unbearable pressure pushing on him that forced the events of yesterday.

The memory of one particular summer day with her drifted to the surface, vivid and full of warmth.

He was twelve. They'd been at their favorite spot by the river, where the trees hung low and the water was shallow enough to wade through. Joy had jumped in first, splashing him as she laughed, her blond hair shining like gold in the sun.

"Come on, Eli, stop being such a scaredy-cat!" she'd called out, her laughter ringing across the water. "You're not gonna melt!"

"It's cold," he'd muttered, hesitating at the water's edge. He'd always been more cautious than her, his bold and fearless sister.

She rolled her eyes and splashed him again, sending water flying into his face. "If you don't get in, I'm gonna come get you!" she threatened, and he laughed, knowing she wasn't kidding. Before he knew it, she was charging toward him, her arms outstretched, water flying around her as she ran.

He'd tried to dodge her, but she'd caught him, both of them tumbling into the water, laughing and splashing as they wrestled in the river. It was one of those moments that felt timeless, like they were the only two people in the world.

"I wish we could stay like this forever," she'd said, lying back in the water, her face tilted up to the sky. There was a quiet, contemplative look in her eyes, one he didn't see often. "Just you and me, Eli, doing whatever we want."

Eli, floating on his back beside her, feeling the warmth of the sun on his face, replied, "Yeah… me too sis."

She'd turned to him, her face serious, a rare softness in her gaze. "Eli, promise me something?"

He'd looked at her, feeling the weight of her words. "What?"

"Promise me you'll live your life the way you want. Don't let anyone push you around. Be brave, Eli. For me."

He'd nodded, his throat tight. "Okay."

As he lay in the boat, the memory washed over him, filling him with both warmth and longing. And he felt that maybe he had started to fulfill that promise. He missed her terribly, missed her light and her laughter. But here, on this boat bearing her name, he felt close to her again, like she was there with him, sharing this peaceful moment, lying next to him. He could almost hear her voice in the wind, urging him on, telling him he was doing the right thing, that he was brave.

The gentle sound of waves against the hull lulled him, his mind drifting as he lay there. Images of Aston began to fill his thoughts—the way his eyes sparkled when he laughed, the warmth of his hand in Eli's, the quiet strength he'd always offered. Aston helped him be brave. Helped him fulfill his promise to Joy. He might not have been able to do it on his own. But with Aston by his side, he was stronger. That said something.

Eli found himself imagining the future he'd never dared to picture before—a life with Aston by his side, where they could build a home together, where he could bring Aston to family gatherings without fear, where his parents would accept him for who he was.

The thought filled him with a bittersweet longing, knowing it might never happen, but he allowed himself to dream, if only for a second.

As the sun climbed higher, Eli let himself drift between memories of Joy, dreams of Aston, and the peaceful lull of the ocean around him. He started to feel calm come over him, as if all the pain and confusion had faded into the background, leaving only the quiet certainty that he was exactly where he was supposed to be right now. Here, alone on the open water, where he felt free. He felt whole. The silence of the void comforted him immensely. All the noise, all the raging confusion and chaos just disappeared. He closed his eyes and let go of his thoughts.

A few of hours later, as the afternoon sun began to wane, Eli jolted awake, thanks to a very light drizzle of rain, and a stiff, cold wind rocking the boat. The water had become choppy. He looked at the darker clouds on the horizon. The weather was turning and he needed to head back.

Thankfully the unexpected and relaxing nap made him a feel refreshed and at peace. His skin was still warm and pink from the afternoon's sun, but his mind was clearer than it had been in days.

The reality of the world waited for him back on shore—the challenges, the hurt, the uncertainty. But out here, he felt he'd recaptured a piece of himself, a reminder of who he knew he was and the strength he carried within him.

With a final glance at the darkening horizon, he pulled on his clothes and sneakers, and raised the sail, feeling the boat catch the wind once more. As he began to head back, the freedom of sailing the ocean grabbed his soul once more.

With the cold chill of the breeze hitting him and Joy's sails full and taut, the salty water splashed droplets of water onto his face and caused his hair to blow free and wild in the wind. He picked up speed, riding the ocean like he owned it.

It was the fastest this little boat had ever gone. A happy grin adorned his face and in this moment, he finally felt whole.

Holding onto the mast, he stood, crouched at the bow, like a warrior heading into battle, one foot perched on the front edge of the boat and rode the wind like never before. He was unable to contain his excitement and began laughing uncontrollably, feeling unadulterated joy.

Whatever came next, he knew he'd face it with courage. For Joy, for Aston and for himself.

"Let's gooooooo! Woooo hooooo!" He screamed enthusiastically at the top of his voice and punched the air with glee.

Chapter Thirty Two

The afternoon sun was high in the sky and a low rumble echoed in the distance. Aston sat on the edge of his bed, looking out the small window of his room. Thick, gray clouds had gathered over their home, churning and darkening as the wind picked up, stirring the trees outside, as if to intentionally make his life even more miserable. He could see the storm building, like the slow tightening of a knot, echoing his internal state. As the first few raindrops began to fall, he sighed and sank back onto his bed, his mind turning over thoughts of Eli, as it had all day. There was a gnawing ache in his chest, an empty, hollow feeling he couldn't shake, and he hated that he was here, feeling depressed and alone, instead of with Eli.

He knew that Eli was hurting. The pain in his lover's eyes last night when Rebecca lashed out at him had been clear as day, an anguish so raw that Aston could still feel it echoing in his own chest. The scene kept replaying in his mind—Rebecca's cruel words, the look on Eli's face, the way he'd stormed off into the night. Aston wanted nothing more than to speak to him. But Eli had asked for space, and Aston had promised he would respect that, no matter how hard it was.

The wind outside picked up quickly, rattling the window panes, as the rain intensified, and a flash of lightning illuminated the storm clouds for a brief, flickering second.

It was all too much. Aston, who had been in complete isolation, shutting the entire world out, except for checking his phone for messages from Eli, suddenly felt trapped. He sat up and paced around his small room, the familiar four walls feeling suffocating. He paused by his dresser, leaning against it, his mind spiraling as he tried to imagine what emotions Eli was going through back at home. Hurting, feeling alone, lost. How were his parents handling the situation? Was Eli still regretting ever coming out at all, cursing the night he'd trusted Aston enough to confide in him?

Aston clenched his fists, feeling powerless. In moments like these, he wished he could fix everything, make things right with a few comforting words or a touch on Eli's shoulder, a silent promise that he wasn't alone. But his love, his comfort—it wasn't enough, and he was beginning to realize that as he longed for Eli's touch once more.

There was a soft knock on his door, and Aston's mom stepped in, her face gentle with concern. She closed the door behind her and crossed the room, leaning against the wall with her arms folded as she watched him.

Instinctively, she knew and said softly, managing a small smile. "What's wrong, sweetie? Shouldn't you be at work already?"

Aston took a breath and let it out slowly, the words spilling out before he could stop them. "I got fired," he said, his voice breaking slightly, the reality of it sinking in.

"What? What happened?"

"Eli… he came out to his parents last night, and it was awful, Mom. They… they took it horribly, and his mom—she just… I don't know, she blamed me. She's always been so strict with him. And it was like she saw me as the enemy."

His mom's expression softened, her eyes filling with empathy as she sat down on the edge of the bed, patting the empty space next to her and pulled him into a hug as soon as he sat down. "Oh, honey," she whispered, holding him close. "I'm so sorry. That must've been terrible, after everything you two have been through."

Aston let himself sink into her embrace, the familiar warmth of her presence a balm to his frayed nerves. "It's not just that," he murmured, his voice muffled against her shoulder.

"It's... I keep thinking that maybe I pushed him too hard. Maybe it's my fault things went so bad. I wanted him to tell his parents so they could understand, so we wouldn't have to keep hiding. But now... now he's hurting, and it feels like it's all my fault."

His mom pulled back slightly, brushing his hair away from his face as she looked into his eyes. "Aston, honey, you did what you thought was right. You were just trying to help him find his way, to support him in the only way you knew how. And that... that's all you could have done. It's what I would have done if I was in your shoes." She gave his shoulder a reassuring squeeze. "It's not your fault that his parents reacted the way they did. That's on them."

"But what if he hates me now?" Aston whispered, the fear clawing at him, raw and consuming. "He wanted space, Mom. He told me in no uncertain terms to give him space. He's never said it like that before... I mean, what if he just... what if he doesn't want me in his life anymore?"

She shook her head, smiling softly. "Oh, sweetie, I don't believe that for a second. Eli just went through something huge—of course he needs some time to process it all. And I know you're feel helpless right now, but sometimes, the best thing we can do for the people we love is to give them space when they ask for it."

Aston nodded, taking in her words. "I know, you're right, Mom. It's just… hard. I want to be there for him, to make it all go away. But I can't do that. Not this time. Not with me sitting here like this feeling sorry for myself."

She nodded, understandingly. "You can't always protect the people you love from the world, baby. But you can be there for Eli when he's ready, and that's what matters most. If he loves you, he'll come back to you. In his own time."

The words hung between them, a tentative hope that things might eventually get better. She leaned in, brushing a kiss over his forehead before standing up. "Everything will be okay, Aston. It's hard to see right now, but these things… they work out. Time makes everything easier."

Aston managed a small smile, squeezing her hand in gratitude. "Thanks, Mom."

She gave him a final hug, pulling him close and whispering into his ear, "Talk to me if you need, you hear?" She got up and began walking to the door.

Aston cleared his throat. "Um, well, actually…" he began, his voice hesitant.

Laura paused, glancing over her shoulder at him. "Hmm?"

"I've just got another quick question. Nothing bad, really."

Laura thought it already sounded bad, by the way he had phrased that sentence. "Yeah?" she replied cautiously, turning around and facing him.

"I'm asking this for a friend…"

Laura immediately knew he was asking for himself. She did not however expect whatever this was to involve both him and Eli.

"If… let's just say that… If someone had some dirt on a friend," Aston said slowly, not able to keep eye contact, "and they were threatening to tell people about something they didn't want to come out, what do you think that person should do?"

The question hung in the air for a moment, thick with unspoken meaning. Laura folded her arms, before walking back to sit next to him once more. Her brow furrowed in concern, her eyes studying his face.

"What's going on here? What kind of dirt are we talking about?" she asked carefully, her tone neutral but cautious.

Aston shrugged, trying to sound nonchalant, but his heart began pounding in his chest. "I don't know… he just said dirt. Something that could really hurt him.
Something that could change how people see them. Maybe even ruin their life."

Laura's concern deepened, and she was unable to keep it in. "Aston, is this about you? Or Eli?"

"No," he replied quickly, shaking his head, but the words felt like they weighed a ton. "I'm just asking for someone else that I met… A customer at the marina," he sheepishly added.

She was not convinced, her gaze narrowing slightly as she leaned in. "It sounds serious. Are you in trouble? You can tell me."

"No," Aston answered again, too fast, too defensive. He felt the heat of her scrutiny and tried to steer the conversation away, forcing a small smile. "I'm not in trouble, Mom. It's really not about me."

But Laura knew him too well. She recognized the way he was skirting the real issue, the way he was holding something back.

She took a breath, her voice softening with concern. "Aston, if someone is threatening you… or Eli… or even this mystery customer or friend, as you put it, then that's a big deal."

Aston knew he had blown his story by mixing 'friend' and 'customer'. He regretted saying anything in a moment of vulnerability. Now she knew something was up.

"Especially if it's something that could ruin their life. You need to be careful who you trust, and you need to let me help you if this is something serious," Laura continued.

Aston's fingers tightened against the edge of the bed, his knuckles going white. He could feel his mother's eyes on him, waiting for more, but he wasn't ready to tell her the whole truth. Not about the sex caught on video, or the threats Mark had made. He dared not say it out loud.

"I know," he mumbled, keeping his gaze down. "But it's not… It's just hypothetical."

Laura didn't press him, but her expression softened into something more tender, more knowing. She reached out and placed her hand over his, her touch warm and steady.

"The friend… it's Eli, yes?"

Aston's heart lurched, his breath catching in his throat. He didn't know how to respond.

Of course, she'd guessed it. She always saw through him. But he felt like he was betraying Eli's trust by saying anything.

He swallowed hard, trying to stay calm and not letting on that it was the both of them. "I… I didn't say that."

"You didn't have to," Laura replied gently. She squeezed his hand. "I know things have been difficult for him, for both of you. And I know you're worried about him. But whatever's going on, Aston, you need to be careful. I don't think you're talking about his coming out. He is already out to his parents, so how much worse could that get? This is something else."

Aston took his hand back slowly, suddenly feeling exposed, vulnerable. He stood up, a little too quickly. "I'm not in trouble, Mom. Neither is Eli. It's just the issues you know… I promise." He lied mainly to protect Eli. But also, how could he tell her that someone had recorded them while they had sex on a customer's boat. He really regretted saying anything now.

"Aston—"

"I've got it under control, mom!" he interrupted, his voice firmer than he felt. He turned toward the door, desperate to escape the conversation. "I'm just gonna go for a walk. I need some air."

Without waiting for her to respond, he grabbed his jacket and headed out the bedroom door, leaving his mother sitting on his bed, her concern hanging in the air like a cloud that refused to lift.

"Aston, it's storming and it's getting dark. You can't go out now."

Aston stopped and sighed, realizing that his flustered state was not allowing him to think clearly. He stepped back into his room and looked at her and gestured towards the passage. She tried to lighten the mood by playfully furrowing her brow and giving him a stern look.

"Mom…"

"Okay, I get the picture! I'll let you be." She stood up and walked past him slowly, keeping eye contact, being more playful now, pointing a playful finger in his face as she passed, trying to make him feel more comfortable. She knew he had bungled the delivery of whatever he was trying to tell her. And he knew that she knew something was up.

"You talk to your mother, young man. No matter what. And be careful."

"Yeah. Thanks… mother," he said, playfully rolling eyes. He felt foolish for mentioning 'the friend'. But his mother's words echoed in his ears, and all he could think about was Eli. The weight of the secret they shared felt heavier than ever.

As she left the room, Aston closed the door and sat on the floor, leaning back against his bed. He dropped his head back and stared at nothing as the storm outside began to pick up further, rain pattering against the windows, lightning flashing intermittently. He hoped his mom was right, that things would calm down, that Eli's parents would soften, and that they could find a way back to each other.

Chapter Thirty Three

The morning sun filtered through the living room curtains. Aston slumped on the couch, scrolling aimlessly through his phone, feeling restless. He wasn't really paying attention to anything on the screen, but it was a distraction from the steady hum of conversation between his mom and Alex in the kitchen.

He could hear their laughter, the occasional clink of plates as they set out breakfast. He hated how comfortable Alex seemed in their home now, as if he belonged there. Aston bit the inside of his cheek, trying to push down the irritation bubbling inside him.

"Hey, Aston!" Alex's voice broke through his thoughts. He looked up to see the older man standing in the doorway, hands casually tucked into his jeans pockets. "You want some coffee? Your mom made extra."

"No thanks," Aston muttered, eyes darting back to his phone.

Alex hesitated, then stepped into the room anyway, taking a seat on the chair across from Aston. "So, any plans for the day?" he asked, trying to sound upbeat.

Aston shrugged, still avoiding eye contact. "Might head out for a bit."

Alex nodded and smiled, as if that was the most fascinating answer he'd ever heard. "Nice. Get some fresh air. Good for clearing the mind." He paused, clearly waiting for Aston to continue the conversation, but when it became clear Aston wasn't going to say more, Alex pressed on. "You know, I used to go hiking a lot when I needed to clear my head. Nothing like being out in nature."

Aston glanced up briefly, his expression unreadable. "Yeah, cool."

Silence stretched between them, awkward and heavy. Alex seemed determined not to let it get to him though. "I've been thinking of taking your mom to that Italian-styled restaurant near the beach. Have you heard anything about it?"

Aston let out a soft sigh, finally locking his phone and standing up. "I haven't, no." He stood, grabbed his jacket off the back of the couch, pulling it on with quick, irritated movements. "I'm heading out now."

"Alright," Alex replied, watching him. "Enjoy."

Aston gave a brief nod, slipping his shoes on by the door and walked to the kitchen. Alex followed him through.

"See you later, Mom," he called out toward the kitchen.

Laura appeared, "You're going out? Where to?"

"Just…out," Aston replied vaguely, opening the door.

"Okay, sweetie. Be careful."

Aston squeezed past Alex and left without another word, shutting the door firmly behind him. The sound echoed in the quiet house, leaving Alex and Laura standing there, exchanging a glance.

"Well," Alex said, rubbing the back of his neck. "I think that went okay, right? We chatted a bit."

Laura chuckled softly, though her eyes were filled with worry. "Yeah, I guess. At least he didn't bite your head off."

"Small victories," Alex grinned, leaning against the counter.

But he noticed the tension in Laura's shoulders. "What's wrong?"

Laura sighed, glancing toward the door where Aston had just left. "I'm just worried about him. He's been… off lately. He asked me something strange. He was talking about a friend, but I don't know. It didn't feel like he was telling me the whole story." When she said 'a friend', she gestured with air quotes using her fingers.

"What did he ask?" Alex's voice softened, concern filling his tone.

"He asked what you should do if someone had dirt on a friend and was threatening to expose it," Laura explained, her brow creased. "He said it wasn't about him, but…" She trailed off, shaking her head. "But it's about him."

Alex frowned, leaning against the counter. "That does sound…odd. Do you think he's hiding something?"

"Yeah, I do," Laura admitted, her voice quiet. "I just don't know what."

Alex folded his arms. "The words he's using sounds a lot like blackmail. Which is pretty serious, if true."

He thought about it for a second and then continued, "But maybe it is about a friend. Let's not jump to conclusions until we know for sure. Maybe it's to do with his boyfriend, Eli?"

Laura nodded slowly. "Yeah, I've been thinking the same thing. But he shut down quickly last night. He wanted to say something, but didn't know how. I don't want to push too hard, either. I'd rather he comes to me. I made it clear that he can talk to me whenever."

"Yeah, I'm also available if—Actually scrap that. I doubt he will open up to me about anything. I'm in the dog house for dating his mom, remember?" he smiled. But then got serious again and added, "But I am here for you both. Just saying."

"Thanks, Alex," said Laura, looking out the kitchen window.

Alex reached out, placing a reassuring hand on her back. "He's a good kid. Whatever's going on, I'm sure he'll come to you when he's ready. Just… keep an eye on him."

Laura leaned into his touch, grateful for his calm presence. "Thank you. I just… I feel like I'm losing him sometimes."

"You're not," Alex assured her, his voice firm. "You're his mom. He'll come around."

Aston walked through the streets of Clearwater, hands jammed into his jacket pockets, the cool breeze tugging at his hair. His mind was racing, turning over his conversation with his mom from the night before. He didn't mean to let things get so out of control, but everything was a mess. Eli was hurting, and Mark's threats were still hanging over their heads like a guillotine.

He had to know how Eli was doing. He couldn't just sit back and wait.

Before he knew it, his feet had carried him to Eli's house. He stopped at the gate, staring up at the familiar building, feeling his stomach twist with nerves. Part of him wanted to turn back, but he couldn't. He had to know. He had been banned from seeing Eli, but that didn't stop him. He had to at least find out how his man was doing. He hoped that Eli's parents, especially his mother, were calmer. Maybe they had time to process and were more accepting. He had severe doubts, but there was no way to find out. Eli was not answering his texts, and he couldn't bear the silence any longer.

Aston walked up the path, his heart pounding in his chest. He knocked on the door, hoping it was Eli who opened the door, and not his mother.

Chapter Thirty Four

The front porch looked exactly the same as it always did, but it felt different—charged with an unspoken tension that sent chills down his spine. He knocked on the door once more, the sound echoing in the silence. After a moment that stretched like an eternity, Rebecca, opened the door.

She looked older, wearier, as if the weight of the world was pressing down on her shoulders. Her eyes were red-rimmed, and a frown creased her lips. Her voice low and heavy. "Go away or I'll call the cops."

Aston swallowed hard, desperation bubbling to the surface. "Please Mrs. Taylor. I need to see Eli. Please, I just want to make sure he's okay. Then I'll go, I swear."

"You're not welcome here, Aston," she said bluntly, the words harsh and unyielding.

Aston stepped forward, his heart racing. "I'm not leaving until I see him. You can't keep trying to control him like this. He's his own person. He has to live his own life."

Rebecca's gaze hardened, and for a fleeting moment, Aston caught a glimpse of anguish behind her anger. But it was gone just as quickly, replaced by something colder.

"It's no longer an issue," she said, her voice flat. "Eli took the that small boat out the morning of the storm. He never came back."

Aston's world shattered. The words hung in the air, heavy and suffocating. "What do you mean?" he stammered, unable to process the implications of her statement. "What are you talking about?"

"He drowned," she said, and there was no kindness in her tone. "They found his body a few miles down the coast." She turned away, as if to retreat from the conversation altogether.

Aston couldn't move, his body becoming overwhelmed with raw emotion. "You're lying to me. You just don't want me to see him," he said, desperate for that to be the truth.

Before turning her back to him, she said, "It's your fault my Eli is dead." Tears formed in her eyes. Her reaction was a mixture of bitterness, anger and heartache.

Aston took a step back, knowing from the look in her eyes that she was not lying.

"No…"

Rebecca turned her back to him, her shoulders shaking slightly. "You need to leave. Now. Never come back here."

She closed the door behind her as if he wasn't even there.

Aston labored a step back, the enormity of her words crashing down on him like a tidal wave. Tears welled in his eyes as disbelief and horror twisted together in a sickening knot. His throat tightened and pained as he swallowed.

Aston felt as if the ground had given way beneath him, leaving him teetering on the precipice of despair.

"Eli…" He whimpered softly, but it felt like his name echoed into the void. He turned and began to walk slowly. The walk quickened into jog and eventually into a full blown sprint as he ran from the house, the world spinning in a blur around him. He sprinted in the direction of the docks, his heart racing with panic, confusion and fear. Heat and pain bellowed from his legs and body, running with a pace he never knew possible. He pulled off his hoody, and dropped it behind him on the street, without stopping.

The air was thick with more impending rain as he reached the shoreline, dread wrapping around him like a shroud. He stumbled onto the dock, his footsteps heavy on the worn wood, eyes frantically scanning the water, the beach, the workshop yard, praying for a glimpse of Joy, for any sign of Eli. But what he found instead was a damaged shell of the boat they had worked on together—*Joy*. She had been pulled onto the sand, her mast snapped at the bottom, a jagged collection of splinters where it once stood proudly tall, now lying flat, the sails torn and the hull cracked.

His breath hitched as he approached the wreckage, finally slowing his pace, as his legs began to fail him. A deep sense of despair washed over him, as if the outgoing tide itself had pulled away his hope. "No, no, no," he murmured, dropping to his knees beside the broken boat. This couldn't be real. It had to be a nightmare from which he would wake at any moment.

Aston didn't initially notice the large figure that appeared from the office, walking slowly toward him. It was Eli's father, his face etched with sorrow, eyes hollow and distant.

Aston felt an icy grip of emptiness clutch his heart. Samuel walked directly past him, not acknowledging his presence, and then stopped a few paces away, staring out at the ocean with a shared and profound emptiness.

"And a jogger found his body washed up on the beach a few miles down the coastline," he said, voice devoid of emotion.

Aston's world crumbled further around him, the air thick with grief and disbelief. "No," he whispered, the word slipping from his lips like a prayer. He shook his head in denial.

Samuel didn't look at him. "Take the time you need, Aston… But then you should leave. You shouldn't come back here. You'll only find despair," he said calmly, his tone a dull echo of the pain that filled the space between them. He turned and walked off without saying another word.

Aston sank to the ground beside the wreckage of Joy, his mind that had been racing with memories of laughter, love, and light, now replaced with complete darkness. He sat there for a moment and stared at the name *Joy*.

He turned and leaned up against the boat, and looked like a crumpled mess beside it, not able to move, except for the uncontrollable sobbing that quickly and completely enveloped him.

Finally, after what felt like an hour, his body was not able to expel anymore tears. He forced himself up, feeling weak. He walked down the docks and past the workshop.

Memories of their time together flashed into his mind. He wandered around aimlessly.

Then his eye caught the paint tin and brush they had used to paint Joy's name onto their boat. He didn't know why, but he walked over and reached for them, and made his way back to Joy.

With trembling hands, he painted Eli's name beside Joy's on the boat, his heart shattering with each stroke. The paint glided over the wood, a tribute to a life that had been so full of potential. Eli, who had been full of dreams and laughter, was now just a memory.

"I'm so sorry, Eli," he whispered, as he completed the dot on the letter i of his name. A final tear streamed down his face once more as a wave of emotion suddenly smashed into him. "I'm so fucking sorry. I love you."

He dropped the brush into the sand, his chest heaving with grief. It was a pain unlike anything he had ever known, an all-consuming darkness that threatened to swallow him whole. It was different to how he felt with his dad. Now, guilt gnawed at him, sharp and relentless, whispering that if he hadn't pushed Eli so hard, if he hadn't pressured him to come out, maybe this wouldn't have happened.

If he hadn't pushed for the truth, maybe Eli would still be here, laughing and smiling, alive. If he hadn't met him, they would not have made love that afternoon.

He would still be alive if it wasn't for you pressuring him.

"I promised to protect you," Aston choked out, his voice breaking. "I should have been there. I'm so sorry. I failed you."

He felt a profound emptiness, a void that echoed the loss of the one person who had seen him for who he truly was. The world around him faded, and all that remained was the ache in his heart, a deep-seated longing for the man he loved. The reality of his surroundings fading as he lost himself in grief.

With trembling hands, Aston grasped at the edges of his chest pain, trying to make sense of it all. He could hear the distant waves crashing against the shore, a reminder of the world that continued to turn despite his shattered heart. In that moment, he felt utterly alone, lost in a storm of sorrow that would not relent.

The sun began to set, painting the dark clouds in the sky in hues of orange and pink, but Aston couldn't appreciate its beauty.

Instead, he sat beside the broken boat, the names of Eli and Joy forever etched in his heart, mourning not just for Eli's death, but for the life they could have shared, the future that had been ripped away from them both.

As the darkness descended, he realized that nothing would ever be the same again. Eli was gone, and the weight of that truth settled like a heavy fog over his heart, an insurmountable loss that would haunt him for the rest of his life.

In that quiet moment, as the waves lapped at the shore, he made a silent vow—to remember Eli, to cherish the moments they had shared, and to carry the weight of his absence with him always. The pain would never fade, but he would find a way to honor Eli's memory, to live a life that would make him proud.
But even as he thought this, the reality of his grief settled in, a reminder that nothing could bring Eli back, and he was left with the shattered remains of a love that would never be fulfilled.

But for now though, he struggled to move. All he could do was sit in the cold sand, broken and bereft, and let the waves wash over him as the tide slowly came back in.

Chapter Thirty Five

The wind was sharp this night, cutting through the trees as if nature itself bad been in mourning. The moon hung high and full in the sky, casting its pale light over the quiet coastal town of Clearwater.

Everything had changed since Eli's death. Days blurred into one another, but the pain was always there, lingering like a bruise that never faded. Aston couldn't shake the image of Eli's face—the way his eyes sparkled when he laughed, the warmth of his hand in his own. And now, all of that was gone, snatched away by a cruel reality that Aston wasn't ready to accept.

Mark Benson. You mother fucker.

That name burned in his mind, louder than anything else. It wasn't just the threat that haunted him; it was the fact that Mark had set everything in motion. If he hadn't threatened Eli, if he hadn't cornered him with those cruel words, maybe —just maybe—things wouldn't have spiraled out of control.

Aston couldn't sit with that any longer. Something had to be done. Mark had to pay.

Aston's hand tightened around his black hoodie that he had retrieved on the way back home that horrible evening. He slipped it over his head. His movements were deliberate, slow, as if each step solidified the decision in his mind.

He had never done anything like this before, but in the void of his grief, it felt like the only answer. His sneakers were soft on the floor as he crept out of his room, past his mother's door, and down the stairs. The house was silent, but his heart was pounding, his pulse roaring in his ears. He had to be quiet—he didn't want to answer any questions, didn't want anyone to stop him.

The coastal air hit him like a slap in the face as he stepped outside, the weight of what he was about to do heavy on his chest. The docks were a good fifteen-minute walk, but tonight, it felt like forever. Each step echoed with the memories of Eli's final days. He couldn't stop thinking about the fear in Eli's voice, the shame that had been forced upon him by Mark. Aston clenched his fists in his pockets, jaw tight with rage. This wasn't just for him—it was for Eli, too.

When Aston arrived at the docks, the world seemed to quiet around him.

There was no one in sight, just the soft lapping of the water against the boats, and the distant hum of a generator somewhere far off. He knew the area well. He slipped into the shadows, moving with a purposeful stride toward the boat storage lot behind Taylor's Charters, where Mark's boat was being stored behind the chained and locked gates.

The wall surrounding the lot wasn't high, but it was enough to keep out the curious.

Aston grabbed onto the edge, muscles straining as he hoisted himself over, landing with a soft thud on the other side. The parking lot was mostly empty, save for a few small fishing boats scattered around. In the center of the lot, Mark's boat sat—a sleek, expensive vessel, the kind that screamed privilege. It gleamed under the dim security lights, looking smug, baring extensive hull damage, but otherwise untouched by the chaos and turmoil it had caused.

Aston's breath came in short bursts as he crouched low, scanning the lot. His heart raced, and his mind felt clouded.

He wasn't here to be subtle; he was here to make a statement. Moving quickly, he made his way to the workshop at the edge of the lot. He made his way to where the fuel was stored.

The door to the workshop was locked too, but a quick shove with his shoulder dislodged it just enough for him to slip inside. The smell of oil and grease hit him immediately, a pungent scent that reminded him of the summer days spent here with Eli. He shoved the thought away, forcing himself to focus. In the dim light of the workshop, Aston found the fuel canisters near the back wall, stacked haphazardly on a shelf. He grabbed one, feeling the full weight of it in his hands.

Before continuing, he grabbed a wrench, stepped onto the boat, being careful not to get into the line of sight and smashed the Go-Pro camera off its mount, sending it to the floor, destroying it with a single, swift motion.

He moved quickly now, dousing the boat in the pungent smell of gasoline, the liquid splashing onto the polished wood and metal surfaces. He hesitated for a moment when he reached the soft seating area where he and Eli had made love. But he had no time to waste. With purpose he doused everything until the fuel canister was empty. He dropped it to his side, the empty sound it made as it hit the wooden deck echoing the feeling of emptiness in his heart. His hands were shaking, but he didn't wait to allow himself to second guess what he was doing.

This wasn't just revenge—it was retribution. He was finishing what Mark had started, hopefully making him feel a minuscule amount of the pain he had caused.

Aston climbed off the boat and stood back, his breath ragged, staring at the boat now slick with fuel. The air was thick with the smell of gasoline, suffocating in the still night. He fumbled with the matches in his pocket, that he had snuck out of the kitchen drawer, fingers trembling as he struck one against the rough surface of the box. The tiny flame flickered to life, casting a faint glow across his face.

His breath intensified. A moment of hesitation, an image of Eli flashed into his mind and he tossed the match towards the boat. It flickered at it cartwheeled towards the fuel drenched boat.

"Fuck you and your Friday deadline, you massive piece of shit."

The boat immediately burst into flames, the explosion way fiercer than Aston had anticipated. He stumbled back three steps, retreating as the heat screamed furiously into his face, falling to the concrete. But within seconds, he was up again, taking a few more steps back, mesmerized by the sight, intensity and heat of it all.

"Burn, you bitch."

Reflections of the flames danced against his face, a lone hooded silhouette standing in front of an inferno of rage.

The flames amplified with a roar, the fire licking greedily at the fuel-soaked boat, sucking in the air feverishly, like it couldn't get enough. For a moment, Aston just watched, his eyes wide, entranced by the destruction unfolding before him. The fire danced wildly, the boat consumed in a matter of seconds, the blaze reflecting in the glassy surface of the nearby water.

It got hotter as the seconds went by and Aston stepped further back until he reached the workshop wall. But then, something shifted in the air—an unsettling silence amongst the crackling of the blaze.

Before Aston could fully register it, a faint, mechanical sound pierced the quiet. His breath stopped as he glanced around, his eyes widening in realization.

The alarm. In his haste to get retribution of some kind, no matter what form that took, in this case, Mark's burning boat, he had not thought of the alarm. His compromised state becoming apparent. His heart raced.

His feet stumbled backward as he made for the shadows, trying to disappear into the darkness of the docks.

But it was too late.

The sound of sirens cut through the stillness, growing louder and more frantic as red and blue lights flashed in the distance, closing in on him. Panic surged through Aston's veins. He turned, breaking into a sprint toward the wall he had climbed earlier, his heart pounding in his chest.

Just as his hands reached for the top of the wall, the blinding flash of a flashlight caught him. "Stop! Don't move," a voice commanded.

It was a flight or fight moment and Aston chose flight. He pulled himself up onto the wall and just as he was about to jump over the other side, the taser terminals gripped into his back and he felt the jolt of electricity coursing through his entire body. The pain was intense, but it was the most alive he had felt in the last couple of days. He fell forwards, over the wall and onto the grass on the other side, with a dull thud.

His heart raced as the footsteps closed in around him.

Hands gripped his arms, and within moments, handcuffs bit into his wrists with a ratchet sound. The weight of his actions crashed down on him, suffocating, inescapable.

The flames from the burning boat flickered in the background, as Aston was shoved into the back of a police car, his mind numb as the door slammed shut.

Aston's court appearance came days later, but it felt like a blur. The judge's voice was a distant echo in the sterile courtroom as he heard the words "house arrest" and "released on bail." The gravity of what he had done hadn't fully sunk in, even as the monitoring bracelet was fastened to his ankle, the cold metal a constant reminder of his confinement.

Back home, the house felt smaller, suffocating even. Laura tried to comfort him, tried to understand, but Aston didn't want to talk. He retreated into his room, the walls closing in around him. He sat on the edge of his bed, staring at the floor, head in his hands.

The fire had burned Mark's boat to ashes, but it hadn't brought Aston any peace. Instead, he was left with the charred remains of his own guilt, the weight of his actions settling deep into his bones.

Chapter Thirty Six

Three weeks had passed since his first court appearance, but to Aston, it felt like years. Each day had dragged on, filled with sleepless nights and agonizing self-reflection. Every time he closed his eyes, he saw Eli. Every time he let his mind wander, he was back at the dock, watching the storm roll in, the boat's broken mast a tragic monument to his greatest failure. And then Mark's face would invade those memories, and the crushing guilt would return, reminding him that no matter how justified his anger had felt in the moment, he had crossed a line he could never uncross.

Now, sitting in this courtroom again, the culmination of his actions was upon him. The sentencing. His future. It all hung in the balance, and the weight of that realization settled heavily on his shoulders.

The room was sparsely filled—only a handful of onlookers, a few reporters hoping to catch a dramatic story, and in the back, his mother, Laura, sat with her hands clasped tightly in her lap, her face drawn with worry, Alex beside her, his arm wrapped around her shoulder. She had been there for him through everything, trying her best to be a comforting presence, but even she couldn't fully reach him.

He had built high walls around himself, isolating from the world, from everyone who loved him. He felt like he didn't deserve their kindness, not after what he had done. Laura questioned herself if there was anything she could have done differently too. She felt like she had failed him somehow. But it made no difference now, even if there was something she could have done.

The prosecutor rose to speak, her heels clicking sharply on the polished floor as she approached the judge. Her voice was cold, professional, each word carefully measured as she laid out the facts of the case.

"Aston Carter's actions were reckless and dangerous," she began, her gaze briefly flicking toward him. "While we understand that emotions were running high due to the tragic death of Eli Taylor, this does not excuse the severity of the crime of arson. The defendant's actions showed a complete disregard for the law, and we urge the court to consider a sentence that reflects the seriousness of the crime."

Each word landed like a blow, compounding the guilt that already weighed so heavily on Aston. He kept his gaze focused straight ahead, unwilling to meet the prosecutor's eyes, or anyone else's for that matter. He didn't need to look to know that everyone was judging him, even those that pretended not to.

He could feel the weight of their scrutiny.

The judge sat quietly as he listened to the prosecutor. His expression was inscrutable, giving no hint of the decision that loomed ahead.

Aston's lawyer stood next, clearing his throat before addressing the court. He was a middle-aged man with kind eyes, someone Aston's mother had hired in the hope that he could make the judge see Aston for who he truly was—a grieving, broken boy who had lost control in a moment of unbearable pain.

"Your Honor," the lawyer began, his tone calm and deliberate, "we do not deny the seriousness of this incident. However, it is important to understand the context in which these events took place. Aston Carter was in an extreme emotional state following the tragic death of his closest friend, Eli Taylor. The loss, combined with the stress of the situation, led to a moment of poor judgment."

Aston flinched at the words. "Poor judgment" didn't begin to cover it. It felt too light, too easy a way to describe what he had done. Aston was not that person. He never in a million years would have thought he was capable of something like this.

And then his mind shifted to the words "closest friend". As if that even began to describe what Eli meant to him. His lawyer pressed on.

"Mr. Carter deeply regrets his actions and has shown genuine remorse throughout this process. He has no prior record, no history of previous crimes, and he poses no threat to society. We ask the court to consider leniency in its sentencing. Mr. Carter acknowledges that he was not in his right mind due to the tragic loss of his friend."

The room seemed to hold its breath as the judge leaned back in his chair, his hands folded thoughtfully in front of him. Aston felt numb, the silence stretching on, each second feeling like an eternity.

Finally, the judge spoke, his voice deep and authoritative, filling the courtroom.

"Aston Carter," he began, and Aston felt his entire body tense. "I've taken into consideration everything that has been presented to this court—the circumstances of your actions, the emotional state you were in, and the impact of the loss you suffered. I don't doubt that you are grieving, and I don't doubt that what happened on that dock was the result of a culmination of emotions that you were struggling to process."

Aston's hands tightened into fists under the table, his nails digging into his palms. He forced himself to breathe slowly, trying to remain calm, though his pulse quickened with each word.

"That being said," the judge continued, his tone growing more stern, "what you did was serious. The law cannot turn a blind eye to that. However, I also recognize that you are young, and that this was an isolated incident. You are not a hardened criminal, and there is still a chance for you to make amends and learn from this."

Aston's breath caught in his throat as the judge paused, the weight of his next words hanging in the air like a guillotine poised to drop.

"I am sentencing you to 190 hours of community service," the judge declared. "You will be placed on probation for one year. During this time, you will be required to attend anger management counseling, as well as grief counseling, to ensure that you are receiving the support you need to process the trauma you have experienced. If you violate the terms of your probation or fail to complete your community service, you will face further legal consequences, which could include jail time."

The words washed over Aston in a wave of disbelief. Community service. Probation. No jail time. It was lenient—far more lenient than he had expected. His lawyer had warned him to prepare for the worst, but now, hearing the sentence, a mix of relief and confusion swirled inside him.

The judge's voice softened slightly as he looked directly at Aston. "I hope you understand the gravity of this situation, Mr. Carter. This is your opportunity to make things right—not just for yourself, but for those around you. Don't waste it."

Aston nodded numbly, though the words barely registered. His mind was spinning, caught between the relief of escaping prison and the unshakable guilt that clung to him like a second skin. He didn't feel like he deserved leniency. He didn't feel like he deserved anything. Jail time would have felt more appropriate. Not for the burning of Mark's shitty boat. Fuck Mark… It was the pressure he himself had put on Eli that he felt remorse for. And knowing he could never undo what he had done was the life sentence that he had imposed on himself.

The gavel came down with a sharp crack, signaling the end of the proceedings. The tension in the room broke, and Aston's lawyer placed a reassuring hand on his shoulder.

"You got off light," he said quietly. "This could have gone much worse."

Aston swallowed, his throat dry. "Yeah. Thank you," he murmured, though the relief he was supposed to feel never came.

As the courtroom emptied, Laura thanked the lawyer and then approached Aston, her face a mixture of concern and relief. "It's over," she said softly, pulling him into a tight hug. "You'll be okay now. We'll get through this."

Over. This will never truly be over. The only person it was over for was Eli.

Aston stood stiffly in her embrace, hands in his rented suit's pants pockets, his mind numb. He didn't believe her. Sure, the legal battle was over, but the war raging inside him was far from won. And it was un-winnable. He still had to live with what he had done. He still had to live with the memory of Eli, of all the moments that had led him to this point.

The guilt weighed heavily on him, refusing to lift even as the world around him tried to move forward.

The following months blurred together, each one dragging on in a monotonous cycle of court-ordered appointments and community service tasks. Aston threw himself into the work, scrubbing graffiti off walls, picking up trash from streets, doing anything to keep his mind occupied.
The physical exhaustion was a welcome reprieve from the endless loop of guilt that played in his head.

No matter how hard he worked, no matter how many hours he spent trying to atone for what he had done, the guilt remained, gnawing at him relentlessly.

He thought often of Eli—of his laugh, his smile, the way he had made Aston feel understood, even when the rest of the world seemed against them. And now Eli was gone, and all Aston had left were memories tainted by the knowledge that he had pushed too hard, that his insistence on confronting their demons had driven Eli into a storm he could never escape. Like a programmed robot, he checked off each hour monotonously, going through the motions, paying for a penance that could never be repaid.

Late at night, when the world was quiet and he was left alone with his thoughts, Aston wondered if he would ever feel whole again. The ankle bracelet had finally been removed, but he still felt shackled.

He wondered if the pain would ever dull, if the guilt would ever fade. But deep down, he knew without a doubt that the scar left by Eli's absence would never heal.

The judge had given him leniency, a chance to move forward, but Aston wasn't sure he could, or how to take it. He didn't feel like he deserved it.

And so, he worked. Day after day, hour after hour, hoping that one day the weight of the guilt might become just a little bit lighter.

But for now, it was all-consuming.

Chapter Thirty Seven

The light breeze had a soft chill that afternoon, brushing through the leaves and carrying with it the scent of the ocean. Aston had been wandering aimlessly around town, with no destination in mind, trying clear his head. It had been months since Eli's death.

Today, his feet led him to the docks. They came into view as he rounded the bend, and for a moment, he hesitated. He hadn't set foot near them since the day he wound out about Eli's drowning, as if avoiding the place would somehow erase the memories—the guilt. But now, the sight of them drew him in. He knew he shouldn't go, but he couldn't turn away.

He walked closer, and his eyes fell on Joy. The boat was no longer a proud vessel in the water but a broken shell, hidden beneath the boardwalk as though it had become an embarrassment for the tourists. The paint on the hull had begun to chip away, and a faint layer of algae coated the once-sleek surface. She looked like a ghost of her former self, decaying and forgotten. The sight of it tore something deep inside Aston.

This boat had been Eli's sanctuary, his escape. Now, it was abandoned. A memory of times past.

He glanced over at the building that used to house the Taylor's business. The windows were stripped of the blinds, displaying the dark, gloomy shell of an empty office inside. Faded paint framed a brighter rectangle on the exterior wall, where the "Taylor Charters" sign had hung just months ago.

Aston turned his attention back to Joy, and he stepped closer, careful, hesitant. His breath caught in his throat as he saw Eli's name on the bow, painted in bold letters next to the fading scrawl of his sister's name. The sight of it made his stomach turn. The memory of painting it there—the sorrow and love behind that moment—now felt like a cruel reminder of everything that had been taken from him. Of everything he had lost.

He took a few steps forward, taking a deep breath and reached out, his fingers brushing against the cold, rough surface of the boat. His eyes stung as the flood of memories washed over him—days spent with Eli, the quiet moments together. And then, as always, the guilt showed itself, souring the moment of fond memories.

He blinked, his vision blurring. He felt foolish for being there, for standing in front of a broken boat as if it could give him any solace. It couldn't. Nothing could.

Just as he was about to leave, he heard a familiar voice behind him and jumped.

"Can't stay away, huh?"

Samuel's voice was low, steady, but tired. Aston's heart skipped a beat, his entire body freezing in place. Aston turned, his stomach twisting into knots as he made eye contact with Eli's father.

Samuel looked older. The lines on his face had deepened, and his shoulders sagged under the weight of grief. His once-strong, sturdy frame now seemed frail, as if the loss of his son had hollowed him out. It obviously had. He wore a heavy coat, though it wasn't cold, and his hands were shoved deep into his pockets, similar to how Eli used to hold himself.

Aston immediately took a step back, retreating, guilt flooding him. He wasn't supposed to be here. Rebecca and Samual had made that perfectly clear.

Aston stammered, his voice barely above a whisper. "I'm sorry. I know I shouldn't be here. I didn't mean to—"

Samuel held up a hand, stopping him. "It's alright," he said quietly, his voice gruff but not unkind. "You don't need to apologize, Aston."

Aston hesitated, unsure what to do. "I… I didn't mean to come here today."

Samuel sighed, glancing past Aston to the boat under the boardwalk. "Neither did I, but…" His voice trailed off, and for a moment, the two of them stood there in silence, the only sound the gentle lapping of the waves against the shore.

"I do sometimes. There were a lot of happy memories that happened here. I'm drawn to this place," Samuel admitted after a while, his eyes glancing at the boat adorning his children's names. "Just to help me… remember."

Aston didn't know what to say. The weight of their shared grief hung between them like a physical presence, but it wasn't something that words could easily touch.

Samuel's gaze shifted to Aston, and for the first time in a long while, there wasn't anything behind his eyes but sadness. "I miss him," he said softly. His voice cracked, and he cleared his throat. "Every day."

Aston's throat tightened, and he nodded, unable to find the right words. It felt wrong to speak. Wrong to even be there, standing near Eli's father after everything that had happened.

"I know you miss him too," Samuel continued, his voice a little stronger now. "You don't have to say it. I can see it." He looked back at the boat. "We all do."

Aston swallowed hard, his guilt threatening to overwhelm him. "I… I feel like it's my fault," he confessed, not sure why he felt he needed to say that, his voice barely audible. "I pushed him. I… I thought that if he came out to you and his mom, that things would get better. But instead…"

Samuel's brow furrowed, and he let out a deep breath, and he spoke quietly. "I've thought about that day a thousand times. I've gone over everything I said… and didn't say. Everything Rebecca said. I've wondered what would have happened if we'd handled things differently." He shook his head slowly.

"But you and I blaming ourselves won't bring him back."

Aston closed his eyes, the guilt heavy in his chest. He had been holding onto that blame for so long, it had become a part of him. A dark and heavy force pulling him down. Letting it go seemed impossible.

"I should have stopped her," Samuel continued, his voice softer now, tinged with regret. "Rebecca. I should have stood up to her more that night. I knew… I always knew Eli was gay. Just didn't want to accept it."

Aston blinked, surprised by Samuel's words. He hadn't expected this—this admission of guilt from Eli's father. He had always assumed that Samuel had sided with Rebecca, that he had been blind to Eli's struggles.

"How… how did you know?" Aston asked, his voice hoarse.

Samuel smiled faintly, though it didn't reach his eyes. "A father knows," he said simply. "I may not have understood everything, but I could see the way he looked at you. The way he was with you. The way he changed when you were around. I should have done more to help him, to support him." His expression darkened. "But I didn't. And now…"

He didn't finish the sentence. He didn't have to.

"I can't know for sure, but I think Rebecca knew too. That's why she pushed so hard for him to find a girlfriend. Maybe hoping that it would spark a connection and get him to be the person she wanted. But forgetting about what he truly wanted. Which was you. And only you. You made him happy."

Aston just listened, staring at Samuel.

They stood there in silence for a long time, the weight of their shared guilt pressing down on them. Aston looked back at the boat, at the name Eli painted on the bow. It felt like a memorial now, a reminder of what they had both lost.

"I do miss and think about him every day," Aston whispered, his voice barely audible. "I don't know how to move on."

Samuel nodded slowly. "Neither do I," he admitted. "But maybe we don't have to. Maybe it's okay to carry that with us, as long as we don't let it destroy us."

Aston looked at Samuel again, trying to process the words. He had spent so long blaming himself, convinced that he didn't deserve to move on.

"How is Eli's mom doing?"

Aston was unsure if he should ask, but the question had been weighing on his mind for weeks. The unknown answers to the questions swirling in his mind were heavy.

Samuel's expression remained blank. "She's... struggling," he said carefully. "She blames herself too, though she'll never admit it. She's... angry. At herself, at me, at you. At the world, really."

Aston nodded. He understood that anger all too well. No matter her role in this, she had a right to be angry. They had lost both their children. Whatever Aston was feeling, her and Samuel must be feeling it double the amount. Joy, and now Eli.

"I don't know if she'll ever forgive herself," Samuel added quietly. "Or if she'll ever forgive you. But... that's not something you can control. She has had it rough. We all have I suppose. But she is not a bad person, Aston. Life just sometimes has a way of breaking people down. Don't let this break you down."

Aston swallowed hard. He didn't know if he could ever forgive himself either, but maybe that wasn't the point. Maybe it wasn't about forgiveness. Maybe it was about learning to live with the pain, the regret, the loss.

The sun had begun to sink in the sky, casting shadows over the docks. Aston looked back at the boat one last time, at Eli's name. He felt a small sense of peace.

"What are you going to do with the boat?" Aston finally asked.

"I have no use for it. If you want it, it's yours."

And with those words, Samuel turned and walked off, his footsteps heavy on the wooden dock. He walked slowly down the road until he turned the corner and disappeared. And that was the last time that Aston ever saw him.

Chapter Thirty Eight

The afternoon air was cooler than usual as Aston walked home, his conversation with Samuel replaying in his mind. The quiet streets of Clearwater offered no comfort as his feet carried him back to the house.

When he reached the house, he saw the blue sedan parked in the driveway and sighed. As he put his hand on the front door handle, Aston hesitated, staring at the worn wood as if it might offer him some clue about what waited inside. Last person he wanted to see now was Alex. But when he opened the door and stepped inside, what he saw stopped him in his tracks.

His mom and Alex were standing in the living room, wrapped in a warm embrace, their faces close as they shared a gentle kiss. It wasn't anything dramatic, nothing like the passionate scenes you saw in movies, but it was intimate, tender. A softness in the way they held each other that spoke volumes about the connection they shared. For a moment, they didn't notice Aston standing there, his heart racing as a flood of emotions he couldn't fully process surged through him.

The confusion hit first. Then the anger.

"What the hell, mom?" Aston blurted, his voice louder than he intended, but he didn't care.

Laura pulled back from Alex, her eyes widening in surprise and guilt. "Aston—"

Aston ignored her, glaring at Alex instead. "What are you doing here again? You're always here these days."

Alex raised his hands in a calming gesture, his voice soft and measured. "Aston, take it easy. I—"

"No!" Aston snapped, taking a step toward them. His pulse hammered in his ears. "Don't tell me to take it easy. What the hell are you doing? You think you can just waltz in here and replace my dad?"

"Aston, stop," Laura pleaded, stepping between him and Alex, but Aston didn't back down. The anger was bubbling up inside him, threatening to boil over.

"I'm not trying to replace your dad, Aston," Alex said, his voice calm, but Aston could see the tension in his jaw, the unease in his eyes. "I'd never try to replace your dad. I'm just—"

"Don't lecture me," Aston interrupted, his voice shaking with the force of his emotions. "You have no right. You could never be my dad, no matter how hard you tried. You're just here because you didn't stop at a stop sign. That's all!"

"Aston!" Laura's voice was sharper now, her face tight with frustration. "That's enough. Go upstairs."

Aston stared at her, disbelief and hurt crashing through him in waves. He shook his head, his hands balled into fists, and he stormed up the stairs. The door to his room slammed behind him with a loud, resounding bang that echoed through the house.

Downstairs, Laura let out a heavy sigh, rubbing her temples as she turned back to Alex. "I'm sorry," she murmured, her voice soft with guilt. "He didn't mean that."

Alex shook his head, offering her a gentle smile.

"It's okay. I know he didn't. It's difficult, I completely understand," he said quietly. "He's going through a lot. I get it. I'm not upset."

Laura sighed again, looking up the stairs where Aston had disappeared, her heart heavy with the weight of her son's anger and despair. "He seems so broken. I just wish he could understand."

"He will. He is a good kid." Alex said softly, stepping closer and pulling her into a comforting embrace. "He just needs time. He's been through a rough patch, that's for sure. Can't really blame him."

Laura leaned into him, grateful for his support even as the tension hung in the air.

Chapter Thirty Nine

Upstairs, Aston lay on his bed, staring at the door he'd slammed shut, his heart still pounding, anger and confusion twisting inside him like a knot he couldn't untangle.

He closed his eyes and tried to push the noise of it all from his mind, but the guilt lingered. The grief for Eli, the burning anger that had consumed him that night—it all twisted in his chest, refusing to let go. His thoughts were interrupted by the distant sound of a car pulling up to the house. He opened his eyes and listened. The engine turned off. There was a pause, then the soft click of a car door.

Someone was here. Aston felt a sense of curiosity of who it could be, but was too tired and ultimately felt indifference to find out who it was. Not much interested him at the moment. Just the ceiling that he was staring at. He closed his eyes once more.

Downstairs, there was a knock at the door. Laura, not expecting anyone, wondered who it could be. She opened it tentatively. The man standing in front of her wasn't anyone she recognized. He was tall, broad-shouldered, and his expression was cold, calculated.

There was something about the way he stood there, the way he looked past her into the house, that made her immediately wary.

"Can I help you?" Laura asked, her voice steady, but her grip tightened on the door handle.

"I'm looking for Aston Carter," the man said, his tone rough, almost indifferent. "Is he in?"

Laura frowned, her eyes narrowing. "Who are you, please?"

"I'm the guy whose boat he burned to ashes. He needs to pay for what he did," Mark said flatly.

A chill ran down Laura's spine. So this was the man Aston took his anger out on. She squared her shoulders, trying to keep her calm, but her voice raised slightly. "You've had your day in court. Aston has paid his dues. And you need to leave. Right now."

Mark's expression didn't change. He leaned slightly toward the doorframe, refusing to move. "I'm not leaving until I talk to him."

Laura's heart started to race. She could feel the threat hanging in the air, thick and suffocating.

Just as her mind was scrambling to figure out what to do, a calm, firm voice cut through the tension.

"Is there a problem here?"

Laura turned her head. Alex was standing behind her, his presence immediately filling the space. He had heard the exchange and sensed the fear in Laura's voice. He stepped forward, positioning himself between her and Mark, his eyes locked on the younger man.

"You Aston's dad?" Mark asked, looking at the man standing in front of him.

"That's none of your business," he replied, his tone calm but authoritative. "Laura, why don't you head back inside? I'll take care of this."

Laura hesitated for a moment, her eyes darting between the two men. She trusted Alex, but there was something dangerous about the way Mark was holding himself, the tension crackling beneath his cool exterior. She nodded slowly, stepping back into the house, but she kept close, watching through the small window beside the door.

Alex shut the door behind him and stepped outside, facing Mark squarely.

Alex was taller, broader, and his calm demeanor only seemed to make the moment more intense. "So, what is it you want?" Alex asked, his voice low but steady.

Mark crossed his arms over his chest. "Your kid needs to pay for what he did. That was my boat he torched. You think he can just burn it to the ground and get away with it?"

Alex studied him for a long moment, his expression unreadable. "Get your insurance to pay for your boat." he said quietly.

Mark's smirk faltered slightly. "I didn't have insurance. So he needs to pay what's owing to me."

"That's pretty dumb to own a boat with no insurance, don't you think?"

Mark stared at him.

Alex's gaze hardened. "You've obviously heard about what happened to Eli Taylor?"

Mark's face paled slightly, the cocky veneer slipping, "I heard… Doesn't change the fact that my boat was torched," he said, coldly.

Alex took a step forward, his voice firm but calm. "Eli is dead. And I have a feeling that you had a part to play. A part that contributed in a big way to what drove him to that ultimate death. So if you think you can come here, harass Aston, and pretend like you're some sort of victim in all of this, think again. Aston burned your boat, yes, but he's already paying for it. And Eli has paid the ultimate price. You? You'll have to live with the fact that your actions played a part in a young man's death."

"Oh please. I had nothing to do with Eli's death," said Mark, coldly.

Alex considered his next words carefully. After thinking about what Laura had said, and what Aston had done, the pieces had begun to fall into place and he had an idea that Mark had somehow been involved, leading to the escalation of events. Not knowing exactly how though. But he felt he knew enough, and he decided to test his theory on Mark and gauge his reaction. He could immediately see that Mark was the kind of person who would only respond to threats. Just like any bully.

"Let's get one thing straight. I know everything." Alex said calmly. "And I don't care what you have to say. What matters is what you did. And what I'm telling you now is this: if you ever come near this house again, if you ever try to contact Aston or harass anyone else in this town, I'll make sure you regret it. I'll personally fuck you up. Your boat? Consider that your penance for being an asshole. Get over it. Move on with your life, because if I hear you're stirring up any more trouble, I'll personally make sure the cops know about your bullying… If you want a fight, you got one. But it will be with me, not with some kids. And I promise you, you don't want to get into a fight with me. Physical, or legal. I can do both… well. Don't test me."

Mark's eyes hardened, but Alex could see the flicker of concern behind them, as Mark looked him up and down, considering the threat. Alex could see that he was getting through to him. To seal the deal, he leaned forward slightly and whispered, "Oh, and let's not forget about the small matter of blackmail. I've got a good lawyer I can contact, if you wanna go there."

Mark's mouth opened slightly, but no words came out. Alex had taken a chance, but from Mark's reaction, he knew he had hit the nail directly on the head.

Mark took a step back, his eyes blinking nervously.

"Whatever," he mumbled, the fight seemingly draining from him. He took a couple of steps back and then stopped. "Just know that I never meant for the kid to die."

Alex didn't respond. He just stared at him, his gaze steady and unflinching. The silence stretched. Alex gestured with his head towards Mark's truck. Mark got the message. He turned, his shoulders slumped, and he walked back to his car. Laura watched on from the living room window. Mark climbed in, his hands fumbled with the keys, and then the engine roared to life and he drove off.

Alex stood there for a few moments, watching until the vehicle disappeared around the corner. Only then did he turn back to the house. When he opened the door, Laura was waiting for him, her eyes wide with concern.

"What happened?" she asked softly, her voice barely above a whisper.

Alex closed the door behind him and gave her a reassuring smile. "Don't worry. He won't be back here again."

Laura exhaled a long breath she hadn't realized she was holding, and without thinking, she wrapped her arms around him in a tight embrace.

Alex held her close, his hand gently rubbing her back as he whispered, "It's fine. You're safe. Aston's safe."

Laura pulled back, her eyes glistening with relief and gratitude. "Thank you," she whispered. "Thank you for being here for us."

Alex smiled softly, brushing a strand of hair from her face. "No problem, Laura. And I apologize for what happened earlier with Aston. I didn't mean—" he said, his voice full of quiet conviction.

"You have no reason to apologize. I'll chat to him. He'll stop hating on you one day, I promise," she forced a smile and got one back in return.

In the bedroom above them, Aston retreated from the open window.

Chapter Forty

The house had grown quiet. Too quiet.

Laura, sat at the small kitchen table, a cup of tea growing cold in her hands. It was late afternoon and Alex had just left and she stared at the swirling liquid as though it held some secret, some answer she was desperately searching for. But it didn't. It was just tea—lukewarm and flavorless. A perfect reflection of the hollow silence that had filled their home since Eli's death. Aston was no longer the boy he used to be. She knew it would take time, but the longer it took, the more she worried about her son.

She sighed and set the cup down, her eyes drifting toward the staircase. Laura pushed her chair back quietly and stood, her fingers lingering on the worn wood of the table for a moment before she walked out of the kitchen and up the stairs. Pausing outside Aston's door, she listened. The silence on the other side was deafening. She raised her hand to knock, hesitated, then gently rapped her knuckles against the wood.

"Aston?" she called softly. No answer.

She waited, hoping he might acknowledge her presence. But the silence stretched on, heavy and impenetrable. Laura's heart clenched in her chest. She had seen her son suffer before, but never like this. Not since the day his father had died.

Laura slowly opened the door. The room was dim, the curtains drawn tightly against the daylight. Aston was lying on his bed, face lit up by his phone screen.

"Aston," she said softly, her voice filled with concern. "Can we have a chat?"

Still, no response. His thumb continued scrolling the phone screen, as though he hadn't heard her at all.

Laura stepped closer, her heart sad at the sight of him. He looked so small, so lost, lying there in the dim light. These days there was always a hollowness in his eyes that she hated seeing. It was like the Aston she had raised—the vibrant, passionate boy she knew—had disappeared, leaving behind only this shell of a person.

She sat down beside him on the bed, the mattress creaking softly. For a long moment, neither of them spoke.

The air between them was thick. Laura struggled with how to start what she wanted to say.

"I know you're angry. And I know you're struggling with everything that has happened. It's been a lot of changes for us," Laura said gently, her voice barely above a whisper. "I know that what's going on with Alex and I must be hard. But Alex is a good guy. And I know your anger isn't only about him. It's about Eli and what happened. Pleas try not to take all of that anger out on Alex. He is really just trying to help us. I'm not saying don't be angry. It's natural to be. Eli was taken from you. Your dad was taken from us."

She knew words would not change the fact that he would carry some of the weight of this tragedy on his shoulders forever, thinking that he could have somehow prevented it.

"Sweetheart," she whispered. "Even though you feel responsible in part for what happened to Eli, at the end of the day, it was an accident. Eli decided to go out that day. Not you. What happened to him wasn't your fault. You were just trying to help him. Always remember that. You need to start thinking what Eli would have wanted for you. And I know he would want you to be happy. Take the time to grieve. Feel it, process it.

But leave yourself open to be able to look after you as well. I want my Aston back too. I need that guy. I need him badly."

"I promised I would protect him" Aston muttered finally, putting his phone down, his voice barely audible. "And I didn't."

"Not all promises can be kept. No matter how much we believe the words when we say them. That is life, unfortunately. You loved Eli. And he loved you. That's what matters. Not what happened after, not the mistakes or the choices. What matters is that you cared for each other," she said softly, her voice steady and strong.

Aston remained silent.

"And I know it's hard," she continued gently. "You once told me that Eli deserved to be happy. Now I'm telling you that you do too."

"I don't know how to anymore," he whispered, his voice raw. "I don't know how to move forward from this."

Laura felt her throat tighten again, and she reached up to brush a tear from her cheek.

"I felt the same when your dad passed away. I know you did too. But we moved forward. Never forgetting him, but not letting life's circumstances hold us back from living our own lives. I don't have all the answers," she admitted, her voice shaky. "But I do know that shutting yourself away like this… it's not the way. Eli wouldn't want that for you. He would want you to keep living. And moving forward is not forgetting. It's honoring those we love and loved. We owe that to them."

Aston closed his eyes, his jaw tight as he fought back emotions that threatened to spill over. For a moment, the room was silent again, the only sound the soft ticking of the clock on the wall.

"And if I don't know where to start?" he finally asked, his voice barely a whisper.

Laura smiled faintly, though it was tinged with sadness. "One step at a time, baby," she said softly. "That's all you can do. Just take it one step at a time."

Aston looked down at his hands, his expression conflicted.

"I've been thinking," she said carefully, her voice gentle. "I know you were not welcome at Eli's funeral.

That was wrong of Rebecca, no matter the circumstances. You had a right to pay your respects. You needed your closure too. So I've been thinking. Maybe there's a way to honor Eli's memory. Something that would help you move forward, but also keep him with you. Doing something for him and therefore, for yourself, might help you get that closure."

Aston frowned, his brow furrowing. "What do you mean?"

Laura took a deep breath, choosing her words carefully. "Well, Eli loved the ocean," she said softly. "Maybe go down to the beach sometime. Write something to him. Put the note in a bottle and throw it into the ocean. Something like that. Just talk to him. Have your own ceremony. Something personal. Just you and the memory of him. Of course, I'll be there with you if you want. But think about it. Do something for him. It might help you. I'm just throwing thoughts here. I don't have all the answers. Just trying to help."

Aston's eyes scanned his hands, and Laura could see the wheels turning in his mind. She knew he wasn't ready to commit to anything yet, and that was okay. He had lost two of the most important people in his life, only a few years apart. And he was still young.

She understood how difficult it was for him. But the idea had been planted. And that was enough for her for now. She had no intention of pressuring him out of his grief. That would happen over time. But she just wanted to get him to start thinking about the future and finding some sort of closure.

"I'm not saying it has to be right away," she added quickly. "Just something to think about. A way to keep him with you, without carrying all this guilt and anger."

She reached out and gently squeezed his hand, offering him a small, reassuring smile.

"I just want you to be okay," she whispered. "You've been through so much, and I want you to know that I am always here for you."

Aston nodded and changed the subject, feeling his emotions tugging at him.

"I saw what Alex did just now. Sending Mark on his way… Like a boss," Aston managed a small smile.

Laura's eyes lit up seeing the smile, something that she longed to see more from her son again. She smiled back at him.

"Alex doesn't seem that bad… He still can't drive though," continued Aston.

Laura's smile grew to the edges of her face, her eyes glistening. "I agree with you on both counts," was all she could muster, nodding and gave a little laugh.

"I love you, Mom. And you do deserve to be happy too. I'll try give him a chance," Aston whispered.

"Thank you. I love you too, sweetheart. More than anything." She leaned forward, taking Aston into her arms and hugging him tightly.

Chapter Forty One

The following morning was dull and overcast. The air was heavy with silence, punctuated only by the faint ticking of the clock on his bedside table. It had been weeks—weeks of solitude, weeks of numbness, weeks of sinking deeper into the hollow pit of guilt that seemed to consume every part of him. The world outside carried on without him, and yet, he couldn't muster the energy to care. All he could think about was Eli's death, the storm, the boat. His part in it all.

He hadn't gone to the docks since that day he saw Samuel. Since he had stood there, staring at the remains of Eli's boat—the boat with his sister's name on it, the boat Aston had once touched as if it were a part of Eli's soul, now shattered, like their future. The image haunted him, and no matter how many times he tried to shove it from his mind, it always crept back in, a relentless, suffocating reminder of what he had lost. Of what he had done.

His phone buzzed from the bedside table, the screen lighting up for the briefest moment before it dimmed again, leaving the room in a muted haze. He didn't bother checking. He hadn't responded to any messages in days. Maybe weeks. Time had blurred into one endless moment.

There were no sharp edges left, no milestones to mark the passing of days. Just the weight of everything that had happened, crushing him.

He had shut everyone out—his mother, his friends, even his therapist that his worried mother had organized to try help him through this difficult time. But no one could understand. No one could feel what he felt. The only person who had known him, truly known him, was gone. And it was his fault.

And of course, he blamed himself for everything. For pushing Eli too hard, for being selfish, for not seeing the signs. He should have known. He should have stopped Eli from going out that morning. He should have been there with him, instead of hiding in his room, trying to figure out what their future held. In reality, he was not able to, but his mind wouldn't allow him to see that. It continuously told him it was all his fault. Now, there was no future. Only this endless void of guilt and regret that felt never-ending.

A quiet knock on his bedroom door startled him out of his thoughts, though he didn't move. He didn't want to talk to anyone. He just wanted to be left alone. The knocking persisted, soft but insistent. Finally, after what felt like an eternity, Aston forced himself to speak.

The door creaked open slowly. He didn't look up, already expecting to hear his mother's voice, another round of gentle urging to eat, to talk, to "let her in." He couldn't. He couldn't handle any of it.

Instead, familiar voice broke the silence—one that wasn't his mother's.

"Aston?" Ava's voice was quiet, tentative, as if she wasn't sure if she should be there.

He got up, surprised to see her standing in the doorway. Ava. Her curly hair was pulled back into a messy ponytail, her eyes wide with concern. She looked different—but then again, everything was different since Eli's death. She stepped inside, hesitating at the threshold as if unsure whether she was welcome.

"I knocked a few times," she said, offering a small, awkward smile. "Your mom let me in. I'd hoped you wouldn't mind me coming to visit you."

Aston swallowed hard, the lump in his throat tightening. He didn't want to see her. He didn't want to see anyone. Especially not Ava.

She was a reminder of everything he had failed to protect—Eli's future, his happiness, everything that might have been. He looked down, staring at the floor. "Hi, Ava."

Ava didn't move. "I know you probably are not in the mood to see me. But I couldn't just… I couldn't stay away. I also wanted… needed to talk to you."

Silence stretched between them, thick and suffocating. Aston's heart pounded in his chest, the urge to tell her to leave growing stronger with each passing second. He really did not want company. It wasn't her fault, it was him. But he couldn't bring himself to say the words. Something about the way she stood there, her vulnerability palpable, kept him from pushing her away completely.

"I know what you're going through," she said softly, breaking the quiet. Her words hung in the air. She couldn't possibly know. No one could. But then she continued, her voice wavering. "I mean, I don't know exactly what you're feeling. But I lost him too, Aston. He was a good friend. Initially, I actually thought I might have had a chance with him. But yeah. I could see how you two were together. I never had a chance, did I? He was always yours."

Her words touched him. He hadn't let himself think about anyone else's pain. Not really.

He had been too consumed by his own, thanks to the overwhelming guilt. But now, hearing Ava's voice tremble as she spoke Eli's name, the reality of it crashed into him all over again. Eli wasn't just his loss. Eli was Ava's friend too. And his parents.

"I didn't know what to do," she continued, her voice thick with emotion. "I didn't know how to reach out to you. After everything… I thought maybe you wouldn't want to hear from me. But I've been really hurting too, and I—" She broke off, her breath hitching. "I didn't want either of us to be alone in this. Well, let's just say that I felt like I needed to come over. You weren't answering any of my texts."

The honesty of her words slowly cut through Aston's defenses as he listened to her. For weeks, he had convinced himself that his grief was his alone to bear, that no one else could possibly feel the depth of pain that he felt. But now, Ava was standing in front of him, also grieving, also lost, and it forced him to confront something he had been trying so hard to ignore.

He wasn't alone in his grief. Only in his guilt.

Aston took a shaky breath.

His eyes flicked toward Ava, and for the first time since Eli's death, he allowed himself to really see her—not as a reminder of what had been lost, but as someone who was hurting too.

"I miss him," Aston whispered, the words slipping out before he could stop them.

Ava nodded. "I miss him too."

They stood there in silence for what felt like an eternity, the shared grief between them filling the space. Ava's presence was both a comfort and a reminder of everything that had been taken from them. Aston's throat tightened, the guilt swirling inside him once again. He had been the one to push Eli, to confront the truths Eli wasn't ready to face. He had pushed too hard, too fast, and now Eli was gone.

"It's my fault," Aston said, his voice cracking under the weight of the confession. "I should have stopped him. I should have… done something.

Ava shook her head, as she stepped closer to him. "You can't blame yourself for what happened."

He wanted to believe her. He wanted to take those words and wrap them around his heart like a shield, protecting him from the guilt that gnawed at his soul. But he couldn't. It was too late for that.

"I pushed him. I pushed him to come out, to face everything. If I hadn't—"

Ava cut him off, her voice firm despite the tears building in her eyes, seeing him struggle. "You didn't do this, Aston. You loved him. You cared about him. That's not what hurt him. That's not why he's gone."

For the first time in weeks, the tightness in his chest began to loosen just a tiny amount. Her words hung in the air, and though the guilt still clung to him like a second skin, something about what she said began to chip away at the darkness inside him.

After a while, Ava spoke again, her voice softer this time. "You loved him, Aston. We both did." And with the statement, she stepped forward and put her arms around him. Aston wasn't sure if it was for his or for her benefit. But it didn't matter. He returned the hug and they stood there in a silent embrace, sharing the grief and loss together.

And maybe that was a start.

In the days that followed, Ava continued to reach out to Aston, gently coaxing him out of the darkness he had retreated into. At first it was only short visits. But as the days went on, she spent more time coming over. Eventually, they would spend hours talking, sometimes about Eli, sometimes about nothing at all. There were moments of silence, where they simply sat together, sharing the weight of their loss without needing to fill the space with words.

With Ava by his side, he found that the guilt no longer felt quite as unbearable. It was still there, lurking in the shadows, hitting him like a baseball bat at random intervals, without warning, but it didn't consume him continuously in the same way it had before.

Slowly, bit by bit, he began to open up again. To let people in. His mother. His friends. Even his therapist.
The process was slow, and some days were harder than others, but he was trying. And that was more than he had been able to do before.

Ava had become an unexpected lifeline in his darkest moments, and though their relationship had once been defined by the expectations of others—by Eli's family, by the world around them—they had found something deeper in the aftermath of the tragedy. They had found understanding. Compassion. Connection.

It wasn't perfect. But it was something real. Something that mattered. They were helping each other simply by being there.

And for the first time in what felt like forever, Aston allowed himself to believe that maybe, just maybe, he could begin to move forward. Not forget—never forget—but live with the memory of Eli in a way that didn't tear him apart each and every day.

It was a long road ahead. But he wasn't walking it alone.

And that made a difference.

Chapter Forty Two

Aston stood in front of the mirror, staring at his reflection with a mixture of resignation and fatigue. His face had grown leaner over the past few months, the once vibrant spark in his hazel eyes dulled significantly. He buttoned up his shirt, each movement slow and deliberate, like someone trying to convince themselves to keep going despite the weight pulling them down.

Grief counseling. Another session loomed. Another hour of dredging up painful memories, of sitting in a circle with strangers, all united by the invisible thread of loss. Listening to their stories but focussing on his. Over the past few months, it had become a routine. Mandatory, part of his probation—190 hours of community service and counseling, the judge's orders. But it wasn't the hours of cleaning parks or painting benches that weighed on him; it was the group therapy sessions and the anger management groups.

Anger management, Aston scoffed to himself. He never considered himself an angry person. He never used to lash out, not until that one fateful day. That moment, when rage had consumed him, felt so far removed from who he was.

And yet, here he was, lumped together with people whose lives had been shaped by their tempers. He didn't fit in there, and he hated it.

But the grief counseling sessions were different. It wasn't about controlling his anger—it was about managing the sadness, the crushing guilt that gnawed at him from the inside. Grief was an emotion he understood deeply, one that had been his companion since the day Eli died. Since the day his father died.

The counselor, a woman named Sharon, had a kind demeanor. She never forced anyone to talk but encouraged them when the time was right. Aston had shared his story in small pieces over the months, each fragment of his pain slowly revealed as if he were peeling back layers of his heart.

He finished dressing, grabbed his jacket, and left the house, walking the familiar path to the community center where the sessions were held. The streets were quiet, and the autumn air carried a crispness that cut through him, making him pull his jacket tighter around his frame.

As he approached the door to the building, he paused, feeling the familiar sense of hesitation that always came just before a session.

There was still a part of him that resisted these meetings, that wanted to avoid the discomfort of facing his feelings head-on. But he had learned, through trial and error, that avoidance only made the grief heavier. So, with a deep breath, he stepped inside.

The room was already half-filled with people when he entered. The circle of chairs felt too intimate, as always, but he took his usual seat near the edge, greeting the few familiar faces. And a new one. Sharon walked in, followed by a young man. Her calm presence immediately grounding the room, taking a seat and gesturing to the man to sit next to her. She welcomed everyone, her gentle eyes scanning the group as they settled in.

"Before we begin today," Sharon started, her voice soothing, "I'd like to introduce someone new to our group. This is Jordan."

She gestured to the young man. Aston's eyes flicked toward him, and something about the way Jordan carried himself—shoulders slightly hunched, hands nervously gripping the strap of his bag—caught Aston's attention. He looked like someone who was just as lost, just as broken, and unsure of where to go from here.

Jordan was tall, maybe a couple of inches taller than Aston, with dark hair and piercing brown eyes that seemed to hold a weight of their own. He glanced around the room before his gaze briefly met Aston's, and in that instant, there was a flicker of recognition. Not of each other, but of the shared pain that had brought them to this place.

Jordan sat directly across from Aston.

"Jordan and I have spoken before this and tonight he has decided that he feels ready to join us on our shared journey and share his story. Jordan, whenever you are ready, you may begin."

There was a pause, a moment of quiet, before Sharon gave him a reassuring nod.

Jordan hesitated, but when he finally spoke, his voice was soft but firm. "Hi… I'm… uh… I'm Jordan," he started, his words faltering slightly. "I lost my dad two months ago. He had a heart attack. It was… sudden."

Aston felt a pang of sympathy as Jordan's words hung in the air. He immediately understood. Eli's death hadn't been a heart attack, but the way it had blindsided him felt just as cruel.

"He was healthy," Jordan continued, his hands twisting together in his lap. "At least, that's what we all thought. One minute, he was fine… and then he wasn't." His voice caught, and he paused, swallowing hard. "I was there when it happened. Tried to do CPR, but… it didn't work."

The room was silent as Jordan spoke. Aston watched him closely, feeling a strange sense of connection. He hadn't expected to feel this way—he never did when new people joined. But there was something in Jordan's story that struck a chord with him, something that made Aston want to reach out.

"It's been hard," Jordan admitted, his voice cracking slightly. "I keep thinking… if I had done something different, maybe… maybe he'd still be here. And that's all I would like to say for now, if you don't mind."

Jordan swallowed hard and looked down, stopping himself before he allowed the emotions to take over. Aston felt his chest tighten. He recognized the guilt that Jordan felt. The endless loop of "what ifs." He knew that feeling too well.

Sharon gave Jordan an encouraging smile. "Thank you for sharing that, Jordan. I know it's difficult to talk about these things, especially when the loss is still so fresh."

Jordan nodded, his eyes downcast. He didn't say anything else, but the way his shoulders slumped told Aston everything he needed to know—Jordan was drowning in the same kind of feelings that he struggled with.

As the session continued, Aston found it hard to focus on the others as they spoke. His mind kept drifting back to Jordan, to the look of quiet devastation on his face. When his turn to speak came, Aston hesitated, unsure of what to say. He had already shared so much of his story over the past few months, but today felt different. Today, he didn't want to talk about his grief; he felt he needed to reach out, to help someone else shoulder the burden they were carrying. And for the first time, he did not speak about Eli. He spoke about his father. He spoke for someone else's benefit.

"I lost my father too, Jordan," Aston finally said, his voice steady but quiet. Jordan's eyes flicked up and locked with Aston. "Almost three years ago now. It wasn't as sudden, like with your dad, but… it was still unexpected."

Aston felt like it was just them two in the room. The shared burden of both losing their fathers recently making an immediate and strong connection between them. He stared at Jordan, who matched the stare with those piercing brown eyes.

Aston could see the pain there, the same kind of helplessness that had haunted him for so long. It was like looking into a mirror.

"And I know what it feels like to blame yourself, for stuff," Aston continued, his voice softening. "To think that maybe if you'd done something differently, things would have turned out differently. But the truth is, sometimes there's nothing we could have done. Sometimes things just… happen, and we can't control them."

Jordan's gaze lingered on Aston for a moment, and then he gave a small, almost imperceptible nod. It wasn't much, but it was enough to let Aston know that his words had reached him in some way and had meant something.

After the session ended, Aston found himself lingering outside the building, his hands shoved deep into his pockets as he waited for something—he wasn't even sure what. He had never been the type to approach people, especially not in a place like this, but Jordan's story had stirred something in him. Maybe it was the shared guilt, or maybe it was just the recognition that they were both trying to navigate through the same kind of darkness.

The door to the community center opened, and Jordan stepped out. Aston hesitated for a moment before stepping forward.

"Hey, Jordan," Aston called out, his voice steady despite the nerves prickling at him. Jordan turned toward him, his brow furrowed in mild surprise.

"Oh, hi… Aston, right?" Jordan replied, his tone cautious but not unfriendly.

"Yeah, Aston. Pleased to meet you."

"Pleased to meet you, Aston."

Aston removed his right hand from his pocket, and they shook hands and stood awkwardly for a second, not knowing what to say. Aston thought for a second and then spoke.

"Sorry about your dad," Aston said, feeling slightly uncomfortable, as he put his hand back in his pocket. "Losing someone close to you like that… it messes with your head."

Jordan gave a small, but genuine smile. "Yeah. It really does." His face was kind and he seemed to appreciate that Aston had waited just to tell him that.

For a moment more, they stood in awkward silence, neither of them sure what to say next. But it was Jordan who broke it.

"Thanks for what you said in there," he admitted, his voice quiet. "I guess… it helps to know I'm not the only one who feels this way."

Aston nodded, feeling a sense of relief wash over him. "No problem," he said simply.

Jordan looked at him for a long moment, and then smiled, larger this time.

"Maybe we could grab a coffee sometime?" Jordan suggested, his voice tentative. "You know… get to know each other a bit… and share more. I don't really like these group things. Took Sharon ages to convince me to come here tonight."

Aston smiled, a genuine smile that felt foreign after so many months of sadness. "Yeah," he agreed.

"I'd like that. I don't enjoy these either. I'm unfortunately forced to attend due to the judges orders."

"Judges orders?" enquired Jordan, raising an eyebrow, but not dropping the smile.

"Long story. I'll share it with you over that coffee, perhaps."

"I look forward to hearing about it."

They chuckled together.

"Thanks again, Aston. Nice meeting you and thanks for reaching out."

"Great to meet you too, Jordan. I look forward to seeing you again. Bye for now."

"Goodbye."

As they parted ways, Aston felt something different. Aston glanced back at Jordan, only to catch him glancing back at him as well. It put a smile on his face and a small, but significant spring in his step.

Chapter Forty Three

The sun filtered through the slit in the curtains in Aston's room, casting soft golden stripe across his bed. It was early, but he was already awake. The familiar sounds of seagulls and the distant roar of the ocean filled the air, but this morning they felt lighter somehow—less heavy than they had in months.

He reached for his phone, his fingers brushing over the well-worn case, glanced at the screen before placing it back down without unlocking it. No messages, no notifications. No anxiety gnawing at him this morning. The feeling of dread had begun to ease. Slowly, incrementally, but unmistakably.

Today, like so many days recently, he would meet Jordan.

They had grown close, almost without Aston realizing it. Their friendship had started with small moments, quiet conversations during grief counseling, lingering chats outside the community center after sessions. Coffee at the mall. Jordan had been hesitant at first, as had Aston. They were both navigating their own seas of pain, each carrying burdens they hadn't quite learned to share fully. But with time, something shifted.

A rhythm formed between them—a shared space where silence wasn't uncomfortable but comforting.

The first few times Jordan attended the group sessions, he barely spoke. He'd sit, arms folded, eyes down, participating just enough to avoid any attention. But Aston noticed the small ways he opened up—leaning in when others shared stories, nodding in agreement when someone spoke about the unpredictable waves of grief that could pull you under at any moment. When Aston talked about Eli for the first time in Jordan's presence, it had been quiet, a little hesitant, but honest.

"I was… I guess you could say, I was in love with him," Aston had said one day during the group. He hadn't planned to reveal that, hadn't even known he was going to say it, but there it was, out in the open. He said nothing more, but Aston looked up, catching Jordan's gaze across the circle, and there was no judgment, no pity. Just understanding.

Jordan stayed after the session that day. They'd walked together, not saying much at first, the silence between them filled with something unspoken yet comforting.
It was that day, Aston knew, they'd moved from being just acquaintances to something closer. And over the weeks, they grew into a solid friendship.

As the months passed, Jordan attended the final few of Aston's mandatory grief counseling sessions, more out of solidarity than necessity. "If you're going, I'm going," Jordan had joked one afternoon, slinging his bag over his shoulder as they left for one of the last group meetings.

It wasn't just the sessions, though. Jordan also began tagging along to help with Aston's community service. They spent afternoons together painting fences, cleaning up parks, and picking up trash. With Jordan there, the hours went by faster, filled with easy conversation and banter. The work, which had felt monotonous and frustrating at first, became almost therapeutic. Jordan had a way of making even the dullest tasks feel bearable, sometimes even fun.

"I think you're doing more of my community service than I am," Aston teased once, wiping sweat from his brow as they sat on the tailgate of a pickup truck after a long day. Jordan shrugged, his usual easy smile crossing his lips.

"Just here for moral support. And to make sure you don't get into any more shit, Troublemaker."

Aston chuckled. Trouble. It felt like another lifetime ago now—the rage. He hadn't thought about that day as much recently.

Grief had lessened, and had overshadowed any anger, and with each passing day, the memory of that moment had softened, replaced by something quieter, more introspective.

Aston hopped onto the top of a low stone wall at the edge of the beach, his legs swinging lightly above the sand below. Jordan joined him leaning back on his hands, his gaze fixed on the horizon. They had just finished another exhausting day of community service. They'd spent most of the day picking up trash along the shoreline, clearing debris washed up from a recent storm. It was tiring work, but Aston, with the help of Jordan, was ticking off the remaining hours of his sentence.

Aston wiped the sweat from his forehead with the back of his hand and glanced over at Jordan. His friend looked as tired as he felt, but there was a lightness to his posture, a kind of relaxed ease that Aston had always admired. It was like Jordan could find peace in any situation, no matter how tedious or frustrating. Aston wished he could be more like that.

They sat listening to the distant crash of the waves against the shore. The beach was mostly empty at this time of day, just a few families packing up their things and heading home, leaving Aston and Jordan in their own little world.

The peace of the moment was comforting, and Aston found himself grateful for the quiet companionship.

Jordan broke the silence first, his voice soft. "You doing okay, man?"

Aston hesitated, unsure how to answer. He'd been getting that question a lot lately.

"I don't know," he finally said, his voice low. "Some days, it feels like I'm getting better. Other days… it just hits me all over again."

Jordan nodded slowly, his gaze still fixed on the waves. "Yep. One minute you're fine, the next, it knocks you on your ass."

Aston laughed, but it was a hollow sound. "Yeah. It definitely does that."

They lapsed into silence again, the rhythmic sound of the ocean filling the space between them. Aston's mind wandered back to Eli, to their last few days together.

"What you said the other day at group… I didn't know you and Eli were so close," Jordan said after a while, his voice tentative, like he wasn't sure if he should bring it up.

Aston hadn't really talked about it, not in any real way, and the weight of it was difficult.

"We were…" Aston started, then paused, struggling to find the right words. "We were more than just friends. I don't think anyone really knew. Eli was… he was afraid of people finding out. Especially his parents. He wasn't ready to be out, and I tried to respect that."

Jordan's gaze shifted from the waves to Aston, his expression gentle. "I get that," he said quietly.

Aston looked at him, surprised by the sincerity in his voice. "You do?"

Jordan nodded slowly, his hands fidgeting in his lap. "Yeah. I get it more than you know."

There was a pause, a beat of silence. Aston wasn't sure what Jordan was getting at, but there was something in his tone, something in the way he avoided looking directly at Aston that made him think this conversation was about to go somewhere deeper.

"What do you mean?" Aston asked straight out, turning his body slightly to face Jordan.

Jordan took a breath, his shoulders rising and falling with the effort. "I'm gay, too," he said, his voice quiet, almost tentative, like he was testing the waters.

Aston blinked, caught off guard by the admission, but was not too surprised. He had a feeling. He had known Jordan for a while now, but Jordan had never mentioned anything about his sexuality. It wasn't something that had ever come up between them, and Aston had just assumed that Jordan was straight, like most of the other guys in town. But somewhere deeper down, he somehow had an inkling.

"Okay… Cool," Aston replied, processing the revelation and wondering where this was going.

Jordan nodded, a small, wry smile tugging at the corner of his mouth. "Yeah. I don't exactly go around advertising it, especially not in a place like Clearwater. But yeah, I am."

Aston didn't know how to reply. He hadn't expected this kind of confession today from Jordan, but at the same time, it made sense. Jordan seemed like the kind of guy who kept things close to his chest, who focussed more on others than himself. In some ways, Aston understood that. He had been the same way for so long, especially before Eli.

"I didn't know," Aston said, feeling a little dumb for not realizing it sooner. "I mean, I never would've guessed, I suppose."

Jordan chuckled softly, the sound warm and genuine. "Yeah, well, like I said, I keep it low-key. Clearwater's not exactly the most welcoming place for guys like us."

Aston nodded, understanding all too well. He'd seen how the town could be—small-minded, conservative, clinging to old traditions. It was part of why Eli had been so scared, why he'd kept their relationship a secret for so long. And it was part of why Aston still wasn't sure how to move forward now that Eli was gone.

"Yeah," Aston murmured, staring out at the water. "People can be so closed minded."

"Look, Aston," Jordan said after a while, his voice soft but steady. "I just want you to know… I like you. I've liked you for a while now, actually. But I didn't want to say anything because I know you're still dealing with everything with Eli. And I don't want to make you feel like you have to feel anything back… you know. Just felt I needed to tell you. I'm sorry if it's inappropriate timing. You're just such a good person and I thought you would want to know. Well, I wanted you to know, anyway."

Aston's heart skipped a beat at Jordan's words, a mix of emotions swirling inside him—surprise, confusion, maybe even a little fear. But the reason for the confession was out. And while a part of him was flattered, maybe even curious, the rest of him was absolutely not ready. Not yet.

"Jordan, I... I appreciate you telling me," Aston said, his voice hesitant. "But I'm not ready for... for anything... Not after Eli."

Jordan nodded, his expression understanding. "I figured. And that's okay. Again, I'm not saying this for any reason but myself. I just wanted to be honest with you about how I feel. Just get it off my chest more than anything else. I feel lighter that you know."

Aston looked down at his hands. He appreciated Jordan's honesty, but at the same time, it felt slightly overwhelming. Everything with Eli was still so raw, so fresh, and he wasn't sure what this meant.

"I like you too," Aston admitted, his voice quiet. "But I just... I'm still trying to figure everything out, you know? With myself. But you're a good friend."

Jordan reached out and placed a hand on Aston's shoulder, his touch warm and reassuring.

"I get it, man. You don't have to explain. We're just two gay friends. We can just be friends forever, if that's what you need. I'm totally cool with that."

Aston felt a sense of relief wash over him at Jordan's words.

"Thanks," Aston said, his voice sincere. "I'm glad you told me, Jords."

Jordan smiled, his eyes warm and full of understanding. "I'm glad I told you too. It's a weight off my shoulders. I need friends too, you know. You and Ava… you guys are that for me. So, whatever you need, I'm here, Troublemaker."

Aston smiled back. Jordan's presence was like a lifeline, something steady to hold onto as he tried to navigate the way ahead.

They sat there for a while longer, watching the waves roll in and out, the sun sinking lower on the horizon. He was content with this—a quiet moment with a friend who understood. They understood each other and were both better for it.

Chapter Forty Four

It wasn't long before Ava joined Aston and Jordan more often on their expeditions. They hadn't been close after Eli's death. But once Jordan became a regular fixture in Aston's life, and after Ava reached out to him that day in his bedroom, Aston eased and began letting people back in. And Ava seemed to naturally re-enter the picture. They met at a coffee shop one afternoon, and the three of them fell into conversation with surprising ease. Ava, with her kind heart and genuine care, had a way of making others feel comfortable. She had been through her own grief and confusion over Eli's death, and though their relationship hadn't been romantic, she carried her own sense of loss for someone who had grown to be a good friend. She did however share with the boys that she had recently met a guy who she felt could be something more. Both Aston and Jordan were happy for her.

The three of them spent more and more time together, sometimes meeting at the coffee shop, sometimes wandering down the beach, occasionally sitting near the marina where Eli and Aston had worked, legs hanging off the pier, but never getting too close.

The conversations flowed easily, a blend of past memories and future plans, punctuated by the natural camaraderie they shared.

One afternoon, as they sipped iced coffee by the window, Ava brought up the idea.

"You know…" she began, her voice tentative but hopeful. "I was thinking. Maybe we could… I don't know, do something for Eli? Like, something meaningful."

Aston looked at her, his brow furrowed. Remembering it was something his mother had mentioned too. He wondered if she had anything to do with the suggestion. That maybe she had spoken to Ava. He didn't know the answer, but it didn't really matter. He wanted to find out what Ava had in mind. "Like?"

Ava paused, glancing between Aston and Jordan. "His boat… Joy. She's still sitting there, rotting away under the boardwalk. I was thinking… maybe we could rebuild her. Restore her, you know? Like you and Eli did. It could be something we all do together. For Eli. And for us."

Aston stiffened at the mention of Eli's boat. Joy.

It had been months since he'd last seen it—he had often purposefully avoided that part of the beach, unable to bear the sight of her in that state. The idea of restoring it felt overwhelming, like reopening a wound that hadn't fully healed. He glanced at Jordan, looking for some sign of how he should feel.

Jordan smiled softly. "I think it's a great idea," he said, his voice calm but encouraging. "It could be something… meaningful. A nice project. I would love to go sailing one day too."

Aston felt a surge of resistance rise in him. Joy represented everything he had lost. Could he really face her again? Could he rebuild something that had been so entwined with his memories of Eli? He wasn't sure. But Jordan's eyes were steady on his, and in that gaze, Aston saw a quiet strength—an understanding that sometimes, facing the things that hurt the most was the only way to truly heal. And Jordan was there to help him through it.

"I don't know," Aston muttered, his fingers gripping the edge of the table. "It's just… it feels like a lot."

Ava reached out, placing her hand gently on Aston's arm. "We'll be with you, Aston. No pressure, but I think it would be a beautiful thing."

"Can I have some time to think about it?" asked Aston.

"Of course," said both Jordan and Ava at the exact same time. They all smiled and the atmosphere was that of relaxed camaraderie. The idea had been floated.

And so it began.

A few weeks later, they found themselves standing in a straight line next to each other on the beach, staring at the wreck of Joy under the boardwalk. The sunlight filtered through the slats of the wooden structure above them, casting long shadows over its damaged hull. The boat was a shell of what it had once been—weathered by time, salt, and neglect. Yet, as Aston stood there, with Ava and Jordan beside him, all he could see in his mind was the restored boat that he and Eli had worked on. And she was beautiful.

He walked closer, running his fingers along the faded wood, tracing the outline of Eli's name on the bow. The memories came rushing back—days spent with Eli working together, the day on the water, laughter echoing against the waves, the warmth of the sun on their faces. But this time, instead of heartache, Aston felt something else. He felt gratitude. He had loved Eli. And for all the pain and sadness, there had been so much joy too. So many moments of happiness that could never be erased.

Aston stood back up and Jordan stepped up beside him, silent but present. He knew that this was a significant moment for Aston, a turning point of sorts. Without a word, Jordan placed a hand on Aston's shoulder.

Aston blinked, and took a breath. A breath of hope, of healing. The project before them wasn't just about rebuilding a boat—it was about honoring Eli's memory, about reclaiming something that had once been lost, and about finding a way forward.

"I think we can do this," Aston said quietly, his voice thick with emotion but steady.

Jordan smiled beside him. "Yeah, I think we can."

Ava, standing on the other side of the boat now, grinned. "Not think… We are gonna do this!"

Chapter Forty Five

Aston sat on the porch steps, gazing absently at the street ahead. He wasn't sure when it happened exactly, but things between him and Alex had softened some. The tension had eased since that day—since Alex had stood up to Mark. Aston still wasn't sure how to feel about his mom's relationship, but he had to admit, Alex was proving himself to be a decent guy.

The front door creaked open behind him, and he heard the familiar heavy steps of Alex approaching.

"Hey, Aston," Alex greeted, his tone light, though there was always a sense of cautiousness when they spoke. "Everything alright?"

Aston looked up from where he was sitting and nodded. "Yeah, just thinking."

"Mind if I sit?"

Aston shrugged, and Alex dropped down next to him on the porch, his broad frame dwarfing the small wooden steps.

They sat in silence for a few moments, watching the occasional car pass by. It was peaceful.

Aston cleared his throat. "Hey, um… do you think that maybe you could drop me off at Jordan's place later?"

Alex's eyebrows lifted slightly, clearly surprised but pleased. For the first time, Aston was asking him for something. "Yeah, of course!" He grinned, reaching into his pocket and pulling out his keys like he'd been waiting for this moment forever. "Let's go. I've got nothing else on today."

Aston gave a half-smile and stood up, slipping his phone into his pocket. The awkwardness that used to hang between them had definitely lessened—at least now they could sit together without feeling like strangers. It wasn't like Aston was suddenly best friends with Alex, but he didn't feel that simmering resentment anymore.

They climbed into Alex's blue sedan, the engine humming to life as Alex backed out of the driveway. The silence wasn't uncomfortable, just quiet, like they were both figuring out what to say.

As they drove through the town, Aston stared out the window. The familiar streets of Clearwater rolled by, the ocean glimmering in the distance.

It had become home, in a strange way, even if it had been the place where so much had gone wrong.

They were approaching Eli's house now. Alex's hands tightened slightly on the steering wheel, as if he realized too late what route he'd taken. Aston's gaze fell on the lawn. It was overgrown, untidy—the way it had been left for months now. The house was empty, with a "For Sale" sign hammered into the dirt. Except now, the sign had been had a red sticker over it: **Sold**.

Aston's chest tightened at the sight. All he had heard was that Samuel and Rebecca had moved away after Eli's death, but seeing the house like this—a shell of what it used to be—made it all the more real.

Alex glanced sideways at Aston, seeing the way his shoulders slumped. He didn't say anything but reached out and patted Aston's shoulder twice, a simple, reassuring gesture. Aston glanced at him, caught off guard, but gave a small smile in return.

The Taylor family had indeed left Clearwater shortly after Eli's funeral. Samuel had taken the loss of his son harder than anyone, becoming a ghost of the man he once was. He had tried to hold on, for Rebecca's sake, but there was too much guilt. Too much sorrow.

Rebecca, once sharp and controlling, had withered under the weight of their loss. Her bright red hair, which she had always kept immaculately styled, had become limp and dull.

They had sold the house, packed up their lives, and left town for good. No one knew exactly where they had gone, but rumors swirled about them heading somewhere up north, to try to rebuild in a place where the memories of Eli and Joy weren't as suffocating.

The lawn, once meticulously maintained, was now wild and untamed, like the remnants of their family.

Alex cleared his throat, breaking the silence. "So, how's the boat repair going?" he asked, trying to steer the conversation away from the heavy thoughts.

Aston shrugged, still staring out the window as they passed Eli's house. "It's tough. We don't have all the tools we need, so it's been slow."

Alex nodded thoughtfully. "What do you need? I've got a bunch of power tools in my garage. You're welcome to use whatever I have."

Aston looked over at him, surprised. "Really? That'd be great. We could definitely use some better stuff. We've been making do, but it's been a pain."

"No problem," Alex said, smiling. "We can stop by my place if you like, and you can grab whatever you need."

Aston felt a weight lift off his shoulders. It wasn't just about the tools—it was the fact that Alex was offering to help, no strings attached. This felt like another step forward. A part of Aston couldn't deny that it was nice having someone around who cared.

"That's very kind of you. I'll make sure we look after them. Thank you," Aston said sincerely. "It'll really make the project a lot easier."

Alex glanced over, his smile widening. "You should have asked me earlier. You need help, you just let me know, okay?"

Aston nodded, appreciating the gesture. He hesitated for a second, then said quietly, "And… thanks for making my mom happy again."

Alex looked taken aback for a moment, his face softening at the comment.

He didn't speak right away, as if weighing his words carefully. Then, he smiled, his voice gentle. "Your mom makes me very happy too, Aston. I'm lucky to have her in my life."

Aston didn't reply, but he felt a strange sense of relief wash over him. He hadn't fully realized until now how much it had bothered him—how much he worried about his mom being alone. He still missed his dad, and he always would, but seeing his mom smile again… that was something special.

They pulled into Alex's driveway, and Aston followed him into the garage, where Alex showed him a collection of tools neatly organized along the wall. Aston picked out a few that would make the boat repairs easier—power drills, saws, clamps.

After loading up the tools into the car, they headed back out. The drive to Jordan's house was short, but the atmosphere in the vehicle had shifted. The tension that had once filled the space between them had lessened.

As they neared Jordan's house, Alex glanced at Aston. "You sure you're good?" he asked, his tone serious but kind.

Aston gave a small nod. "Yeah, I'm good. Thanks again for the tools. And, y'know… everything."

Alex smiled. "Anytime, kid."

They pulled up to Jordan's house, and Aston hopped out of the vehicle quickly, grabbing the tools from the back.

"Can I help you carry?"

"Naa, it's cool. Thanks."

Jordan came walking out of the house and Alex greeted him with a friendly smile. Jordan was excited to see the tools they had and thanked Alex.

Aston popped his head down to the open window and gave Alex a genuine smile. "See you later. And thank you again."

"Take care," Alex replied, watching as Aston and Jordan headed up the driveway to Jordan's front door.

Alex reversed out the driveway and drove down the road. "Yay, me," he whispered, grinning. Today was the best day. Aston was accepting him. And it felt good.

Chapter Forty Six

The weeks that followed were filled with long days of hard work. Rebuilding *Joy* was no small feat—the boat had been left to rot for too long, and there were moments when it felt like an impossible task. But with every nail hammered, every plank replaced, Aston felt a little bit of his own healing begin to take shape.

Jordan became a constant presence during those days. They spent hours working side by side, sometimes in silence, sometimes in deep conversation. They talked about everything—about Eli, about their fathers, about the strange ways life had brought them together. There was no pressure between them, no expectations. Just a quiet understanding that they were both moving forward, even if it was slowly, even if the path was uncertain.

Ava was there too, less often now, as she was starting to spend more time with her new boyfriend, but her presence was a steady source of warmth and energy. She had a way of lifting the mood, of reminding them that this project wasn't about sadness—it was about honoring life, about celebrating it.

She often brought snacks or iced coffees, and during their breaks, they'd sit in the sand, laughing and joking like old friends.

As the weeks flew by, *Joy* began to take shape once again. The boat started to transform into something new—something that represented their friendship.

The final day came on a warm, sunny afternoon. The three of them stood on the beach, looking at the newly restored *Joy*, her hull gleaming in the sunlight. The boat wasn't perfect—there were still scars from the damage, marks that couldn't be erased—but that was part of what made her so beautiful. She was a testament to the hard work they had put in, to the resilience they had found within themselves. Aston did the final part of the job. Restoring the names on the bow, with a fresh lick of royal blue paint.

Joy and Eli.

Aston stepped back and looked at the boat, and felt a deep, genuine sense of peace and pride. He thought back to the day he and Eli had taken the boat out together, the way the wind had filled the sails for the first time, the laughter that had filled the air as it did.

Those memories would always be with him, but they no longer hurt the way they once had. Now, they felt like a gift—something to carry with him as he moved forward. And they were going to be adding to those memories.

Ava clapped her hands together, breaking the silence. "So, when are we taking her out on the water?"

Aston grinned. "As soon as the paint dries. She's ready."

They stood there for a while longer, waiting impatiently, the three of them, looking out at the ocean as the sun hung high in the morning sky on the most beautiful day Aston had experienced in a really long time. The future was still uncertain, but Aston felt okay with that. He had found something new in the wake of his loss—friendship, hope, and maybe even the possibility of love.

The waves swished against the shore, and Aston took a deep cleansing breath, taking in the refreshing ocean air.

This is for you, Eli, he thought.

Jordan placed his hand gently on the small of his back, and Aston closed his eyes for a moment, letting the warmth of the closeness fill him with peace.

It was a simple gesture of support, but one that carried so much weight. It was the same thing Aston had done for Eli once, on the days when Eli had struggled under the pressure of his own insecurities. Jordan gave Aston a quiet smile.

There was something between them now—something unspoken but undeniable. Whether it would one day turn into more, Aston didn't know. But he was okay with that too. For now, it was enough to know that neither of them were alone.

Aston moved his hand and placed it on Jordan's back. He looked at Joy, and a small smile grew on his face and he knew in that very moment that everything was going to be okay.

- **The End** -

CLEARWATER
A novel by Egan Sheridan

Thank you for your time.

Please feel free to get in touch:
@EganSheridan
EganSheridan@gmail.com
http://sites.google.com/view/EganSheridan
http://www.amazon.com/author/egansheridan

Egan Sheridan.

If you enjoyed this book, kindly consider leaving a positive review on Amazon. It would be greatly appreciated.

More books by Egan Sheridan:
(Available on Amazon)

Get Wet: A College Experience

Shower

Shower Club

Breaking Brad

Two Weeks in Provence

Once Upon a Time in the Closet

Bathhouse Brian

Coming soon in early of 2025:
19/46: A Hot & Steamy MM Age Gap Romp!

© Copyright Egan Sheridan 2024

Printed in Great Britain
by Amazon